Advanced Praise for *A New Love*

"Katerina Katsarka Whitl _____ ʰility to bring back to life characters _____ ᵢnce and history. In putting flesh bᵃ _____ ʰat great books have always done— _____ .ᵤᵣᵢes (and our own stories) anew. *A New Lᵢ* _____ ᵤₙₜ shaped by solid scholarship and beautiful storytelling. You'll see the life of its characters—and of the early Church—as you never have before."

—**Greg Garrett,** author of *The Prodigal* and *Entertaining Judgment: The Afterlife in Popular Imagination*

"Katerina Whitley takes readers into the sweeping landscape of first-century Greece—and into the minds, hearts, and homes of the earliest Christians. Through the magnetic figure of Paul the Apostle—and the passion of his faith in the risen Christ—Whitley weaves a story of transforming love in a world turned upside down by these new believers. A beautifully written, inspiring book, with finely drawn characters and an authentic window into ancient settings, *A New Love* is a must-read for anyone fascinated by the origins—and the life-changing power—of the Gospel."

—**Nancy Fitzgerald,** former editorial director of Morehouse Publishing

"Helena, a Greek girl living in Roman-occupied Corinth during the first century, is infused with the proud inheritance of Greek myths and poetry. Can the Apostle Paul articulate Christ's message in a way that permeates her mind and heart as her sheltered soul is tormented by love and shattered by brutality? Can Helena awaken to new life through the people of The Way? In this moving story of confusion, danger and love, author Katerina Whitley skillfully brings the reader's heart along with Helena's as she seeks to understand God."

—**Nancy G West,** author of award-winning *Suspense* and the *Aggie Mundeen Mystery Series*

"Katerina Katsarka Whitley's novel, *A New Love,* is not primarily a historical romance but rather a "loves" story. The young-girl-figures-out-who-she-truly-loves plot, set in the Greco-Roman world of the first century, is the loom on which Whitley weaves the more powerful story about how the new idea of God as Love began to change the world. We see a wide range of people—women and men, slaves and rulers, craftsmen, artists, laborers—coming into contact with converts to the new religion of Christos and being touched, and changed, by the Love that lies at its heart. One of those people is a young Greek woman, Helena, whose world falls apart early in the book, then slowly and painfully takes a new shape as she finds a haven in the home of Phoebe, a Greek Christian, meets Paul the Apostle, and experiences firsthand the selfless love they say comes from Christ. This is an intriguing read for 21st-century Christians who rarely think about the day-to-day lives of early Christians."

—**Jane W. Blackburn,** Director of Libraries, Appalachian Regional Library

Praise for Previous Books

"*Around a Greek Table* is extraordinary in the sense that Whitley describes Greek cooking with the same unbridled passion she has demonstrated in her books on faith, her writing in Episcopal publications over past decades, and her popular dramatic readings that are based on research into the powerful voices of biblical women."

—**Jerry Hames,** long time editor of Episcopal Life and Episcopal Journal

On *Waiting for the Wonder:*
"Beautiful prose, reading like poetry, which tells of the advent of the promise of peace to the world and the birth of a Savior. Each essay is in the voice of the biblical figures which surround the wondrous birth… This book is a welcome celebration of goodness, a message of hope and anticipation that each of us longs for, especially at Christmas."

—**Mary Popham,** author *Back Home in Landing Run*

Also by Katerina Katsarka Whitley

*Around a Greek Table: Recipes and Stories Arranged
According to the Liturgical Seasons of the Eastern Church*

*Light to the Darkness: Lessons and Carols,
Public and Private*

Waiting for the Wonder: Voices of Advent
(also available in Audio Book)

Walking the Way of Sorrows: Stations of the Cross

Seeing for Ourselves: Biblical Women Who Met Jesus

Speaking for Ourselves: Voices of Biblical Women

Katerina Katsarka Whitley

A NEW LOVE

A Novel of the First Century

New Beginnings
An Imprint of Material Media LLC
San Antonio, Texas

To my husband, Rudy, who was with me throughout this book's journey. Now, maybe, he will ask St. Paul: "How much did she get right?" And they will smile together.

*A glossary of Latin and Greek words
is found at the end of the novel (page 271).*

A word about the spelling and pronunciation of Greek words and names

I have found it difficult to accept the predominant Latin spelling of Greek words, especially when the originals are found in New Testament Greek. I have used the Greek ending *-os* in place of the Latin ending *-us* throughout this book, except in cases when the name had a Roman origin. For example, I have preferred Erastos to the accepted Latinized Erastus; Dionysos instead of Dionysus; and for nouns of the neuter gender, the *-on* ending instead of the Latin *-um* as in *peristylion* instead of *peristylium* and *prektron* instead of *prectrum*.

I have also preferred the Greek *kappa* to the Latin *c* in names of Greek origin: hence Makedonia instead of Macedonia; but where the spelling might confuse, I opted for the c, as in Corinth, instead of k, except when I use the original Greek as in Korinthos or Korinthia.

The Greek letter χ (chi) is pronounced like a rough *h* which I denote with the combination *kh* as in *kharis* (grace) and *khêrai* (a greeting). Greek today, unlike the classical, has but one *e* sound pronounced like *ee*.

To avoid confusion between the *ee* and *eh* sounds I have used accents. For the sound of *ee*, as in agapē, I employ the straight line above the ē. Whenever the Greek sound is an *eh*, I have designated it with the circumflex over the *e* as in Kenchreaê.

Katerina Katsarka Whitley ~ January 2016

Contents

Prologue

Pavlos is dead. The news spread in Korinthia like the fire that was burning Rome. *Pavlos, our brother, is dead.*

The musician Helena heard it like a drumming in her head but it would not register into reality. She looked at the men, women, and children gathering in the cave inside the hidden recesses of the rock Acrocorinthos, at the people of Corinth's troubled *ekklesia*, this fractious company now united in their sorrow. *Pavlos, our brother, is dead.* They had been led there by Phoebe who knew the ancient sacred places on the mountain, Phoebe who had brought the news of the terror that was unleashed in Rome when Nero went mad in it. Would the madness spread east, to the communities of faith Pavlos had established in the provinces?

But now *Pavlos is dead.* The sad news echoed in the cave. The rumor spread as rumors do: the People of the Way in Rome, those called Christians, were being used as kindling or thrown to the beasts. Was this the end of time as Paul had predicted? Helena looked at the frightened faces of those who were now forming circles of family groups; she recognized those who had truly loved Paul and those who had tried to make his life miserable. *Yet he loved us all,* she thought, *he loved us all.*

Her dear Phoebe, her adopted mother, as she had come to think of her, had undertaken the difficult journey a month before, leaving from the port of Kenchreaê to travel to Rome in order to visit Paul in his prison, to take to him offerings of food and blankets together with greetings from his friends in

Corinth. She had found him in good spirits, looking forward to his trial where he planned to proclaim the gospel publicly to the Romans. He was convinced that he would be released, his hope strong that, finally, he could fulfill his dream of going to Spain. She saw that he was full of love for all his "children" as he called the people of the *ekklesiae* he had started. His good humor and kindness extended toward his jailers who seemed mesmerized by him. "They are not quite certain that Paul is human," Phoebe had written to Helena. "They think him a kind of demigod because he never complains and he treats them like brothers."

When the time came for Phoebe to return to her people in Kenchreaê, she went to bid him farewell. "Be of good cheer, Phoebe," he told her. "They are treating me well. I have daily opportunities to witness to God's grace." He had taken her hands in his and looked into her eyes, his own deep-set and dark but filled with love and that strange light that always reminded her that there were memories in Paul of something that was beyond this world. She had asked him once, "Paul, have you entered the other realm?" and he had understood immediately and had said simply, "Yes, but I don't have the words—I cannot speak of it, Phoebe." And she had not pursued it.

Now, in his prison room, where he seemed content to be, he held on to her hands and said, "Phoebe, if it be the Lord's will to take me to himself before he returns, you must look after my children. You must not allow them to quarrel among themselves. And you must not allow them to seek martyrdom. The Lord Christ needs all of you alive and strong—one in him. Take care of my children, Phoebe."

She had known then that she would never see him again on this earth. With deep sadness she had said her farewells to him, her mind full of messages from him for so many in Corinth and Kenchreaê—each one of them remembered by name. She then set upon the return journey, traveling by carriage to Brindisium. Before reaching the port on the Adriatic, she was overtaken by Urbanus, one of the rare Roman brothers who could afford a horse. He had ridden fast and hard to bring her the terrible message: Rome was burning. "Nero may have started the fire," he whispered; "he has always wanted to rebuild Rome, they say, but now he is blaming the brothers for the fire. They are being burnt and killed indiscriminately." Phoebe, pale, barely able to stand, started to ask the question, "And Paul? . . ." but her friend shook his head. "The prison is gone. Nothing but ashes left. There is no sign of Paul—just burnt bodies, unrecognizable." He urged her to leave immediately, to carry the frightful news, to warn the converts in the province of Corinth and the rest of Greece that the persecution was coming. The end was near, but Paul, who had waited for it, had not lived to see it. *Will the Lord return to save us?*

She knew of a cave in the Acrocorinthos, the small mountain that rises like a rocky father to cover the elegant, vibrant city, a capricious daughter. The cave had been claimed by her ancestors as a place for the worship of Aphrodite. She would take her friends there to hide them, to keep them from being burned, from being thrown to the beasts.

Phoebe stopped in Kenchreaê long enough to warn her people, then continued on to Corinth. Now, exhausted, she stood up among them, in the shelter she had chosen for them and told them of her journey and of Paul's words to her.

"My dear brothers and sisters *en Christô*," she started, and memories of Paul's words filled their minds. "Our beloved brother in Christ has left us, but I know he is still with us, as the Lord he loved is with us. I was so sad on that ship crossing the Adriatic to return to you. Every time the waves hit us I thought, *It will be easier to die than to face this sorrow,* but then Paul's words came back to bring me to myself. I ask you now to remember his words. Let us repeat them aloud to one another."

Like a litany, voices rose from the dark, one after the other:
*"Oh death, where is your victory? Oh death,
where is your sting?"*

*"Faith, hope, love, these three. But the greatest of
these is love!"*

"Owe no one anything but to love one another."

On and on the remembered exhortations filled the cave. The time now came to break bread together, to share it and then drink the wine from the common cup. "In remembrance of me," they whispered to one another. "Do this in remembrance of me."

Then, as the dark fell all around them, they huddled together and they remembered where and who they had been fifteen years before when Paul first appeared in Corinth.

Locations Mentioned in the Book

1. Corinth
2. Kenchreae
3. Thessaloniki
4. Amphipolis

5. Thassos
6. Neapolis
7. Philippi
8. Beria

9. Naxos
10. Kriti
11. Kos
12. Sounion

Chapter 1: Helena

As soon as Helena opened her eyes she remembered not that it was her eighteenth birthday but that she wanted to die. The bruises from the rape were now visible, but it was the pain inside her that burned like a fire that wouldn't be doused. *I will seek revenge and then I'll die. But how can I die when Ares loves me?*

In the middle of the night, summoned by the steward Alexandros, Claudia had found Helena moaning and immediately sent for the physician. Then Alexandros ordered all the hovering slaves away from her room, but he stayed nearby to guard her.

Later, as Helena found herself waking from a sickly daze, she heard Claudia's normally cool, aristocratic voice spiking with emphasis: "*I* will deal with my husband, Helena! He will pay for this, I promise. But you must not tell Ares what happened to you. You must *not* tell him. When he comes to see you I'll have the slaves send him away. They will tell him you are sick, but he must *not* see you in this condition. Do you understand? Show me that you do."

Helena was tossing on her defiled bed. The linen with the bloodstains had been ripped away, but she still felt dirty and torn. *I always will.* Fever was burning her, yet her desire for revenge felt more like a fire. She nodded painfully to Claudia that she had heard her, then beckoned to Alexandros.

The head slave approached in his reserved, assured manner. Slender and upright, his close-cut hair turning silver, he looked like an aristocrat, not a slave. Since her father's death only his steady presence had given her a measure of protection in this household. "Alexandros," she whispered, "don't let him come near me again," and he knew she meant Claudia's husband, not her beloved Ares.

From the doorway, Claudia's voice sounded harsh. "Place a slave here to guard the door," she ordered the steward. "I'll deal with Gaius." And with a last troubled look at Helena, she stormed away.

Alexandros placed a cool, wet cloth on Helena's brow. "I swear on the memory of your father, Helena, I will not let the master trouble you again."

"*Trouble* me? Such a mild word, Alexandros." She saw him flinch, his fifty years now showing on his tired face, and then the physician's powerful sleeping potion pulled her once more into darkness.

She woke up hours later, in the afternoon of her birthday, still burning with pain and a passion for revenge. As the memory of the night hit her again she heard a noise that spoke of rescue. Shouting outside. Ares' voice. "You *will* let me see her or I swear, I'll tear you and this house apart!" Suddenly there he was, knocking the slave at her door speechless with one furious blow, rushing into her room. She cried out and he gathered her in his arms, staring at her, seeing the bruises on her arms and legs. His face darkened.

"Who did this to you?"

"Gaius Marius Sylvanus," she blurted out without thinking.

"He violated me like a slave."

And at that, Ares cried out in rage and rushed from the room, leaving Helena weeping with helpless fury, calling his name. Her drugged body felt too heavy to leave the bed. Then her will abandoned her altogether and she couldn't stop her eyes from closing. What had the cursed physician given her?

When she awoke again, it was dark outside, and Claudia, holding a candle, was glaring down at her. "You foolish, willful girl," she started, having regained her cool voice—the aristocratic Roman matron in full force.

"Where's Ares?" Helena struggled to sit up.

"Did I not warn you? Why didn't you obey me?"

"Where did Ares go?"

Claudia glowered. "You needed to tell him the truth, didn't you? Like the foolish boy that he is, he exploded and went straight for Gaius. It took three slaves to stop him and all of Alexandros' persuasive powers to convince him to leave the villa before Gaius and his lackey saw him. Why didn't you listen to me, you silly girl? No man needs to know his betrothed was raped."

"Claudia! Someone has to avenge me. Why did you stop Ares?"

"You fool," Claudia now showed her worry. "That would mean Ares' death. Don't you understand? Do you want him to get killed?"

Helena hid her face into her pillow to muffle her screams. *It is Gaius who must die. But Ares? Ares can't die. How can I live if Ares dies? Oh, Ares, don't leave me. Come back! Come back!*

She was falling into a black hole. *Was this madness?* She cried until even her voice was gone.

She hid in her room, her mind wild. *Hades has come for me,* she thought. *Call me Persephone.* The only one allowed in her room was Alexandros who offered her food that she rejected. She drank only water. Every time he entered, she asked, "Where's Ares?" And each time he replied quietly, hiding his worry, "I don't know, Helena."

Two days later, Ares' letter arrived.

Chapter 2: Waiting

"Ares writing from Kenchreaê to Helena," his letter began. *"The morning will find me on the Eirēnē sailing for Alexandria. Greatly troubled since your father's death, Helena. The fault lies with me. My impotence in removing you from the cursed house of Gaius and Claudia has brought me to despair. He has defiled you, and I must avenge you. What will happen to you when I kill him? Only Alexandros' persistent question stopped me. I must go away for the safety of us both. Forgive me. I shall return as soon as I have earned enough treasure to rescue you from there. With love always, Ares."*

She was numb but didn't know whether it was from grief or fury. She stood rigid, looking straight ahead, and Alexandros saw the change in her. He had always admired her beauty, so different from Claudia's. Helena's seemed to emerge from joy, Claudia's from perfect grooming. Now Helena's joy was gone, as if blown away, the way lamplight was extinguished when one opened a door suddenly. The girl before him was still lovely to look at: a slender, lithe body that moved with grace, a face that Praxiteles would have enjoyed copying; high forehead, large gray eyes, abundant black curls that escaped from their ribbons to caress her cheeks, a mouth that used to smile so easily. Now all that beauty was still present but cold, lifeless. It saddened the slave who had loved her like his own child.

She handed the letter to Alexandros who read it in silence. "I must show this to Claudia," he said, his eyes averted, grooves of worry on his forehead. She said, "Nothing matters now, except the death of Gaius Marius Sylvanus."

"But not by your hand, no, Helena!" Alexandros whispered anxiously. "*Swear!* In the name of your father, swear to me you will not do it. Do not endanger yourself. Think of your father. His grief, if he knew."

"What about *my* grief?" she cried out, the numbness gone, the tears present and bitter as they had been daily since his death a month before. "How could my father kill himself when he knew I'd try to follow him?"

Alexandros, feeling his guilt, had no response to her heartbreak. He left quickly, but first he gave orders to the hapless slave not to move from his place at her door. So Helena sat on her bed and waited for the next blow from the semi-goddess who pursued her, Moira, the cruel, Moira the ever-present. She felt enslaved by Moira. Instead of harsh Fate, however, Claudia's two children ran inside and tried to pull her to her feet. Her affection for them made her forget herself for a moment and she obeyed their call. "Play for us, Helena. We love your music. We heard you're sick so we came to make you well with your music. Isn't that beautiful? To make you well with your music?"

She started to say, *I'll never be made well again,* but how could she reveal this to the children? Their lives could not possibly turn out like hers. They had a mother who was rich and who loved them despite their lecherous father. Helena picked up her *kithara* and the children sat at her feet. The little girl handed her the *plektron,* Helena ran it quickly over the strings, closed her eyes and played a melody she had loved—sad and wistful. The children sat still and quiet. "Sing, Helena," the boy begged her, "sing for us." But the song, a funeral dirge for the Trojan women, made them weep and, after a while, with tears burning her own eyes, she plucked two more plaintive notes and lowered the instrument.

"Helena, why are you sad?" the girl, Claudia Sylvana, asked as young Marius looked on, his thin face serious. "Do you miss your father?"

"Yes," she answered, touched by their care, "and I miss Ares also. Do you know that he has sailed for Alexandria?"

They comforted her as children can do by their presence, but soon they forgot her sorrow and pulled her with them downstairs, through the atrium, to their favorite garden behind the kitchens. Their nursemaid must have followed them for she appeared carrying a scroll. "The mistress wants you to read to them," she said and thrust a scroll of Euripides' works to the startled Helena. "The children have been depraved of lessons lately," and Helena almost succumbed to laughter hearing the nurse's failed attempt to imitate Claudia. *Depraved!* The voice in her mind cried. *It's only their father who is depraved. The verb may be wrong, but the diction,* she thought, *was almost right.*

She had read faithfully to the children for the past two years, ever since she had moved, together with her father, to this Roman villa where he acted as tutor and mentor and she as the resident musician. Since her father's untimely death, Helena had taken over the children's education, and the unorthodox arrangement was tacitly approved by Claudia. The children memorized easily, wanting to please. Demosthenes, her father, had praised Helena's "consummate skill" in reading aloud, in those happy days when he was with her and she, eager to please him, had recited the tragedies he had taught her with such pride and patience.

Helena unrolled the papyrus of *The Trojan Women.* "It's

a very sad play," she told the children, "but this is how I feel today. Would you like to hear it?"

They nodded eagerly. Claudia Sylvana, in her precocious manner, said, "Mother says that Erastos was the best Hecuba in all of Greece. Do you agree, Helena?"

She was puzzled. "Erastos? Who is he? I don't think I recall the name."

"He used to visit us a lot," the little girl continued, "when he acted at the *Theatron*—don't you remember? But he hasn't been here in a long while. He promised he'd take me to see a play. I want him to keep his promise. Don't you think he should?"

Helena shrugged but talked to them as to equals. "I used to love the theater when my father took me with him to see the great plays. That's before we moved here. I'd memorized most of them as you are doing now. But that was a long time ago, when I was about your age, Claudia Sylvana. I think my father attended the theater only with your mother since we moved here."

"Mother says," and here the little girl mimicked with wicked accuracy her mother's high-class accent: "'Erastos *hates* what's happening to the theater. He despises the Roman mimes, so he has stopped acting.'"

Helena smiled despite herself. She started reading aloud, the words of the Trojan women appropriate laments in her ears, matching her sorrowful mood with their own cosmic mourning. After an hour of this the children grew restless and decided their current concerns were much more enjoyable than the enslavement of women centuries before. "The Greeks were not very nice," the boy declared and Helena agreed: "Just as bad as the Romans," she said firmly and led them back to their nurse.

The days now were filled with an agonized waiting. When would Ares arrive in Alexandria? Would the ship take two weeks or a month to reach its destination? She knew that he had left at a dangerous time. The autumn months were not propitious for sailing and that troubled her even more than his sudden departure. She knew his impatient nature, his fiery temperament that was matched by his arresting face and dark, burning eyes. She recognized, of course, that after her thoughtless blurting out of Gaius' guilt, Ares would try to harm the hated Roman. But Helena had never expected his running away. And it was all her fault. She shuddered when she thought of the dangers of early November in the treacherous Aegean. *What if I lose him? What if I lose him? I'll be all alone, cut off from all who knew me as a child. And then I'll be lost forever.*

She hid in her room, except on the days when Alexandros informed her that the master was not in the villa. Then she emerged only to play with the children. They had finished the recitation of *The Trojan Women;* they were now on the last scene of Euripides' *Helen* and, reading it to them, she was trying desperately to believe the contrived happy ending.

But then one day Alexandros appeared, and all her premonitions came to the fore. The children wanted to stay with her, but Alexandros motioned them to go away. He approached her, his face serious and sad. Her heart did such a painful flip that she bent her body in two and stayed there looking at her feet, the blood rushing to her face, blinding her eyes. "Helena, *korē*," he began but she cried out, "He's dead, isn't he?" She heard her own voice tearing the stillness around her and then the sound of the children's feet as they stopped running to listen to her cry.

Alexandros knelt in front of her, his head close to hers, and he said, very quietly, "Helena, we received word. The *Eirēnē* has sunk. My messenger from Kenchreaê arrived this moment. The news is not good. The *Eirēnē* never reached Alexandria. Ah, Helena!"

Helena, stunned, raised her head to look at him, her eyes wild, begging him to agree: *They have made a mistake.* "How do they know?" she began, but there was nothing in his eyes to help her hold on to hope. *They must have proof,* but she did not want to know about it. She reached up and tore the ribbons from her hair. It fell on her shoulders loose and mournful. She ran to the kitchens and grabbed a sharpened knife, Alexandros close to her, his hand outstretched, ready to intervene. She pulled at clumps of hair again and again and, with that sharp knife, without pity, she slashed at the black curls. They fell to the ground together with her tears. She handed the knife to Alexandros and, like a blind person, climbed to her room. There, with a head shorn in mourning, she let out a high keening wail that went on and on in waves throughout the day. Those who heard the heartbreaking sound covered their ears. The only thing keeping Helena alive was her hope for revenge.

Chapter 3: Erastos

Twelve months earlier, on a sunny, clear February day, in the year that eventually would be counted A. D. 50, Erastos stood on the Bēma of the Agora in Corinth and surveyed the city he loved. He felt important, now that he had civic duties, but he still missed his days in the theater, those cherished seasons when the works of Sophokles and Euripides were still worshiped by the Corinthian public. The incoming Romans from the provinces of the empire had changed all that; their disgusting mimes had made his decision final. He would no longer act.

The Agora was teeming with people. An Athenian dignitary had arrived in Roman Corinth, and the city, loving a party and expert at showing off, was putting on a show. The marble and gold statues on top of the Agora's Propylaea glistened and winked in the sun. It was Aphrodite's festival, and her statue, festooned with flowers, taunting in its beauty, stood in the middle of the lower level of the agora. The *stoas*, with their rich shops, had dozens of people milling around or shopping, waiting to pay attention to whichever part of the show they preferred.

When a lovely sound arose in front of the Bēma, and the crowd hushed for a while, Erastos looked for the source of the music. A girls' chorus, in full view of the dignitaries sitting on the Bēma, was singing a song to Aphrodite. Of course, he thought, today was the goddess's festival, which explained the presence of so many lovely girls. The goddess indeed had bestowed her gifts on her favorites. He marked her immediately as the most appealing of the musicians, her delicate face framed by a mass of long hair that had been dressed elaborately on top of her head, reminiscent of drawings on Athenian amphorae. Blue ribbons showed through the dark curls. Her tunic of soft and flowing silk was long, covering her body but leaving one shoulder and her slender arms free, the folds of the cloth clinging on her in a way only sculptors had perfected on marble women. She handed her *kithara* to a companion and bent her body back to adjust the strap of a sandal.

Erastos' heart gave a lurch. He had seen that very movement on a sculpted pediment on the temple of Athena Nikē on the Akropolis. The statue now came alive before him and he was smitten through the heart with the bittersweet arrow of capricious Eros. *So much for mythology's formulas and comforts,* he thought. The beautiful musician reclaimed her *kithara* and held it with long fingers, her back straight and supple. Even in her stillness, energy emanated from her, and from that moment on Erastos became a captive of feelings he had known only through the words of poets and tragedians. In his acting life he had reeled from the power of love but only on the stage; the moment he changed characters, the emotion was wiped away. The question rushed through his brain: *Is this what the real thing does to a man?* The girl sang with a smile on her lips, her suppressed mirth ready to explode into laughter, and Erastos determined to know more about her.

When there was a pause in the music so that an Athenian

philosopher could speak, he saw that she was playful, laughing and joking with her companions. They were chaperoned by a distinguished-looking Greek who acted as the master of the chorus. Erastos, despite his conservative views, approved of the relaxed Roman habits that had lifted the ancient strictures on respectable women who now could perform in public festivals. He waited to see who would accompany the beauty out of the open Agora. The Greek master went to speak to her and she gave him a radiant smile, reaching out to touch his arm as he returned her smile. His pride and affection for her were obvious. But immediately he retreated as the Roman Gaius Marius Sylvanus descended from the Bēma to meet the girl and lead her to the Lechaion Road where his private litter was waiting. The curtains were open and inside Erastos spotted the Roman's two children who squealed with delight when they saw her. Their mother, Claudia, was nowhere in sight. The beautiful musician climbed in, and the slaves moved quickly then, taking her away from the Agora.

As usual Erastos avoided Gaius Marius Sylvanus but determined to see Claudia, the Roman's wife. Since the couple entertained frequently, this was not difficult to accomplish and within a few weeks Erastos had his invitation.

Claudia was one of the most important women in the upper strata of Roman Corinth. A passionate sponsor of the arts, she had become a close friend to Erastos and had contributed financially to several of his famed productions. He now remembered her generosity with gratitude. Claudia's taste was faultless, unlike that of the newly rich who displayed Roman vulgarity with their wealth. Her villa rose on the edge of the city near the Lechaion Road with its quick access to the western port. It was spacious and surrounded by vineyards. With the amenities and proximity to the city of an urban *domus*, it also gave off the luxury and comforts of a villa in the countryside. The walls and entrance gleamed with Greek marble and colorful mosaics etched its elegant façade. As he approached the gate, feeling strangely nervous, Erastos wondered if while inside he would earn a glimpse of that lovely face with the laughter barely hidden in the mouth, the lithe girl of the athletic posture. The familiar gatekeeper greeted him and informed him that Gaius Marius Sylvanus was *in situ*.

I'm not one of his lackeys, Erastos started to say. *It's Claudia I've come to see.* Yet, he knew that his good manners would not abandon him even in front of Gaius.

In the atrium, where the guests had gathered, Erastos noticed that Claudia looked a bit drawn, though her proud bearing was in full force and her hostess's welcome impeccable. Was it grief that clouded her eyes? He perceived a change of atmosphere in the household. The steward, Alexandros, was more reserved and caustic than usual, the serving slaves exceptionally quiet. During dinner, as the guests reclined on the couches of the *triclinium*, Erastos looked at the host. Never fond of Gaius, he now saw him at his most unattractive and wondered again how a person of Claudia's stature could have married him. The man's formerly handsome military looks were smudged on the flushed face that betrayed an inordinate love of drink, his features made heavy by what one could only call debauchery. As the night progressed, the host became loud, eating and drinking too much, while Claudia hardly touched her food. Throughout the meal she kept a wary eye on her husband.

Erastos shared her lack of appetite that evening and Claudia, noticing, reverted to her teasing manner with him, but he thought it sounded forced. "Is it possible," she asked archly, "that our famous actor is finally in love? I cannot think of anything else that would rob you of the appetite that never seems to alter your elegant figure."

Erastos felt his face turning red so, to hide it, he bent near her and whispered, "You may be close to the truth, Claudia, but

I beg you, do not announce it to *hoi polloi*. Could I speak to you privately?" Bemused, she agreed.

But before the last course was served, he felt a violent flutter under his ribcage when the young musician who had not left his thoughts even for a moment approached the *triclinium* with several slaves in tow. "Helena, our muse!" Gaius, already inebriated, raised his arm toward her as he boomed the welcome. "Play something for us! Pleasure us with your Greek songs." *Ye punishing gods*, Erastos thought, *she can't be an hetaera, can she?*

Claudia quickly left her couch and moved near the girl who stood away from the tables and the couches of the *triclinium*, her eyes lowered, her *kithara* held before her like a shield. Claudia whispered something in her ear, Helena nodded, and then closed her eyes. She caressed the *plektron* over the strings and the sound drifted and bounced over the mosaics of Dionysos and Pan, making them dance. The listeners were forced into quiet, something Erastos had not encountered before at the many banquets he had attended. Helena, with her voice and stillness, had imposed silence upon all, but the song was infinitely sad, a dirge. Erastos, surprised, looked at Claudia whose eyes were filling with tears. The girl's features seemed to have closed down. Gone was the mirth of the singer in the Agora. Immediately after her song ended, she turned without looking at any of the guests, the slaves closed ranks behind her, and she disappeared. Before anyone could protest, three slaves started a lively Greek song, joined by others who moved into a dance. After a stunned silence, the noise, laughter, and conversation resumed.

Claudia motioned to Erastos and he followed her to the atrium. They sat next to each other on the edge of the *impluvium,* its waters glistening under the full moon that illuminated the marbled enclosure through the wide opening in the ceiling. "So tell me, Erastos," she started, but he stopped her. "No, Claudia, you tell *me*, who is that enchanting creature you call Helena? She can't possibly be a slave, an *hetaera*?"

"Oh, you poor man," she said looking at him closely, a smile of pity on her lips. "You're smitten, aren't you? Is this the girl who has stolen your cold actor's heart?"

"I saw her last month at the agora, with your husband and the children. She was singing in a chorus. I need to know more about her, Claudia."

"I could tease you, Erastos," Claudia said, "but it would be cruel. Helena is not a slave; she's our ward, but she's spoken for. She is betrothed and, I'm afraid, deeply in love."

He tasted his disappointment but swallowed the bitterness. *The curse of the gods to an actor who excelled as a hypocrite? Eros playing tricks on me?* He tried to laugh and failed. He confessed: "I find her mysterious and appealing. What's her story?"

Claudia didn't get a chance to answer. The demands of a hostess were upon her, and now her loud husband was calling for her. She gave Erastos an apologetic smile, whispered, "Later," and returned to the *triclinium*.

Erastos left, despondent, having no answers to his questions about Helena and wondering why her song had caused Claudia to weep.

Chapter 4: Flight and Shelter

The bitter realization that Helena, the only girl who had ever captured his heart and imagination, belonged to another led Erastos through various emotions he had experienced only on behalf of others—on the stage, hidden by a mask. Now the feelings were personal, they were his, and there was no mask to hide him. His mother, Chloe, was not particularly sympathetic. In the past she had tried to arrange marriages for him with every elegant, rich young Greek woman of Corinth, and now she thought it funny that her son had been entranced by the poor ward of a wealthy Roman. But her heart was tender where he was concerned and she was a master of diversion. Intellectually curious, she kept up with all the new trends in Corinth; nothing seemed to escape her avid curiosity. A week after Erastos' visit to Claudia, his mother called him to her *tablinum*. She observed her handsome son with critical affection. He was tall but seemed taller because of his excellent posture. His hair, cut just below his ears, was dark and wavy, his eyebrows sharply defined, his eyes a deep brown that softened his rather severe expression. When he spoke, people stopped what they were doing to listen. *No wonder he was such a fine actor,* she thought with motherly pride. She avoided thinking of his age. How could he be nearly thirty when she felt so young?

"Erastos," she said, "snap out of this infatuation. There's an interesting new movement budding in Corinth. You need to pay attention. I want you to meet my friend, Phoebe, a woman of exceptional grace and virtue. Were I not so lazy, I would strive to be like her. I've known her a long while; like me, she's a widow. Do you see all these exquisite drapes? They are her work. But listen: She now calls herself a follower of a new Jewish sect, though she herself is Greek. Come, my son. You'll find what she has to say intellectually stimulating. She's coming tomorrow for a visit." Erastos, suspicious of his mother's friends, succumbed to her pleading this time. Before the next evening had ended he had made friends with Phoebe, a woman who was elegant like his own mother, but who seemed to be enveloped by a profound peace while emanating a kindness he had not encountered before. He tried to forget Helena by occupying his mind with new interests, and there was much of interest around Phoebe and her circle.

———— ⌒⌒⌒ ————

Nearly a year passed and on a beautiful winter morning, an unexpected summons from Claudia made him aware of how vividly his memory of Helena still lingered—like a vision that visited him regularly in sleep, she had remained in his life. It had been a long time since he had heard from Claudia. He remembered his friend and was troubled anew by the memory of her worried expression on the night of Helena's performance; he felt ashamed of his year-long indifference.

Claudia had written: *"Erastos, don't refuse me this time. I need the presence of my friends near me tonight. I am loath to be in the company of Gaius and his lackeys without any of my own friends near me. Send word that you accept the invitation."* And he had done so.

Despite her wealth and prominence in the community, this Roman aristocrat had not been the subject of the city's gossip. Erastos was not the only Corinthian who wondered why Claudia had married beneath her, but even the ever-curious Romans stayed away from the subject of the rich woman who had married a military man, now an infamous profligate. *Maybe they are afraid of his reprisals,* Erastos thought. He now felt bad that he had neglected her, for she had been his most generous sponsor during the years of his acting life. So he decided to accept her invitation. He dressed with his usual care, in the good taste Claudia approved of; he donned his toga as a Roman citizen and approached the large villa with some trepidation. It dominated the Lechaion Road at a point in the north where the public buildings ended and private residences began.

The house and grounds appeared as well tended as ever, the well-trained slaves unobtrusive, the guests as boisterous as before but all of them strangers to Erastos. They were not of Corinth's upper classes. The rich Romans of Corinth held on to the habit of bestowing small loans and favors to those who came to them for assistance. In many instances those so favored became acolytes of their mentor, some to the point of servility. Erastos knew that Claudia disliked those who surrounded her husband. She did not seem her usual self when she took his arm and led him to the side. "Help me keep some control over Gaius," she whispered. "He's worse than ever and his drinking bouts are frightful." It was the first time she had divulged anything about her husband to her friend, and this intimacy made him feel uncomfortable.

The dinner was up to Claudia's usual standards, but the tension in the *triclinium* could not be dispelled by culinary pleasures. "Your cook outdid himself with the pheasant this evening," Erastos told her. "I especially like the stuffing of almonds and apples." But Claudia did not comment. She was unusually quiet, and Gaius was drinking his wine neat; after Claudia's note earlier in the day, this seemed to Erastos an ominous vulgarity.

Trays of pastries with layered honey and walnuts were being brought to the table when someone called out, "Let us have music and dancing!" The host turned to his favorite slave, an odious Syrian acutely disliked by the rest of the household, whispered his instructions, and the slave disappeared. Erastos was reclining next to Claudia, so he felt her rising tension and followed the direction of her gaze. Soon, startled, he saw the slave pulling someone by the hand and, with a shock, Erastos recognized Helena. Her face was terribly pale and her lovely dark curls had been cut close to her scalp. "She's in mourning," he thought and marveled at the courage that left such a head uncovered in public.

"Let's have music, Helena, music!" Gaius called out, his words slurred. All of the diners turned toward her. Helena's solemn face was immobile; only her eyes, unseeing, glistened as with a fever. She paused for only a minute. Then she lifted up her instrument and with surprising force threw her *kithara* at the host. It spun around its tortoise shell weight and found its mark on his forehead. He bellowed like a beast. There was something wild about the girl. She looked at no one present, but her voice sliced the silence her act had created. "Gaius Marius Sylvanus, it may be with my last breath, but I will not die before I kill you." Then she turned her back on all of them and moved to the interior of the house, slaves closing in behind her. Erastos saw Alexandros running to catch up with her, and then they both disappeared.

Claudia was already up, conferring urgently with her male slaves. As the confusion spread, her slaves moved quickly to help the drunk and raging Gaius to his feet and to lead him, stumbling and cursing, toward the sleeping quarters. Claudia followed them, and Erastos found himself walking in the same direction. He avoided a stern Alexandros who was returning quickly toward the *triclinium*, sure that the steward would not allow any of the guests to slip into the interior of the villa.

Erastos moved carefully, hiding behind columns in the *peristylion*, trying not to overtake the residents, convinced now that Helena was in danger and determined not to leave her unprotected. He still could not imagine whom she was mourning and what her fury meant, but he had been deeply moved by her outburst. One of the women slaves stopped when she saw him and started to protest, but he improvised. "I'm looking for young Helena. She seemed unwell in the *triclinium*, but then I lost her. Can you tell me where to find her?" The slave, confused and frightened, hesitated, and Erastos was thinking of bribing her when a high-pitched young voice called his name. "Erastos, Erastos, we haven't seen you in months and months," the little girl cried, and Claudia's daughter ran to his arms. "When will you take me to the theater?" He picked her up and admired her. "You've grown up, Claudia Sylvana. Soon you'll be as lovely as your mother."

"But I want to be as lovely as *Helena*," she retorted and Erastos dismissed the slave girl with a motion of his head. He took the child by the hand and led her to an interior garden where a fountain was playing.

"Let's play a game," he said. "Tell me where Helena's room is and I'll promise to take you to the theater as soon as possible."

"Helena doesn't like to be disturbed, you know," the child said solemnly. "Mother says Helena hasn't been very well lately..." She paused and looked up at him. "Helena has been reading to us from Euripides, but now she always cries when she reads."

He didn't say anything. She studied his face before she relented. "As long as this is a game?" she questioned, and he nodded. She assumed a conspiratorial tone. "Across the garden, on top of those stairs, do you see the standing Greek lamp? That's her door. See, it's the third door on the right. She showed me how to count and how to find it. I sit here and watch for her when I want to surprise her."

He picked up the little girl and swung her around so that her feet touched the water of the fountain. She squealed with delight and then, when her nurse appeared, scolding her, she kissed him good night, made sure he repeated his promise for the theater visit and then, satisfied, ran to the woman.

With his eyes on that third door on the right, Erastos found a hidden spot behind the trees of the garden and waited. He was now filled with a profound concern for the young woman who looked troubled beyond her years, for the desperation in her eyes and the hatred in her voice when she addressed the inebriated Gaius. A girl in that condition would be likely to do anything, and he was sure it would be dangerous only to herself.

Hours seemed to pass while the slaves rushed from the atrium to the interior chambers; doors and curtains opened and closed on both stories of the villa, but his eyes never left that third door on the right. Hidden behind a clump of blossoming almonds, he stood still. Torches remained lit on key points of the porticos that ringed the second-story bedrooms, since slaves worked at night doing the cleaning up. Finally, all was quiet.

He was having difficulty keeping his eyes open when a sudden gust that almost extinguished the light of the tall Greek lamp alerted him to movement and he ran from his hiding place to the stairs leading to Helena's door. She emerged from her room as though in a trance and moved quickly away from him toward three wide marble steps that had been hidden from the garden. She was moving quietly, a white shadow. On noiseless sandals she climbed the steps, and Erastos followed.

No one else was about. An eerie silence covered the upper quarters. She paused briefly before a door covered by heavy drapes. She pulled them back, opened the door, and the soft light from an interior torch filtered through the diaphanous curtains that hung above a massive bed. She slipped in behind them, so Erastos did the same. Helena pulled something from beneath her *peplos*, and he saw a dagger glisten in the light of the nearest torch. She lifted her right arm holding the dagger and then bent her head to look down. Close behind her now, he did the same. They both stared at the man's body sprawled before them, face down. There was no question that it was Gaius, but something else was also apparent. If Helena had gone there to stab him, she had already failed. Someone else had been in this same room before her and had succeeded. He sensed her shock and felt the tension in her body as she opened her mouth to scream. Instinctively, he raised his right hand to cover her mouth, while his left circled her waist from behind. "Don't be afraid," he whispered in her ear. "Come with me," and he propelled her away from the canopy and the bloodied bed.

Chapter 5: Phoebe

She made no effort to resist. The man's urgent whisper held no menace. Helena let her arms go limp, he uncovered her mouth, whipped the toga off his shoulders and head and threw it on her trembling body. He took her by the arm and, as they moved together down the marble steps to the lower level, he loosened the dagger free of her clutching hand and stuck it in his belt. The moon, not yet full, was luminous in the cloudless sky, and she saw their elongated shadows on the marble of the atrium floor. No one else seemed to be awake. She wanted to turn, to see who was leading her away from the hated man's sleeping quarters, but she was too dispirited to make the effort. He was moving her from column to column in the *peristylion*. She was surprised at the secrecy, since she was sure that she was being led to her death, but even surprise took an effort. Soon they passed through the common rooms to the vestibule and the front gate. Before they reached the door, he put his mouth to her ear and whispered, "Don't be afraid. I will put my arm around you to fool the gatekeeper. No harm will come to you. Now, do as I ask and pretend." She must have nodded, for he raised the *sinus* to drape it over her hair, like a hood; it covered her face while the rest of the wide garment hung heavy over her body, the end of it dragging the ground.

The man put his left arm around her waist and then, reaching around with his right hand, he pressed her head to his shoulder. "You're a good performer," he whispered. "Try." Her surprise increased, but she did as she was told. His rapid, steady gait changed to the weaving, unsteady one of a drunk, and they moved together to the outer gate.

"Ho, there, Tiresias!" he called out to the guard in a voice that carried, and she thought, *I know this voice.* The guard roused himself, guffawed, and then quickly touched his forehead. This was her moment to escape, for she knew the gatekeeper, but she made no effort to call out to him, to alert him that she was being abducted. It was too late for her. She had lived for revenge for the past three months, and now, having lost the last reason that was keeping her alive, she did not care what might happen next.

They were now beyond the torches of the villa's exterior and walking rapidly south on the Lechaion Road. Because of the moon's light there were still people out on the streets of Corinth and the wheeled traffic, allowed only at night, was making passage dangerous. When they reached the North Market the man pulled her into a grove of pines and stopped. *He's making sure no one else can see us,* she thought, as she waited for death to come. He faced her for the first time and pushed the edge of the *sinus* to the crown of her head so that in the moonlight she must have looked as bloodless as she felt.

"Helena," he said, "I'll not ask you why you wanted to kill him. But I will ask you to try to save yourself. Will you try?" Her body was limp; she was barely standing up. For some reason, maybe because she was surrounded by pines, she remembered the runners Atalanta and Hippomenes, a favorite myth, and she smiled in that forgotten cave inside her that held memories of happiness. The man's large hands were still supporting her at the waist, holding her up. She could smell his anxiety together with the sharp aroma of the pines. *What a strange abductor,* she thought. His voice, even in an urgent whisper, was beautifully modulated, vaguely familiar. If she cared, she would try to remember where she had heard it before. But she did not care. If he let go of her, she would crumple to the ground and lie there until they found her. He shook her gently. "Helena, are you listening to me? Show that you hear me."

She now made the effort and tried to focus her eyes. He was being kind. Maybe there was kindness among men. She dreamed of being with her father, having a discussion about the possibility of kindness in men, but the dream would not stay with her. She had no strength left even for thought. She tried asking, "Who are you?" but opening her mouth and forcing the words out took too much energy. "Come," he said, "we can't linger here. Trust me. I will take you to a friend." She nodded this time, and taking this for an agreement, he half covered her face again. Then he took her by the hand and pulled her among the trees that adorned the public places. She sensed a renewed urgency in his touch and forced her feet to move next to his own as they skirted the *stoas* of the great city.

She had lost all sense of time and direction. They were now in a part of the city she did not recognize—no temples or statues here—in a street with houses that were fronted by shops. He stopped, put her in front of him as though to shield her from curious eyes and knocked a rhythmic beat on the door—*ta-ta-tá, ta-tá.* When it opened, he pushed her inside, slipped in behind her, and closed the door. *This is the end*, she thought, *he's going to sell me as a slave.*

A woman, ready for bed but wrapped in a long *stola*, was holding a lamp. She glanced at Helena with concern, and then, lifting the lamp higher, she raised questioning eyes to the man.

He spoke. "Peace to you, Phoebe. This is Helena. She's in need of shelter for the night."

The woman Phoebe now looked closely at Helena's face and then she cried, "Oh, my poor *korē*. You are ready to collapse. Come, come. I'll look after her, Erastos."

Taking her by the hand she led Helena to the interior of the house, past a small but peaceful atrium, into the rear, where a series of doors led into alcoves and bedrooms. She opened one of the doors and pulled her to an alcove with a bed. "Lie down, Helena," she said, and the girl felt the warm, kind voice touch her where she was raw. "Lie down, and I will send water for you to wash and something for you to sleep in."

She placed the lamp on a ledge in the room; its light fell on the woman's face, and Helena saw Phoebe's long brown braid and kind eyes, and for the first time that night she believed that she was not about to die. Then the door closed, and Helena was alone. "They are either fools or spirits," she said aloud to the lamp and collapsed on the bed.

Only a little later, at the slight sound, she roused from the sleep that must have enveloped her instantly to see a young woman entering, a basin of water in her hands and towels and a gown over her shoulder. Behind her a second girl carried a tray. She laid it on the floor and disappeared. The first servant approached cautiously. "I'll help you," she said, and Helena recognized her Makedonian accent.

Helena pointed to the tray. "Water," she whispered and heard her own voice crack. The girl rushed to put a cup to her lips and Helena drank with gratitude. Then, exhausted, she fell back on the bed.

"Alexandra," the girl said and pointed to herself. "I'll wash off the dust and then you sleep, eh?" Helena submitted to the gentle urging. Alexandra stripped her, washed her quickly and expertly paying special attention to Helena's dusty feet, and slipped a clean gown over the girl's head. But as she was covering her with a soft lamb's wool blanket she realized that Helena was trembling violently. Alexandra held her for a few minutes until the trembling passed, and after adding another blanket, she moved to the lamp. She made as if to put it out but Helena cried, "No, no," and again her voice sounded alien to her ears. She wanted to ask many questions but could not make the necessary effort. The lamp remained lit. Helena closed her eyes and was instantly asleep again.

She's swimming in a deep sleep. Near dawn, the dream visits her again.

She's in the *gymnasion* with the other girls; holding a towel diagonally behind her back she rubs her skin that glistens after the bath. She feels exultant. Her father, a brilliant teacher and trainer at the *gymnasion*, insists that the girls' side as well as the boys' should benefit from the training of the body together with the enlightenment of the mind.

"Oh, Helena," her friend Hermione trills, "young Ares has eyes for no one but you-ou." All the girls laugh, and Helena smiles the secret smile of a girl in love.

"And I have eyes for no one but hi-im," she retorts and the girls give out a hoot of joy.

The scene changes. They are all together, boys and girls, in the fine large *scholē* on the other side of the *gymnasion* where her beloved teacher-father is reciting Homer to them. Helena's lips move with the rhythm of the ancient words, her mind full of images of fleet-footed Greeks, of races and triumphs long gone.

Across from her, Ares ignores Homer and turns his dark eyes on her. She feels his eyes but cannot turn her own to look at him. She's making every effort to see him, but the dream keeps her from turning her head. She struggles to wake, to see Ares again, to see the lean, strong face with the fiery eyes, the beloved face. But she cannot.

The dream changes: She's now in the house—the fancy Roman villa of the Sylvanus family—the children in her charge asleep, and, free after the long day to welcome Ares, she is running to the gate to meet him. She starts to embrace him, when the dream again stops her. Her longing is choking her. She tries again and again to touch the beloved face, but her hands cannot reach him. She cries in her sleep, but the sound comes out as a whimper.

———— ❦ ————

When Phoebe puts a cool hand on her brow Helena is sobbing. "It's a dream, Helena," she hears the deep voice saying over and over until it registers, and Helena gasps herself awake.

"Ah, if only I could…" and then, realizing where she is, she stops. She sees Phoebe and she whispers, "Thank you," and closes her eyes to hide her despair.

The dream has filled her with a longing that she fears will never be assuaged. Still, she would return to the dream if she could. When it does, each time it visits her, she hopes, "This time it will be different, this time I will touch him."

Now, as she closes her eyes in this house where a strange peace covers everything, she thinks, "It's because I did not avenge him; that's why he eludes me." And then the tears come hot and bitter. She tastes them. She knows she's awake and hides her face in the bedding to muffle the sound, even though Phoebe has left the room. "*Aï*, Ares, *Aï*, my love," she wails as the Trojan women did in the play, and she gives herself over to unrestrained weeping.

———— ❦ ————

When Helena woke up she did not recognize the room, and the bed felt different from her own. She saw the tray on the floor and, feeling the dryness in her throat, she sat up to drink the water. She noticed the unfamiliar gown that covered her and then her own elegant tunic and *peplos* folded at the foot of the bed. She sat up, baffled.

She had no idea where she was but there was no doubt that she was famished. She drank more water, ate the almonds that were inviting her from the tray, and then she opened the door to peek out.

A young woman called out the joyful greeting in Greek, "*Khêrai*," and Helena looked in her direction wondering when she would feel joyful again.

"Where am I?" she asked.

"You're in Phoebe-the-Weaver's home. I'm Alexandra. You saw me last night, remember?" When Helena didn't respond, Alexandra offered, "Stay there. I'll fetch Phoebe for you."

Helena waited to see who would appear, but as soon as Phoebe spoke to her, she recognized the warmth of the voice and remembered the kind face that had welcomed her. How long ago?

"What am I doing here?" she asked. "How long have I slept?"

Phoebe stretched out her hands and clasped Helena's cold fingers. "Come," she said, "we'll have a meal and then you can ask me questions."

The girl was grateful that Phoebe guessed her hunger. When they reached the atrium she saw a tripod table laden with fruit, olives, cheeses, freshly baked bread, and honey. Wondering when she had eaten last, she dipped the bread in the aromatic honey, put it in her mouth, and listened to Phoebe who said in Greek now, "You slept through the night and most of this day. You must have been so very, very tired."

Helena continued to eat, unable to remember how she had arrived at this house but, dreading the memories that might creep back, she ignored them. Phoebe touched the girl's short curls. "My poor *korē*," she whispered. "You're in mourning."

Helena, grateful to be in a Greek household, still didn't dare speak, and Phoebe allowed the silence to linger. Finally she asked, "Do you remember anything about last night?"

Helena suddenly blurted out, "I dreamt of Ares again," and her eyes filled with tears.

"You did have a troubling dream. But do you remember anything before the dream?"

Helena shook her head as if to clear it. She lowered her face onto her open palms and spoke through her fingers. "I remember running, running through the city. There was someone with me, but who? I didn't know him. Did he bring me here?"

"Yes. You don't know him? You don't remember seeing him before?" Phoebe spoke with exaggerated care.

"No."

"His name is Erastos." She searched Helena's face. "He was Corinth's most famous actor once."

"Ah, that explains the voice." Something was coming back to her, a man calling out, "Ho, Tiresias!" But of all names, why that one? Why Tiresias? Was he playacting when he called the name of the great seer in the Oedipus story? And then a voice whispering in the dark, a familiar voice—

"You look puzzled," Phoebe interrupted her thoughts. "Did you recognize his voice?"

"I thought I'd heard it before, but I can't put a face to it. What was he doing with me?"

"Do you remember anything that happened before you heard his voice?"

Helena felt afraid, and Phoebe must have sensed it. "Erastos is my good friend," she explained quickly, speaking in short sentences as if Helena were a child. "He's an important man in our city. A good man. He brought you here. Then you saw Alexandra and Evniki, girls of my own household. Weavers like me; they work with me. Would you like to see our workshop later? Good. For now, know that you are safe in our home, Helena."

She saw that the girl was listening carefully but still looked baffled. Phoebe continued. "Yesterday, Erastos thought you were in danger. I don't know why but I trust his judgment. It was well after midnight when he brought you here. You were safe with him. You must know that by now. Please stay here until he returns. Will you do this for me?"

Helena heard all the words but only one made sense— danger. She looked at her hands, her palms open. "Danger?" she asked, something nagging at her but still unclear.

"Will you stay?" Phoebe asked again.

Helena shrugged. "You want me to stay here until this man Erastos returns. Yes. I have nowhere else to go. But I will not go with him."

Phoebe seemed satisfied and invited Helena to see the sprawling house. It was open and comfortable, devoid of mosaics and the luxuries Romans of wealth favored. Like most Greek and Roman homes in the rebuilt city of Corinth, only the front door opened to the street. The rest of the house looked inward, to the atrium, an open space lit from above by an opening in the roof. In Phoebe's home there was a small garden underneath the opening and Helena recognized edible plants among the flowers. On the far side of the atrium, Phoebe had placed stools and small tables where guests could sit in comfort. There were no statues and no mosaics. This didn't surprise the girl, but the total absence of a household altar with the usual *lares* and *penates* did. For a moment she recalled the stark simplicity of her father's house, but she pushed that thought away as soon as it appeared. The *triclinium* was filled with low tables and stools instead of the elaborate couches she had despised in Claudia's home. The rest of the atrium was lined with small rooms where Helena assumed that Phoebe's many guests must sleep.

The front of the *domus* was lined with *tabernae*, the small rooms that served as shops in many Roman households.

At Phoebe's these were workshops and showrooms where beautifully woven cloths were displayed and then sold. One tall warp-weighted loom almost filled the main workshop and there were many baskets, *kalathoi*, used for sorting the wool; in some of the baskets the wool was still rough and un-spun, but the rest were filled to overflowing with lovely, soft-spun skeins of different colors. The smells attracted Helena, but it was the sound of the shuttle being rushed through the threads of the weft and the *knock-knock* of the heddle as the weaver changed directions in the patterns that gave her unexpected pleasure. She stood and watched Evniki, a tall, reserved young woman with long light hair, who seemed totally absorbed in what she was doing; Helena was mesmerized by the movement of the girl's hands, of her knee as it hit the heddle and the even rhythm of the weaving. Out of nowhere, a memory arrived and she felt a sharp longing for her *kithara*, a longing that seemed to belong to another life.

"I'm a musician," she said aloud as if announcing it to herself, and Phoebe smiled. "And a very good one, we hear. Maybe later you will play for us?"

Helena could not respond. She stood still, focusing on Evniki's hands. After a while, she approached the weaver and asked, "May I try this? My mother didn't live long enough to teach me any of the womanly arts. Is it very difficult?"

The Makedonian girl turned and took Helena's right hand into her own. She guided it through the threads. She showed her the difference between the horizontal weft and vertical warp and demonstrated how her knee moved the heddle side to side to change the direction of the weave.

After a while, with a minimum of words, Evniki urged Helena to try it for herself and she started practicing moving the heddle.

"Now," Evniki suggested, "take the shuttle and guide it through the threads from right to left; try not to get it tangled."

Then she showed her the pattern she was following, a winding shape that looked like a river running through the length of it, and explained how she used the different colors without tangling them. Helena was pleased that it resembled the coordination required for playing an instrument. She would have no trouble following this kind of divided attention since making music had taught her to perform different kinds of activities simultaneously. She could have stayed there the rest of the day, but Evniki had work to do.

Phoebe took her to an adjoining room where two smaller looms stood side by side. "Would you like for me to teach you how to follow a pattern?" she asked, and Helena nodded, pleased. She found the movement soothing and was grateful that the effort of following the design occupied her mind enough to push the questions and an indefinable worry to the background. She could not remember the day and night that had just passed. Except for the running. She was used to running, having been an athlete once, a victor in the Isthmian Games, since Father had insisted that she train like a boy. The recollection troubled her, for suddenly she was in a copse of pines again, a voice was whispering urgently to her, but the only words she remembered were Atalanta and Hippomenes, the runners, and the memory of those two lovers stung her eyes with new tears. She smelled the strong resin of the pines and wondered if memory held actual smells. *If only I could ask Father.*

Helena continued her attempts at weaving, and when evening arrived she started feeling comfortable with the movement, with the glance at the very simple pattern Phoebe had drawn for her and the feel of her fingers on the shuttle in pleasant harmony. She had picked up the motion easily enough and the rhythm was something she felt, something that dwelt deep within her. For a few moments she would be almost content, and then something would interrupt the rhythm, and that vague darkness in her mind, a weight that felt like grief, would drop on her again and she would lose all contentment. Phoebe stayed close by, meeting the occasional customer in the other rooms, never letting anyone come close to Helena. And for that the girl was grateful.

Once a fleeting thought entered her mind as she listened to Phoebe's warm, low-pitched voice: *This must be what it feels like to have a mother,* and the new thought startled her.

Chapter 6:
Paul, Prisca and Aquila

On the day after the strangest night of his life, as he came to think of it, Erastos awoke surprised that he had intervened in another's life. He visited the baths, his mind occupied by Helena. He was pummeled and massaged, moving quickly from the *tepidarium* to the *caldarium* and then jumping into the *frigidarium*. "The Romans did something right with the procession of the bath temperatures," he thought as he always did after a visit to the baths. It was his habit to separate what was Roman from what was Greek, eager always to give credit where it was due. Soon he felt awake and invigorated. He dressed and started his usual walk through the city, visiting the markets on his authority as a new *aedilis*, all the while his mind active, trying to understand what had caused him to interfere in someone else's life the night before, even if that someone was Helena. After the years of detachment he had perfected as an actor, it was unlike him to interfere. But then he remembered Paul, Prisca, and Aquila and knew that they would not have hesitated to rescue a person in danger. He decided to visit them.

Erastos still spent the nights at his mother's house, but he hadn't even considered taking Helena there. His mother's house was more luxurious than Phoebe's but Phoebe was a follower of The Way, so the decision had been easy. He had not wanted Helena to be reminded of her previous life. His mother, Chloe, lived in a style similar to that of fashionable Roman women. Erastos paid a quick visit to her quarters to reassure her that he was well, and then he made his way through the open places of Corinth, beyond the temples to the *stoas*, and into the grid of narrow streets that were filled with shops, *tabernae*, and the homes of those who owned these businesses. But there was only one business that interested him—Aquila's workshop.

It was situated in a row reserved for leatherworkers who cut, tooled, and sewed leather bindings that would later be used to make tents, pillows, seats, and many other necessary implements used widely in the commercial city and her trade partners. Aquila and Prisca, his wife, lived behind the shop; these days they employed and housed a man by the name of Paul. It was he who held Erastos' interest—a small man physically but with a sharp intelligence that startled. His hosts seemed to admire him immensely. Aquila was dark and taciturn and Prisca was sunny and bubbling with good humor and lively conversation; they spent their hours either listening to Paul or in deep conversation with him, but their hands were never idle.

Erastos approached and saw Paul sitting near the door of the shop, bent over his leather strips, his quick fingers seemingly working on their own, for it was obvious that his mind was on the two men who were watching him work. Erastos greeted him warmly, overcome with affection for this good man. Paul's smile brought a light that was unearthly to his features which, when in repose, looked sad.

"Ah, Erastos, my friend. Come and meet two of our supporters and friends: Stephanas and Achaicus, brothers from the *ekklesia*. Friends, this is Erastos, one of Corinth's famous men."

Erastos greeted the two, finding Stephanas warm and friendly, Achaicus much more reserved. "Merely a public servant," he said to them quickly, "an *oikonómos* of the city."

"Ah, but he has been Corinth's most acclaimed actor also," Paul added with a mischievous grin as Achaicus and Stephanas showed their surprise. "Strange for a Jew to associate with people of the theater," Achaicus commented and immediately took his leave.

"You must excuse my friend Achaicus," Paul said, laughing. "He is a new convert and he tends to condemn everything that belonged to his old life. He will find his balance. Stephanas here, my sweet brother in Christ, is one of my first children in this city together with all his household."

They chatted while Prisca served refreshments; then Stephanas made his departure, and Erastos was left with his friends. He told them of his adventure in rescuing Helena and then asked Paul the question that had troubled him since the strange night: "The *intent* to kill—how does that compare with the deed?"

"Ah," Paul said with utter seriousness now, "we come to the intentions of the heart! How can we control them but through grace? The will is not enough." Erastos liked the word grace, so beautiful in the Greek—*kharis*—but Paul was meaning something beyond the word's definition; what was it? Before he had a chance to ask him, Paul continued: "This desire for revenge in your ancient culture: is it very strong?"

"It's the chief motivation in many of our tragedies," the former actor explained. "A most powerful undercurrent. Yet, our Greek ancestors understood that revenge was not the right of human beings; they knew that the gods had the final word, with Nemesis."

"'Vengeance is mine, says the Lord,'" Paul interrupted.

"Even my people, who understand so much about the one God, still cling to the retributive saying of 'an eye for an eye.'"

"But the Lord Yeesous has rescued us from that kind of thinking." Prisca entered the conversation eagerly. "Erastos, when he taught in Palestine, Yeesous would repeat these ancient sayings and then he would follow them with these words: '*But I say to you, Do good to those who hurt you.*' You see the difference, my dear friend? Forgiveness and grace. Forgiveness and grace. Forgiveness is ours. Grace is God's gift. Only these would redeem and free your friend Helena."

"Does she recognize me as her friend? No, I doubt it." Erastos was rather sidetracked at this point. "But, listen, Prisca. Would you make an effort to speak to her? Get to know her? Yet on you, dear Paul, I dare not impose—" But before he finished Paul had lifted his hand. "I will speak to her at Phoebe's, on the first day of the week."

Relieved, Erastos set out to visit Phoebe. He was now responsible for Helena and had no idea how to proceed, but it lifted his burden to know that three additional good people also cared for her.

On the following day, when Erastos arrived at her door Phoebe kept him in the front room and spoke softly. "Helena doesn't remember what caused her flight. Or is it she doesn't want to remember? I'm not certain. She says that a man urged her to run but doesn't remember why. I don't think she *wants* to remember, so you must be very careful, Erastos. She has said nothing about herself, except what came up incidentally—that she's a musician and that her mother died too early. But she's young and healthy and looks rested. I wonder how long it had been since the girl had eaten? She was famished."

"Well, I'll take it as a good sign," he said, "but, Phoebe, here's the crucial question—what made her want to kill the Roman? And what comes next?"

Phoebe had already made her decision. "She can stay

here if you agree, Erastos. She has started learning something about the loom and she catches on so quickly. I could offer her employment. Do you think she'll find it insulting? I know nothing about her background. What's your opinion?"

He brightened. "Something to do with her hands, hmm. Maybe this is a solution for now. Thank you, Phoebe. You're a good friend."

"We are here to love and serve one another," she reminded him, speaking as if this was the natural way with everyone, although Erastos knew that it was not. With her usual calm efficiency she led the way to the smaller workshop.

Helena was bent over the pattern Phoebe had drawn for her and did not see them. When Phoebe approached her, Helena lifted her eyes and looked at her and then, startled, glanced at Erastos. He was handsome and fashionable, an attractive man, but the quick glance she gave him was hostile. "Who are you?" she asked him abruptly, sounding like a frightened child. "Do I know you?"

"Did I startle you?" he apologized. "I'm Erastos. I was the one who brought you to Phoebe."

Helena averted her eyes and returned to her weaving. So Phoebe, surprised at the girl's rudeness, laid a gentle hand on her arm. "Helena, would you stop for a while and speak with us? Soon you will not have enough light anyway. Come, there's nothing to be alarmed about."

Helena secured the shuttle among the threads and followed Phoebe to the rear of the house. There was a small garden behind the atrium with a few scattered stools among the plants, and they sat there, the women side by side, Erastos facing them. The silence was awkward, so Phoebe said, "Helena, isn't there something you would like to ask Erastos?" But the girl turned to her mentor and said in a strained voice,

"I don't know this man, Phoebe. I recognize his voice, but I'm troubled that I don't know him. Why was I with him at night?"

Phoebe looked to Erastos for help, but his eyes were on Helena. They were both quiet, he intent on her and she avoiding his eyes. Then he seemed to have an inspiration.

"When you were younger, did you attend the theater?" he ventured, redirecting her attention.

She brightened slightly. "I *loved* the theater. Is that where I heard your voice?"

"It's very possible." He smiled. "You don't remember my face because you have not seen me without my mask."

"You're an actor," she said, unsurprised. "Were you wearing a mask the other night?" Baffled, he turned to look at Phoebe. He mouthed, "Is she making fun of me?" but Phoebe sensed that this girl was not used to subterfuge. He must have come to the same conclusion, for he decided to treat the question seriously.

"No, I was not wearing a mask and we were not at the theater. It was already dark, remember? However, earlier, when it was still light, I was a guest at Claudia's dinner." A question mark hung there between them.

Helena shivered but remained silent, and Erastos looked at Phoebe, who shrugged. He said quietly, changing tactics once again. "Helena, I'm assuming you don't want to return to Claudia's," and the girl turned to Phoebe again, a pleading in her voice making her sound very young.

"Did you say I may stay here for a while?"

Phoebe took the girl's cold hand and held it. "You may stay here as long as you like. If you want to learn weaving, the girls and I would enjoy your help and your company. It's an honorable craft, Helena, and you will be very well compensated."

Helena's large gray eyes were wet with tears that stayed on the edge of her lids but did not overflow. She said, still in her little-girl voice, "I feel safe here. It's peaceful. There is peace in your house, Phoebe."

Erastos, feeling left out, stood up to leave. Abruptly, Helena turned to him. "Tiresias," she said, as if remembering, now sounding like her adult self. "You called out the name of the ancient prophet that night. Why the seer? Why, if as you say, we were not at the theater?"

Perplexed, Erastos stopped. He looked at Phoebe as if to ask, *How can she not remember where we were?* And then he laughed as he understood. "Ah, yes, the gatekeeper at Claudia's villa. I call him by that name because most of the time he pretends not to see, even though he sees everything. He's a Greek slave who understands the meaning of the name. It's a joke we have between us."

But Helena was already walking back to her room. Erastos shook his head in puzzlement. "I don't understand. Does she hate men, or just me?"

"She's suffering some inner torment," Phoebe told him. "She probably has no idea what she's doing or why. It seems obvious the girl is in deep mourning."

"I still don't know anything about her—why she's in mourning, who died, why she's not married. You know, she was betrothed a year ago. At least, that's what Claudia told me. But I did speak to Paul and Prisca about the night's adventure. They will make every effort to get to know her." He opened his palms in apology. "I seem to lay my burdens at your feet, Phoebe."

She smiled. "They are light burdens, Erastos. Helena is very easy to like." And then she bid him farewell. "Until the first day of the week," she promised, and he seemed more hopeful.

Chapter 7: Claudia

On the following day, more troubled than he was willing to admit, Erastos made his way to Claudia's villa. The surroundings were strangely quiet for a place that had recently known violent death. Though Claudia had hired no mourners, the body was on display in the atrium on a remarkably elegant bier. "He was very fond of luxuries," Claudia quipped, and Erastos was shocked at her self-control. She left the visitors, mostly clients of her dead husband, to the care of Alexandros who would allow them, briefly, to proclaim their grief as ostentatiously as they liked, and she led him to her *tablinum*. "Sit with me," she said. "If anyone else pretends to mourn him, I'll throw him out."

He stared at her. "Who killed him, Claudia? Have you found out?"

She didn't avoid his eyes. "Who would *not* want him dead?" she asked bitterly, and Erastos looked around him in alarm. There were always eavesdroppers in Roman homes. She continued in the same tone.

"Don't worry, Erastos, my name is not Clytemnestra. My

husband killed himself. Though I will confess to you that I did not try to prevent him from doing so. In fact I *urged* it on him as the only honorable alternative to what his life had become. That self-righteous hypocrite, Livy, would have been proud of me."

Now Erastos was truly alarmed. "What are you saying, Claudia?"

"Only that my husband had dishonored himself and me and deserved to die. Once, he was a brave soldier in Claudius' army. Then wealth, drink, and women brought him to what you witnessed the other night. All of Corinth knew of the shame he brought on me—did you not? Suicide was the only way out for him. This is the Roman way, after all. I had stopped tolerating his excesses, and that night, after his final banquet, I made it clear that I would no longer protect him from public shame. Then I left him and ordered the slaves away from him. I'm surprised he carried through with it, however. Death by his own hand was the most honorable of his acts. After the disgrace of the last few years of his life…. But I still find it hard to believe that he went through with it."

Her voice was cool, its edges hard, and Erastos was speechless. She asked, "Do you know where Helena is?" to which he nodded and she hurried on, "Tell her to stay away. It's better that she is not seen for a while. His friends are thugs, and several of them were present that night."

But now Erastos was angry. "Claudia, when you were urging your husband to kill himself, did it not occur to you that all the blame would fall on Helena? After her outburst at dinner, didn't you worry about it?"

Claudia shrugged. "At that moment I didn't think of the consequences to her. All I could think of was that I could no longer remain married to him."

He kept remembering Helena's fevered eyes, her utter despair when she was ordered to sing, but he still could not bring himself to ask the questions that troubled him.

She said quietly, "You and I, Erastos, we've known each other for a long while, haven't we? Like a true Greek you cared only for the arts, and I was there to supply the funds for your plays. Yet, you still don't know anything about my background. I am after all as private as you are." She was quiet, looking in the distance. "In Thessaloniki, where I grew up, I was doted on by my excellent father who insisted that I retain full control of my wealth. You can guess why: so that Gaius would not get his hands on it. I wish I had recognized that my father knew more than I did. I was so damnably proud."

She paused and her vulnerability stunned him. He had thought her impervious to the doubts that assailed others. She resumed her telling as if this was something she needed to do. "After we married and moved to Corinth, I still thought myself in love, so I made a terrible mistake. I was generous with my husband and let him have tremendous amounts for his various business ventures. I didn't know until recently that he was a *usurer*." She spat out the word. "He had been lending my money to others—at exorbitant rates. When they could not pay him back, he confiscated properties and lands while I went about promoting the arts in the city. You see the irony? My shame? This ill-begotten money he gambled away. He could never do anything in moderation, you see. Gaius was a person who should never have had money. For this I blame myself. Had it not been for Alexandros' wise management, I would have ended up destitute."

Erastos was so surprised, he could not stir. He saw that her hands were trembling but he didn't dare touch her. She resumed with a struggle. "Helena's father was one of the unfortunate ones. He had borrowed money from Gaius to establish an academy for the benefit of his beloved Helena and her betrothed, Ares. The venture failed. When Gaius took from him all he had, including his honor, the poor man committed suicide."

He saw the tears in her eyes, her stricken face, and tried to find the right words. But years of thinking in the words of the great masters had robbed him of the ability to ask personal questions. How much of what she told him was known to Helena? Before he found the courage to speak he heard the sound—the keys clanging against the *zona* of the chief steward, Alexandros, and Claudia turned her attention from Erastos.

"My lady Claudia," the steward started, looking at Erastos as if to dismiss him, "the *praeficae* have arrived and they refuse to deal with me."

Claudia sighed and stood up. Erastos took her hands in his and said quietly, "You will certainly need *praeficae* for *this* funeral," and at the mention of the hired mourners she smiled briefly and nodded to Alexandros who then walked with Erastos to the exit. Helping him with the folds of the toga, the old Makedon slave whispered: "You need to know: we paid them off." Erastos turned around, but the face of the slave was impassive. Fussing with the folds of the toga he continued, with no change in his voice. "All of them here that night, except for you, sir, were the master's clients; owed him vast amounts of money. Yesterday morning I paid them off to earn their silence. Claudia forgave their debts." Erastos waited. Alexandros stopped folding the toga. "They won't talk about Helena to anyone else. I have their secrets and they know it. No one in this household would hurt our Helena." He turned, and Erastos was left with his mouth open. He then walked to the gatekeeper. "Tell me, Tiresias, how long has Alexandros been with Gaius Marius Sylvanus?"

"With *him*, sir? No, no! He's been with the lady Claudia's family since before she was born. She trusts him more than her own father, maybe. And there's no better mistress in all of Greece."

And at that he stood at attention as another guest approached. So Erastos departed. It was only later, when he had reached the Agora, that the thought struck him, *What happened to the man Helena was to marry? I now know about the father, but what happened to the one who matters more?*

Chapter 8:
Who Are These People?

Helena contemplated the third day of her odd new life as from a distance. She had refused to think of anything that had come before and persuaded herself that she had forgotten those last crucial hours at the villa and afterwards, but now she could not help wondering about the days that lay ahead. *What am I doing in Phoebe's peaceful home? What do I know about these people except that they are kind and not ostentatious? I trust Phoebe without question; I cannot do otherwise.* She wouldn't allow herself to think that a time was coming when she would have to leave Phoebe.

They had stayed up late, talking, but Helena had again avoided revealing much about herself, while Phoebe answered all her questions. The good woman made no attempt to intrude on the girl's reticence but seemed willing to interpret her own world to her guest.

Helena had been thinking about her father; more than ever his presence was very near, and in some strange way this had to do with Phoebe, but why?

She had asked about something else: "Phoebe, you obviously are a pious person, but there are no votive places in your home. No altar?"

Phoebe smiled, "Oh, yes, but it's invisible. We are filled with love for God's Son, Yeesous. Our whole life is an altar to him."

"Are you talking about a new god?" Helena asked, curious about superstitions. She watched Phoebe carefully. *She answers every question with deliberate care and thoughtfulness. My father would have been very impressed.*

Phoebe said, "He is not a *new* god. We see him as the full expression of the One God."

"Do you mean like the *Nous* of the Greeks, of Sokrates' interpretation?"

"The understanding of *Nous* captured part of God's essence, yes, but for the Hebrews, God is the Creator, and at the same time a personal God who cares for them, for us. We who follow The Way find the character of God—who God truly is—we find this God revealed in the person of Yeesous. The name means Savior. Here's the difference, Helena. This Yeesous actually lived in Palestine, not long ago."

"Lived how, like an Olympian, appearing in human form for a short while?"

"No, he's not an apparition, Helena, nor is he anything like an Olympian. Yeesous actually lived as a human being, *anthropos,* in a specific place—Nazareth. It's in the province of Judea. He was born of a human woman, grew up as a child within a family, and when the time came he called a group of followers to himself, like a true Hebrew rabbi, and taught them about the heart of God."

"Oh, I like that. The heart of God. So he was like Sokrates. A teacher with students. But where is this Yeesous now?"

"They killed him for doing good, for saying that he knew God as his own father."

"How sad," Helena whispered and felt a terrible pity for

a good man being punished unjustly. The conversation had now entered a weighted realm that filled her with the most profound sorrow. She said quietly, "Six months ago I would not have believed such cruelty. Now, I do. And it sounds a bit like the story of Sokrates and his unjust death."

"You're quick to see the connection in these stories, Helena. Maybe what we know of mythology and the understanding of our wisest Greeks, maybe that was a preparation for what was to come? Like hints of the eternal? I'm not wise enough to know."

"Hints of the eternal? What an astonishing thought. Yes. I would like to think on this. But how are we to know?"

"How are we to know? We who follow Yeesous have one way of knowing. You see, Helena, there are eyewitnesses who knew Yeesous of Nazareth, and many of them are still living; I find that so assuring and encouraging. My friend Priscilla can tell you about them. These eyewitnesses testify that Yeesous was blameless, that he never hurt anyone, that he did good wherever he went. What I understand from all the stories is this: he was accused by his own religious people of blaspheming because he claimed to know God—apparently this is forbidden to the Hebrews—and he was killed by the Romans for undermining the emperor. He proclaimed a new kingdom, you see."

"A new kingdom? In the midst of a Roman province? How extraordinary. He must have been exceptionally courageous." Phoebe smiled in agreement, and Helena said, "I'd like to know more about this kingdom. Obviously he did not succeed as king; otherwise we would have heard of it."

"So it seems. Those who didn't know him said that he failed. But those who know him consider his death a victory."

"A paradox. And your tenses are unusual, Phoebe. I'm sure you'll tell me more about his life, but how did he die?"

"In the most horrible of deaths—the Roman crucifixion."

Helena felt her breath leaving her chest as if someone had

dealt her a vicious blow. She found that she could not endure hearing the details. Phoebe said, "Early tomorrow morning, on the first day of the week, those of us who love Yeesous will gather to remember him. Our friends will come here before they go to their various activities. We do this once a week. Would you like to attend? There are a couple of people I'm most anxious for you to get to know, and they would like to know you."

How could she say no to Phoebe? "If they are anything like you, Phoebe, I will want to know them."

───── ∽∂∾ ─────

And now it's early dawn. Movements all over the house wake Helena up. She stands close enough to the atrium to see the people coming in, but keeps herself at the entrance of an alcove, hidden behind a drape. The sky is still dark, the stars bright through the opening over the atrium. Torches attached to the surrounding walls light the way for the newcomers. She looks at the people with a curiosity that surprises her with its hunger. From their dress she gathers that most of the women will go to the shops to work when they leave here; two or three look more prosperous, and she recognizes them as Romans. There are several men among them, sleeping children carried in arms, and a few brown tunics that reveal the presence of slaves. Helena knows that Phoebe is at the door welcoming each one of them, but it's Alexandra and Evniki who circulate, making everyone feel at home. New faces are introduced.

There's a murmur that is pleasant to her ears, none of the shrill voices and false laughter she has been used to hearing in her former life. She doesn't dwell on that thought. She senses that something is different in this crowd. It must be because of the air in Phoebe's home—that strange peace she has felt from the beginning—and of the unusually early hour for a gathering.

The atmosphere changes. An impressive woman with

light brown hair braided around her head enters and greets everyone with a strong voice, "Eirēnē, *adelphoi.*" The plural appellation includes men and women as her brothers and sisters as she wishes them peace. Helena, intrigued by the woman's presence, by her greeting of peace, wonders who she is. Then she hears the name Prisca, and the more familiar Priscilla, and watches as many of the women rush to kiss her, while the men are moving aside, looking for someone else. Soon a dark man enters accompanied by a shorter person who at first glance seems nondescript. Yet, there's a stir as he moves among the group, the murmuring stops, and they are all still, their eyes following him. Yes, this is the one they were awaiting. The atrium is now full of people and Helena finds Phoebe whispering in her ear, "The man in the center is Paul of Tarsus, the one who brought us the good news of Christ. I will present you later."

Helena sees this Paul lifting up his arms as he calls out in excellent Greek, "*Kherete!* In the Name of Christ our Lord, *kherete!*" To this invitation to be joyful the crowd responds with the singular, "*Khêrai, Pavle!*"

He turns his eyes to look at all of them. His face seems to glow with an inner light, and Helena feels a lump in the throat. He moves around the circle touching each one, kissing them on the cheek, pausing to say a word or two to a few until everyone is included. They are now connected to him in some invisible way as they begin to find a place to sit down, some on the tiled floor, a few on stools, others on the garden benches. There's hardly room to stand and when the man Erastos enters he finds space close to Helena, but she pretends not to see him, since his presence reminds her of her other life.

Someone has started a song. Helena feels her insides stir, her familiar physical response to music. The song sounds like a hymn to a god. She listens to the words and hears the name of *Christós*, the name *Yeesoús*, the familiar *Kyrie*, Lord. She is deeply moved by the combination of awe and familiarity in the words and sounds. She sees the faces with a sweet glow on them, smiles on many lips, tears running down the cheeks of some of the women. The hymn is addressed to an unseen being. It's the first time Helena has seen worship without an idol, without sacrifice of an animal or offerings of vegetation, so she is both puzzled and entranced. When the hymn ends, there's deep quiet that lasts for minutes and she finds it perplexing that those present are content to be quiet. And now Paul's voice rises. Helena wants to stop listening to the words in order to think about his voice, because she responds to people's voices first, but the quality eludes her. The words take precedence. Paul seems to be quoting:

> *Though he was in the form of God*
> *He did not grab possessively*
> *Onto his equality with God,*
> *But emptied himself;*
> *Taking the form of a slave,*
> *He was born in human likeness.*
> *And being found in human form,*
> *He humbled himself*
> *Becoming obedient*
> *Unto death,*
> *Even death on a cross.*

The idea of *kenosis*, the emptying of God, is so shocking that Helena struggles to understand, to enter into the paradox of Phoebe's words of last night.

"My sisters and my brothers," Paul begins, "I greet you in the Name of the Risen Lord." A murmur rises in an antiphon: "In his Name." Who is this person who bears a name of such power? What does Paul mean about the *risen* Lord? He continues, "I have just returned from Kenchreaê where I traveled with my brother Aquila so that we could bring the good news of our risen Lord to the sailors and their families who live there. Many responded to our message and have been baptized in the new life." A murmur of approval greets his words. Nobody stirs.

The light of a new day enters from the roof and Alexandra and Evniki douse the torches. *Is this my new life? Has it begun?* Helena longs for a new life because the old one is so filled with sorrow and shame that she cannot bear to remember it. She hides her face in her hands and weeps and so she misses much of the proceedings.

Phoebe puts a protective arm around her, as Helena now hears many different voices speaking at one time.

"What are they doing?" she asks Phoebe.

"I think they are praying," Phoebe says. "There are many troubled people here, Helena, people who are poor, weak, or afraid. Prayer helps them deal with their fears."

"Who is listening to them?" She herself didn't remember praying to anyone.

"We are convinced of Christ's presence among us. We know that he hears us and will answer."

"Ah." Helena nods.

A strong voice now rises from the crowd. "*Adelphoi,* our brother Paul is tired. We must not tax his body any longer. Let us sing a song and depart in peace."

"This is Aquila," Phoebe whispers, "Prisca's husband."

A hymn rises from many throats. The people slowly pass by Paul to receive a farewell greeting. Their murmurs continue toward the front of the house and then gradually diminish and disappear. The only people remaining who are not of the household are Paul, Prisca and Aquila, and Erastos. "Come," Phoebe tells her, "our guests want to meet you."

Helena stands before Paul, surprised that he is not tall; a while ago he seemed such a commanding presence. He now looks spent, but he studies her with his intense eyes. She bends her head before him as Phoebe is saying to him, "Helena is a guest in my house, Brother Paul. She has nowhere else to go."

Paul asks, "Helena, have you been here the whole time?"

"Yes," she admits, "but I was hiding. I heard your songs, but I didn't follow the discussion."

"It matters not," Paul says. His voice is now hoarse. "You are searching, Helena, and you will not be turned away. The Lord's patience is infinite."

She is puzzled but strangely comforted. She lifts her eyes to meet his own but now she's astounded by their depth, the lines of suffering on the lean face, the mouth that looks as if it doesn't know how to smile. He places his hand on Helena's head. "May peace go with you, *korē mou*—my daughter," he says, and the feel of his hand sends warm currents traveling through her body while the compassion in his voice touches her to the core.

"Is it true," she asks him haltingly, "that your Lord Yeesous did not despise the outcasts?"

"It is true that he loves them."

A great sigh rises from her depths and she hears herself saying in a small voice, "I like your hymns." Paul's eyes now smile.

"You are in good hands with our beloved sister Phoebe. Trust her." The interview is over. Phoebe takes her hand and leads her to where Prisca, Aquila, and Erastos are standing together. She introduces her to the couple. Instead of using words, Prisca reaches out and pulls her into her embrace. Helena stays in that fold, not wanting to move.

"I'll see you again, soon," Prisca assures her. As Helena clings to her she sees Erastos smiling with approval, but, except for Paul, she finds that she cannot look at any man without shrinking inside.

When she falls asleep that night, the dreams do not trouble her.

Chapter 9:
Erastos and His New Life

Paul and Aquila walked quickly ahead of them toward the leatherworkers' quarter, while Erastos accompanied Prisca at a more leisurely pace through the narrow streets. She said, "What an appealing girl she is, Erastos. I see why you are taken with her. Do you know, I have a strong sense that one day Helena will become a vital person in our community."

"Is this the same premonition you had when you first met me?" Erastos asked her and Prisca laughed. He wondered how she remembered that day; for him, the memory of their first encounter held an almost mystical meaning.

On that day, nearly a year before, he was alone in his dressing room, contemplating his mask. He had assumed the heart-breaking roles in Euripides' *Trojan Women* and the words were playing themselves in his mind:

> *I praise whichever of the gods*
>
> *set firm our life above the bestial and foul.*
>
> *Putting the understanding into us*
>
> *And then our tongue, the messenger of words...*

He was overcome by sadness at the thought that his days as a "messenger of words" were coming to an end and was startled when his servant parted the curtain to show two guests in and then disappeared. Erastos was annoyed. *Who were these people? And where had that sycophantic slave gone?*

The woman said immediately, "Don't be angry with your servant. We bribed him." Her honesty was so refreshing that Erastos laughed. "Who are you," he asked, "and what are you doing here?"

The woman was impressive—long light brown hair braided around her head, the smile ready and unforced, the eyes with depth and laughter in them. Her whole presence said, "Life is good." The man with her was dark, a brooding kind of countenance, an unmistakable reserve. His demeanor said, "It's a sad world we live in."

She said, "May I present my husband, Aquila. I am called Prisca. We are of the Jewish faith."

Erastos retorted, "Why do you introduce yourselves thus? What has faith to do with it? In Corinth, you are free to worship anyone you please. You are Jews, I'm Greek; this is enough."

"It has everything to do with it," the man said in his surprisingly strong voice, "for we were sent to you by our God."

"Which god?" Erastos asked him and heard the sarcasm in his own voice.

Prisca laughed again. "Don't be frightened," she told him. "Our God's intentions are good." She looked into his eyes as if encouraging him. *Frightened?* he wondered with resentment. *I'm not frightened.* But he recognized an unfamiliar tingle at the mention of "our God."

"You must admit," he said aloud to her, his habitual good manners taking over, "your husband's words were most unusual."

"To your ears, yes, they were, but Aquila was merely speaking truth; my husband is a truthful man."

Feeling the strangeness of the occasion, Erastos decided not to argue.

She continued: "I must tell you that we love Greek theater and have admired your performances since our arrival in Corinth. Our years in Rome taught us to enjoy the gifts of the Greeks and the Romans."

"Isn't this unusual for Jews?" Erastos asked her, curious now.

"Not as much as you suspect," she answered, but her husband looked displeased. "Because of our interest, it was not difficult for us to be persuaded that we should visit you."

"None of this makes sense to me," the actor said. "I must inform you that I'm not a religious man."

"Oh, but you are," she said, "you are. No one can speak the words of Sophokles as you do unless he has thought long and hard about the crucial question of the universe."

He felt unseen fingers run up and down his spine. "The crucial question?" he repeated.

"Does God care for his creatures?" she asked quietly, and he, remembering Antigone and Oedipus and everyone surrounding them in that tragic story, shook himself mentally.

"Would you like to walk with me to the city?" he asked them and Prisca countered, "Yes, then come and see where we live."

Thus began the unusual friendship between a formerly successful Greek actor and a deeply faithful Jewish couple. He never again questioned how they were led to him, but it no longer mattered. Prisca was a winsome woman and she soon became a beloved friend. It was she who introduced Erastos to Paul the Apostle, as he called himself; so it was that Erastos was soon hooked by the "Great Fisher of *Anthropous*," as Prisca called her God.

Chapter 10: Demosthenes

Helena's newfound peace was shattered. Paul, who worked tirelessly, apparently expected the same devotion from his followers. He asked and Phoebe agreed to serve the new *ekklesia* he had founded in Corinth's nearby port city of Kenchreaê, to minister to the sailors' families. She gathered the members of her household that now included Helena and announced to them as gently as possible that their lives were about to change. From her comfortable, well-established home and business in Corinth, she would move to Kenchreaê. "But you are not slaves, you are friends," she told them. "I leave it to you to decide whether to follow me or remain in Corinth."

Alexandra and Evniki laughed at the suggestion that they could live without Phoebe. "Of course we'll go with you," Alexandra spoke up for both of them, as she usually did.

"Then stay here with my faithful Aristos until I find a place and send for you," Phoebe told them, and they agreed happily.

Phoebe then looked at Helena. "I'll be staying at a friend's in Kenchreaê, Helena; Junia is married to a sea captain who is absent now, so she offered to house me until I find a place of my own. Would you like to return to your Roman friends or stay here with the girls and Aristos?"

Helena felt a familiar panic rising. "I have no intention of returning to Claudia's," she answered, "but what right have I to stay here? I don't think I can remain in Corinth without your protection."

After promising to consult with Erastos, Phoebe admitted, "I don't like leaving you behind," and Helena thought: *I'll be so good that she will not want to abandon me.*

So it was that Helena set about learning and memorizing the hymns of these followers of The Way. She worked hard in the weaving room and started designing her own patterns, wanting to please the one person who had never asked anything of her. She did not see Paul very often these days, because within a couple of weeks of her arrival at Phoebe's the *ekklesia* had moved to a larger house near the Jewish synagogue, in the home of a man named Titius Justus. The untiring Paul continued his preaching to the synagogue on what they called "the Sabbath" and to the *ekklesia* on Sunday.

Throughout this time Helena refused to talk about her life before coming to Phoebe's; and to her surprise, no one asked her questions about her past. How she cherished their lack of prying. But when Phoebe took her aside to explain why she had agreed to leave for Kenchreaê, Helena recognized the returning panic and acknowledged that she had come to depend on Phoebe's steady and loving presence as she had never depended on anyone since her father's death.

"Why would you go, Phoebe? You have so many good customers here and business is booming."

"It's not because of business, you see, Helena. It has to do with the confidence Paul places in me. Can you understand what an honor this is for me, a woman?"

"You're smarter and more capable than any man I know," Helena protested. "My father taught me to recognize the worth of women, and you are the best of them!"

"What an unusual man your father must have been. Helena, can you talk about him? I would love to know who he was."

How can I talk about him, Helena wondered, *when my heart breaks anew every time I speak his name?*

———— ❧ ————

She had been such a happy child. The house was small but filled with light, and flowers grew among the herbs in the garden. Her father was the one constant presence. The only women she saw were servants who didn't stay long except for an older woman who had been her nurse. She had been told that her mother died in childbirth, but she didn't know what the word "mother" meant. Her father combed her hair, saw to it that her face and hands were clean, told her stories, and read to her from the time she was born. A talented artist he made instruments for her that she learned to play from the earliest years. "We come from a long line of musicians and storytellers," he would tell her. "You have inherited your mother's beauty and you already know most of what I know." She'd put her arms around his neck laughing, "No, Father, no one knows as much as you do." Demosthenes was a serious man, without false pieties but with a deep commitment to living the life of a Stoic.

When she was six a boy came to live with them. He was an orphan from the north, and somehow Helena sensed that her father had rescued the little boy from a dark danger. Now, she was never alone, and the two were taught together. Demosthenes took them to the countryside to let them run and soon they were racing against each other. Helena was exceptionally fast. Ares, who had been scrawny when he came to them, soon grew strong and fit and threw the javelin with accuracy and grace.

Demosthenes was not satisfied with only their physical training. He read to them from Homer and led them through the plays of Aeschylus, Sophokles, and Euripides. He used to say: "When we read Aeschylus, we must bow in reverence. When we read Sophokles, we must lift our hands in praise. When we read Euripides, we must hold on to our heart lest it break within us. I love Euripides because he loved women."

The young people laughed with delight. Ares said, "There's no one like you, dear Demosthenes." Ares was a beautiful child with dark curls and arresting black eyes over a chiseled face, high cheekbones and a square chin. He had started learning to carve stone, so when he was fourteen Demosthenes took him to an old friend in Olympia. The sculptor was to look after him, teach him his art, and find a fit trainer for the boy to compete in the next Olympics. Helena missed him when he left, but now she had a few friends, girls she was allowed to visit in their homes. It was during this time that she realized how unusual her upbringing had been. Most of the girls bored her. None of them had been exposed to what she had read, and their constant preoccupation with marriage drove her to frustration. She confronted Demosthenes. "Why do all the girls think only of marriage?"

"This is what their mothers teach them," he said. "They have kept their daughters hidden, and now they want them to enter the house of a man and be a wife and mother without knowing anything about the world around them." She heard the bitterness in his voice and was surprised.

"Father, tell me about my mother. You have never really let me know anything about her." But she immediately regretted her words because she saw that he was weeping. "Father, forgive me, please."

He took her hands and pulled her down to sit close to him. "Helena, my beloved child, you are fifteen today, the age she was when I married her. The marriage was arranged by our parents, but I loved her immediately. We were both so young, so ignorant of our bodies, of what it meant to be married. You look like your mother, beautiful and fragile."

"Father, I'm not fragile. I'm strong."

"Yes, yes, you are physically strong, but she was not, and I did not know it. She conceived almost immediately, and we had only that one year together, the early months of marriage, and then the waiting for you to come." He turned to her and now his eyes were dry but feverish. "Helena, promise me that you will wait until you are at least eighteen before you marry. Promise me!"

"I have no desire to get married," Helena answered him, laughing. "I have my music, my books, and you. Why would I ever want to leave you, to go with a man I don't know?"

Her father smiled. "Keep thinking so, Helena." Then he grew serious. "Your mother died giving birth to you because she was so young. This is a cruel world for women, Helena. That's the reason I brought you up to think like a man. That's why I taught you to read and let you run in the open and sing in front of others without shame. I want you to be strong, Helena, and not hidden and retiring like other women, but never at the mercy of men."

He was so intense that she dared not laugh. Marriage was not on the horizon for her, not as long as her father lived. When she was sixteen, her father accepted a position in the home of a rich Roman as mentor and tutor to Claudia's children. Helena hated the move, but her father explained that he had a dream for her. "I want to have my own *scholē*, an academy, Helena. You and Ares will be my assistants, and I will know that if something happens to me, both of you will have a means of livelihood. Claudia is offering me a generous salary, has promised a legacy for you, and we can still be together, in our own apartment."

She was almost used to living in the Roman villa when Ares returned from Olympia. When she set her eyes on him, Helena lost her breath. They greeted each other and saw how each had changed in the two years they had been apart. Now, this boy who had been her brother was the young man who made her body tremble. He could not even speak; his eyes said it all. Demosthenes saw them and understood. He took them to his rooms and they sat side by side, both of them feeling like *kitharas* that had been tuned to the breaking point.

"You are both seventeen and you think you love each other," her father said, his eyes kind but troubled. "I'll give you my blessings for your eventual marriage, but not now. I want you both to promise solemnly that you will not marry and you will not lie together before you are at least eighteen." He turned to Ares whose dark complexion turned even darker. "Her mother died because she gave birth at a young age. I don't want this to happen to Helena. I promised her mother that Helena would live, that I would be both mother and father to her. I have already started my *scholē*—working for someone else for now—but soon I will be able to own it and then, after you reach eighteen, both of you can own it with me, and I will see that you are married. Will you promise?"

The two young people looked at each other and then they stood in front of Demosthenes. "I give you my word," Ares said solemnly, and Helena cried, "I promise, Father, I promise." And all three were weeping but content. Ares was living in a room in the *scholē* and her father was spending more and more time in the presence of Claudia. Helena noticed that Demosthenes was very uncomfortable whenever Gaius Marius Sylvanus was in the villa, and that he made every effort to shield Helena from the Roman. One day, when Ares was visiting, Demosthenes again took them to his rooms for one of his fatherly chats. His usual peaceful demeanor was missing, however, and Helena felt a strong premonition of sadness. "Father, has something happened?"

Demosthenes looked at Ares. "If something untoward happens to me, will you care for her?" he asked the boy and Ares immediately professed his desire to walk through flames for Helena. Demosthenes continued: "I want you both to listen carefully. I don't like the way Gaius Marius Sylvanus looks at Helena. I have announced your betrothal to Claudia, and as soon as a business arrangement I have made comes to fruition we will all move away from here. Helena, I have brought you up to be self-sufficient, but we live in a world that does not honor women. We are Greeks living in a Roman world. If you are left alone, without me, without Ares, I don't want anyone, ever, to treat you as an *hetaera*. You have all the gifts men look for in the women they use for their entertainment, but I want you to trust Claudia. She will shield you from other men."

Both Ares and Helena started to protest, but he silenced them. "I only want to make sure you are not ignorant of the ways of the world," he said to calm them. "I see what happens when Gaius and his friends are together, away from Claudia, with other women, and I worry that there are things about this life you don't know. I want both of you to be intelligent and protected. That's all."

⎯⎯ ⌘ ⎯⎯

Phoebe had remained silent while Helena, trembling beside her, was recounting her story. "Do you believe in premonitions, Phoebe? A few weeks later my father was dead by his own hand."

Phoebe prayed without words and after a while said quietly, "No, I don't believe in premonitions, Helena, but please understand that I respect your feelings, your own 'premonitions,' as you call them. You're tired now, my dear. Thank you for giving me a picture of your good father. But I need to think about him. Let's talk some more later. Is that all right?" Yet Helena needed to tell her the rest.

"My father died quite suddenly, you see. It seems, from what Claudia told me, that he had borrowed a large amount of money from her husband, Gaius Marius Sylvanus—may his memory be cursed! Claudia said that my father borrowed the money for the sake of my future marriage to Ares." Her voice betrayed her uncertainty.

Phoebe spoke her surprise. "It doesn't sound like him, Helena, not like the man you've just described. Does it to you? You said Demosthenes was a Stoic. Don't you know that Stoics disapprove of suicide? And isn't it strange that he would borrow money from a man he disliked so intensely? Please, forgive me for asking this question, but how did your father die?"

"He killed himself, that's all Claudia told me. It was after his death that she confessed to me that her husband was a usurer who loaned money at exorbitant rates. Father was going to create an academy for the three of us, you see, but I didn't know he had borrowed money from Claudia's husband. When the venture failed, he stabbed himself with his dagger. So they said." She now sounded exhausted.

Phoebe hesitated, but there was a question she considered crucial. "Helena, something here is very puzzling. How could he commit suicide? A father who loved you so much….All this sounds against his principles. How do you know that Claudia was being truthful?"

Helena was stunned. She knew now that she had avoided asking this same question. She stammered, "Why, why would she lie?"

With a gentleness the girl now recognized as habitual, Phoebe said, "I don't know the woman and I didn't know your father. But—and I ask you, Helena, to forgive me if I'm assuming too much—I've heard that it's very difficult to differentiate between a killing and a suicide, and, again, I repeat: Stoics don't approve of suicide—I'm sure of this. My father also was a Stoic. Why do you believe this woman—this Claudia?"

"It never occurred to me to question her. Why would she lie to me, Phoebe?" She reached back to that terrible moment which she had buried deep within her memory—that night when Claudia came to her room to give her the fatal news. Something had been strange about Claudia. What was it? Helena now remembered the woman's stricken face, the sound of her voice filled with sadness and outrage. She had assumed it was because of Helena's own loss, but Claudia had sounded like someone who had received a grievous blow to her own self.

Helena grasped Phoebe's hand. "I've been a fool. You reminded me of something peculiar, something not right with Claudia when she told me of Father's death. Even at the time it sounded so unlikely, but I was too devoured by grief to notice. 'A venture that failed'? What does this mean? Why was I so gullible?" She sat there shaking until Phoebe put her arm around her to calm her.

"Please, Phoebe," Helena grasped at the slight hope that she would find the truth. "Your friend, Erastos. He's Claudia's friend also; did you know? I don't want to see her or talk to her yet. Would you ask your friend about my father? Would you plead with him to find out?"

"Helena, my dear. Erastos is a good man. You shouldn't be afraid of him. You ask him the questions that trouble you. I'll invite him immediately. I'm sure he will be truthful."

"I'm afraid of all men, Phoebe. The way they looked at me when I played and sang." And then her mind veered to the ever-present horror: *The rape! How can I shake off the fear of that rape?* She made an effort to smile at Phoebe. "But if you trust Erastos, I will also." And so it was agreed.

Chapter 11:
What Is My Purpose Now?

Erastos responded to Phoebe's summons with alacrity, but she welcomed him with a twinge of guilt. *What am I doing to the poor man? Am I encouraging him in something that will never come to pass?*

She led him to her private workroom. "I don't want to take advantage of your kindness to me and to Helena," she began, but he interrupted her.

"Come, come, Phoebe. Don't stand on ceremony with me. I'm the one who brought Helena to you without prior permission. What's happened to her? What can I do?"

"My dear friend, Helena needs to ask you questions..." and at that Erastos laughed aloud.

"The mysterious Helena needs information from me? What have *I* kept from *her*?"

She looked into his eyes and he admitted, "What I've kept hidden is for her sake, not mine."

"Yes, I recognize your reticence. This is about her father."

"But I didn't know her father, Phoebe. I wish I *had*

known him."

"Still, I think you need to hear Helena. Will you?"

He smiled sadly. "I'm afraid, dear Phoebe, that listening to Helena is a pleasure I can never willingly forgo."

They found her standing still and thoughtful before her loom. "She's so beautiful and so sad," he whispered. She reminded him of the exquisite funerary *stylae* of her Greek ancestors as she stood there, vulnerable and pensive. Phoebe said briskly, "Enough work for this morning, Helena." The girl turned and looked at Erastos. "Why does she resent me?" he whispered to Phoebe and then he seemed to absorb Helena's sadness into himself.

"Come, come," Phoebe intervened with false brightness, "Let's go sit in the garden."

They sat as before, Helena and Phoebe side by side, Erastos facing them. *There's no room for small talk with these two*, Phoebe decided, and plunged ahead. "Erastos, Helena wants to ask you about your friend Claudia."

His eyes, full of longing, were on Helena's lovely face, but Helena did not notice. She wasn't looking at him but at her folded hands. She began with difficulty and with that guarded formality she assumed with men. "I understand you have known Claudia for quite some time. I've a vague recollection of the two of you together, but I can't place the memory."

He said eagerly, "I heard you play and sing for her guests once, at a dinner—it must have been over a year ago now—but I noticed that when you played you looked at no one around the *triclinium*, so I'm sure you didn't notice me, and then the servants seemed to surround you as if to protect you from the guests."

"How perceptive of you. Yes, that's exactly what they did for me." She seemed to be looking into a past the others couldn't share. "Did you recite something that evening?" she asked dreamily. "Something from Euripides?"

Erastos looked startled. "If I did, I've forgotten," he whispered, but she continued, "Those words—they were about Eleni of Sparta, weren't they? I heard you declaim them after I left the *triclinium*. Your voice carries remarkably well over marble," and for the first time since he had known her, she smiled briefly. It seemed to cut through him, and of course he did remember. He quoted:

Other women, by beauty fortunate,
Live out their lives. By beauty I perish.

"Those are the words," she said with palpable sadness. "How did you know?"

"I knew nothing," he confessed. "I thought you were one of the most fortunate and beautiful maidens I had ever seen."

"I was *then*, I was fortunate. But your poet's words were prophetic; soon after that day I became an orphan for the second time." She raised her hands and covered her face with her long fingers. Her silence was so long that they were both surprised when she spoke again. "Concerning Claudia. Has she mentioned my father to you? He was her children's tutor and mentor; do you remember meeting him in her home?"

"If your father attended her banquets, I must have seen him, Helena. But I don't seem to remember an erudite Greek at those dinners. I think I saw him with you when you sang with a chorus at Aphrodite's festival. At that time I didn't know who he was. But, no, I don't think I met him at Claudia's."

"No. You would not have met him at her banquets. My father was a faithful Stoic who despised symposia. Besides, he always avoided Claudia's husband and his friends. You might have seen him at the theater, however."

"The theater? Of course! Of course! That handsome Greek who escorted her to the festivals! Demosthenes, wasn't that his name? He was very reserved and let her do all the talking. It was when she sponsored the productions that he came, because her husband hated the theater. Was Demosthenes your father?"

"The handsome Demosthenes," Helena said in a voice full of tears. "I used to tease him about his name. Unlike the famous orator of the same name, my father could always speak well. He was born to be an orator. I used to tell him he belonged in the age of Sokrates, not in this rich Roman province where he had to work for Romans." She spat the last word out.

"He was freeborn, then, was he?" Erastos asked.

"Oh, yes. The Romans left our family alone. Our roots here go back a long, long time, even before that of the cursed Mummius who razed the city. My ancestors never left Korinthia, so when Julius Caesar ordered the city rebuilt, my father's ancestors returned from Sykion and reclaimed their home as their own. My father told me that despite the prevailing opinion not all of Corinth was lost when Mummius went mad in it. And since our people were artists, artisans, and teachers—not soldiers, never soldiers, they were allowed back here and were left alone to live in relative freedom."

Erastos was surprised by her unusually long speech. Helena seemed lost after her historic recounting. Then reality must have returned, for she shuddered.

"What did Claudia tell you about my father?" she asked him.

He frowned in an effort to remember and said, speaking gently. "I noticed that Claudia's face was stricken when she spoke of your father and his suicide; an unusual reaction for the death of a mere tutor, I thought then. She was on the verge of revealing something to me, but we were interrupted by Alexandros. Now, however, seeing you, hearing you, I recall her tears and the sound of her voice, and I think I know the reason. Forgive me if this troubles you, Helena, but I think only a woman in love shows the kind of emotion Claudia revealed over a man who worked for her. I must have known this for a long time, but somehow, I didn't focus on it. How foolish of me. Your father could *not* have committed suicide. I think your Demosthenes and Claudia were lovers and Gaius found out and killed him or had him killed."

She cried out and started pacing, words escaping from her lips, all kinds of emotions fighting on her face. "My father? But he was a man of virtue…Gaius Marius Sylvanus once again, that monster…Ah, he took his revenge on all of us." She was very pale, her gray eyes huge in their sorrow but, after a while, she sat down heavily and agreed. "You must be right. Claudia and my father were very close. I spent much more time with her children than he did. It makes sense now. They took every opportunity to be together, to be alone together. How could I have been so blind?"

"Helena," he asked, "tell us: how did you learn of your father's death?"

"We were living in their villa, you see. Claudia had given us our own quarters, and we were very comfortable. It was last winter, just before the Saturnalia. After I had fallen asleep one night, Claudia came to wake me, to tell me that my father was dead, that he had killed himself because the ship where he had placed all his fortune had sunk."

"And how did she say he did it?"

"'He has fallen on his own dagger,' she told me."

Erastos now trod very carefully. "That dagger, Helena, do you know what happened to it?"

She stood up suddenly. Again, she began her frantic pacing on the marble of the atrium floor. She stopped in front of Erastos and said in a firm voice. "I took that dagger. Alexandros gave it to me, and I kept it in my room as the last memento of my father. Why do you ask?"

"Do you know where it is now?"

She looked at Phoebe, who saw the light of recognition dawn in the girl's eyes. With a clarity that seemed to surprise even herself, Helena said, "I took it out to kill Gaius Marius Sylvanus," and, turning to Phoebe, she added bitterly, "I suppose now you won't want to know me, Phoebe."

Before Phoebe could speak, Erastos asked, "But why, Helena? If you didn't suspect until today that Gaius killed your father, why would you want to kill him?"

She was impatient with him. "Don't you understand? Gaius Marius Sylvanus killed us all. He killed my father, he killed Ares, and then me."

Erastos' brow furrowed in confusion. *Gaius killed her? And someone named Ares?* But then, since she seemed ready to bolt, Erastos simply asked, "Who is Ares?"

"He was my life, and now he's dead," and she buried her face on Phoebe's shoulder. Erastos got up and left quietly.

———— ∽∽ ————

On the next morning, Phoebe found Helena already at the loom, studying the pattern, her hands busy on the weft.

"Good work," Phoebe said brightly. But when Helena turned towards her, Phoebe knew that the girl had not slept at all. Her eyes looked haunted.

"Come," Phoebe said. "No work today. I'm deeply sorry that Erastos and I pried." She led her to her own rooms. The girl was too quiet, too passive, but she still refused to rest or sleep.

"I need you to tell me, Phoebe, what you think of me now, after what you learned last night."

"Think of you, my dear *korē*? Don't you know?"

"You heard me tell your friend what I intended to do with my father's dagger. How can you want to keep me with you after knowing this? I may be a killer."

"Helena, look into my eyes and listen carefully. I told you I'm sorry we pried, but I'm glad I now know you better. You may have wanted to kill that terrible man, Helena, but you *didn't* do it. I don't think you *could* have done it had you had the chance."

"But how do you know? How do you know I didn't kill him?"

"Are you serious, Helena? Don't you know that your patron was dead when you reached his chamber?"

Helena stared at her. "I can't remember, Phoebe," she whispered, frightened. "I've tried, but I still can't remember crucial portions of that night!"

"Then we can make sure you do remember. I will send Aristos to fetch the one eyewitness—once again. Helena, you cannot keep living with this question unresolved. I want you to lie down and rest, and when Erastos returns, I will wake you."

Like an obedient child Helena curled herself on the bed. "Why are you so interested in Erastos?" she wondered aloud. "What more can he possibly know about my life?" But she was drifting to sleep so Phoebe covered her, shook her head, and didn't answer.

It was nearly noon when Phoebe woke her up by calling her name. Helena seemed surprised to discover that she had slept for several hours. She sat up looking confused and groggy. Phoebe handed her a cup of cool water and a wet cloth for her face and then led her to the atrium where Erastos was waiting patiently.

A table with fresh fruit and drinks was already set and, without waiting for them to acknowledge each other, Phoebe said, "Erastos, you and I have wondered how much Helena remembered of that terrible night, the night you brought her here. Now I discover that she still remembers very little. You need to tell her exactly what you said to me after she went to bed in the dark of that night. Start with the banquet. Sit down both of you. Helena, eat something and let Erastos tell you a story."

They had never heard her sound so firm, so they both obeyed. Helena absently was putting fruit in her mouth, as though unaware that she was doing it. As she waited, her troubled eyes rested on Erastos. He took a deep breath, and like the trained actor he was, he prepared to tell his story:

"Helena, it seems to me that I have thought of nothing but the events of that night. I apologize now. I'd assumed that you knew what you were doing."

"What *was* I doing?" she asked. "I remember running in the night, but you told me that already."

"Helena, what I must tell you now happened before I brought you here; it is *why* I brought you here. I told you yesterday that Claudia has been my friend for several years, but you know the Romans: so much of their life is just for show and much of the rest is hidden. I was not aware of your father's role in her household, and I suspect that she hid her love for him quite successfully. I knew her as a very rich, highly cultured woman with important connections to the emperor in Rome and, really, to everyone who has a position of power in Corinth. I must tell you, too, that I have benefited from her connections. What I did *not* know until that night was how terrified Claudia was of what her husband might do in public. I hadn't known anything about their marriage, because I rarely saw them together. A year had passed since I first heard you play in her house but I had not returned there because, in the meantime, I met Phoebe and Prisca and then Paul, so the Roman banquets no longer appealed to me.

"But on that particular day a messenger came with an urgent note from Claudia asking me to attend her dinner that very evening because she would be surrounded by her husband's associates. She sounded unlike herself, rather desperate, and I agreed to go. It was a sumptuous dinner as they always are at her house, but I could sense her tension and I could see that her husband had become a drunk."

Helena had stopped eating and Phoebe saw that tremors were coursing through her body. Erastos glanced at Phoebe in alarm; she now sat closer to the girl and put her arm around Helena to stop her trembling. She seemed to know exactly how to calm Helena down. "Continue," Phoebe told Erastos and he obeyed.

"Someone called out for music and dancing and Gaius motioned to that obnoxious slave of his who seemed to be always with him—do you know the one?"

Helena said, "Yes, the odious Demetrius—that was his name in the household."

"Yes, that one. Gaius spoke to him and the slave left. I was considering how to make a quick departure when I saw the same slave pulling you, no, *dragging* you, through the atrium. He was holding your *kithara* and then he handed it to you and his master bellowed for you to play."

Helena became alert. She lifted her head, clutched Phoebe's hand with her own and stared at Erastos. He whispered, "Do you remember this now?" and she shook her head, "No."

"What you did next, Helena, seemed so strange that only when I realized you were in mourning did it make some sense to me." He continued with some difficulty. "You lifted your *kithara* and threw it at Gaius Marius Sylvanus. And then you called out his full name and you said very clearly, 'It will be with my last breath, but I will not die before I kill you,' and then you turned around and left, Alexandros close behind you."

"I threw my *kithara* at him? Did I hit him?"

"Oh, yes. He was bleeding and bellowing like a beast. It was probably just a scratch on the forehead but he was quite drunk by then and it took several slaves to lead him away. Don't you remember this?"

"I do remember that Alexandros led me to my room. 'For your own safety,' he said, 'don't move from here until I come for you.'"

"Yes, you stayed there for a long while. You must excuse me, Helena, but I followed you and watched from below, from the garden, to make sure nothing bad happened to you after your outburst. You see, everyone at that dinner had heard your threat. But I was the only one there who was not connected to Claudia's husband."

"All I remember is that I was determined to avenge my father's death and the loss of Ares," she said in a small voice. "I had just received news of Ares' drowning. I remember, oh, I do remember, how that felt. I was dead inside, but I was not going to give up until I killed the man who caused all our misery. Did I not succeed?"

He didn't answer directly but continued his storytelling. "After the slaves had stopped their night cleaning, you emerged from your room and walked toward the wide marble steps, the ones not visible from below, and I followed you, Helena. You entered a large room and stood by the bed. I could see you clearly because the torches were still lit. There was no one else around, which was very surprising. You took a dagger from below your *peplos* and you lifted your arm, so I immediately came close behind you, ready to stop you. But then, you looked down and you saw, as I did, that Gaius Marius Sylvanus was already dead."

She was staring at Erastos, mesmerized, listening to his every word. She didn't speak. She pulled her hand from Phoebe's and examined her open palms. "Then I did *not* kill him? So I failed both my father and Ares. No wonder I have no peace." Her voice was bitter, her eyes dull. She asked, "If I didn't kill him, who did?"

"I don't know, but I suspect it was arranged between Alexandros and Claudia. You know them better than I."

"If she did it," Helena said thoughtfully, "no one will give her away. Her slaves are devoted to her. And if Alexandros killed him, she will use all her connections to absolve him of guilt. But the revenge should have been mine." She stood up suddenly and started to leave. Then she stopped and turned to Erastos. She asked, "Why did you bring me here?"

"I had no other choice," he said, surprised at her question. "I thought you were in danger, and I knew my friend here would take you in. I trust the followers of Yeesous."

Helena said to Phoebe. "That name again. I cannot escape your Yeesous." And then she faced Erastos. She was very pale, her voice as tragic as her face. "I thank you for telling me all that you know. But I'm not sure that I can thank you for saving me." And with that, she left them.

Erastos turned to Phoebe in despair. "How do we get through to her? How do the followers of The Way deal with this desire for revenge?"

"Oh, Erastos, you already know the answer. I think this is so ingrained and so serious that we must ask Paul to help her."

He agreed but murmured, "Did you hear her voice when she spoke of the drowning of Ares? Whatever I feel for her, how can I ever break through that barrier of grief? How do I compete with a dead man?"

It was the first time he had spoken of his feelings for Helena and Phoebe respected them by saying nothing.

On the next day Phoebe decided to take Helena with her to Prisca's place where they were sure to find her beloved brother Paul.

She wrapped Helena in one of her long *stolas* and the two of them, accompanied by Aristos, walked through the narrow streets of the noisy city. There was something about Corinth that was energizing, Helena told Phoebe, recounting with sadness, mixed with sudden flashes of remembered joy, the times she had visited the public places with her father and his choirs. She had talked with Alexandra and Evniki enough to discover that her own life had been uniquely enriched by a wise, generous man whose absence had become a perpetual presence of pain in her heart. Since coming to live with Phoebe she had realized that she had never spent much time with women; those she knew had been slaves, only a few of them rich young Romans whom she tended to dislike. She knew that Phoebe had freed the Makedonian girls soon after she bought them and that they had become her family. She said to Phoebe, "I cannot imagine you as a slave owner any more than I could have imagined my father as one." She talked more as they walked side by side than she did in the house, and Phoebe started guessing that, accustomed as the girl had been to rigorous physical activity in her earlier years, she missed it now. The sedentary life expected of women was not for her.

"The life Alexandra and Evniki have revealed to me is very different from anything I've known," Helena said as they were passing by the basilica. "Despite the education my father gave me, I know now that he kept me from the life of the city. His protectiveness echoed the isolation of women in ages past, even though he claimed the opposite. Now here I am, walking through the streets of Corinth with a business woman who is modest and reserved but obviously unafraid. I want to be like you, Phoebe. But you are good, and I am someone who was, no, *is,* willing to kill. Life seems meaningless without vengeance after what was done to me, to my father, and to Ares."

Helena capable of killing? Phoebe refused to consider it. *Paul should be able to answer her questions.* She offered a silent prayer for the troubled girl.

Helena looked depressed when they reached Prisca's place, but the older woman took her in her arms and greeted her with a warmth that coaxed Helena out of her depression.

"I'm so glad you came to see us." Prisca was ebullient. "We've been missing you, Helena. I understand you will accompany Phoebe to Kenchreaê. All of us are very pleased."

Helena was speechless and looked to Phoebe as if to say, *So you have agreed I can go with you?*

Prisca took her by the hand. "Come, let's go to Paul who's anxious to speak with you and Phoebe," and she led them to the workroom where Paul and Aquila were already busy with their strips of leather. There was no other person there, so Phoebe wasted no time in broaching what troubled them.

"My brother Paul, Helena and I have some very important questions to ask you. Will you help us?" Aquila, profoundly private and always sensitive, stood up and quietly moved to the interior of the house. The three women were now alone with Paul.

His eyes smiled at them. "If the Lord has given me light on your questions, I'll be able to help you; my own light is not enough."

"Helena," Phoebe urged, "will you share with Paul what's troubling you the most?"

Helena did not hesitate: "I understand that you, followers of your Christ, are opposed to killing for any reason."

Paul raised his eyes from the work of his hands and said slowly, "Christ is the Lord of *life*, Helena. When one lives in Christ, one lives in life itself; therefore, since there is no death in him, there should be no death in us."

"And what do you do in a city dominated by the Romans and their love of death?"

"Are you talking about their killing others or themselves?"

"Both," she answered, and now her voice faltered. She composed herself before saying quietly, "I do understand that killing is wrong since the law punishes killers, but aren't we required to avenge our loved ones who were murdered by evil men? Our own history and our great tragedies are filled with such stories—the avenging of the blood of a loved one is deeply rooted, is it not? Can Jews be so different from the Greeks?"

Paul abandoned his work. He turned and faced the

troubled young woman. His eyes were sad. "Ah, Helena," he sighed. "No, we are not so different from you. Once, not so long ago, I was a killer of the innocent, but the Lord Yeesous changed me forever."

Helena looked from him to the two older women, but their eyes were fixed on Paul. "I don't understand," she stammered, "you, a killer?"

"I used to be opposed to Christ and his followers," Paul said. "Like you, Helena, and your Greeks, I was convinced that those who committed *hubris* needed to be punished, even by death. In my case, I persecuted Christ's followers because I was convinced that they were breaking God's law; I found them, captured them, and dragged them to the authorities who oftentimes stoned them. This made me a killer also. Someone described me as breathing fire and brimstone."

They were all quiet after his terrible words, and Helena seemed afraid to break the silence, but finally she whispered: "Does—does this mean that *wanting* to see someone dead makes one a killer?"

"This is what Yeesous taught—what the heart desires is as strong, or as guilty, as the act that may result from this desire or intention."

"Then, we are all doomed, aren't we?"

"Without the grace of God, yes. But we live by grace and hope, Helena. What we cannot do for ourselves, Christ does for us and within us."

"It's all too complicated for me, but I need to know this: What stopped you from persecuting Christ's followers, why did they not avenge themselves, and how did you become one of them?"

"Ah," Paul said and now his eyes were full of light. "You asked three questions, but they all have one answer: God's mercy is infinite. The Lord Yeesous himself appeared to me and stopped me from violence and death."

"I thought he was dead." Helena whispered and, confused, looked at Phoebe.

"Yes," Paul answered and his voice was now strong with utter conviction, "but death could not hold him. God called him back to life. This living Lord appeared to me and called me from death to life. As for his followers—they were redeemed of needing revenge. They forgave me, though for a long time they were afraid to trust me. Prisca has personal knowledge of the earthly life of Yeesous, Helena. She was a child in Judea when the resurrected Lord appeared to his friends."

Helena covered her face with her hands and remained quiet for a while. Phoebe sensed a holy energy in the room and wondered if Helena felt it surrounding her. The girl now spoke directly to Paul in a small voice, her face still hidden. "I am filled with hate for my former patron. He killed my father, he violated me after my father's death; and my betrothed, shamed for me and for himself, ran away and then drowned. How can I forget such harm, how can I ever regain my honor when he tried to make an *hetaera* out of me?"

Phoebe cried out as if struck and she saw tears filling Prisca's eyes. "You poor, poor child," they both whispered and reached out to envelop her.

Paul's voice was severe, his anger at those who had hurt her held in check with difficulty. "An evil generation that dwells in darkness," he said. "Who is this man who hurt this child of God?"

"He's dead," Phoebe told him. "Someone killed him, but it wasn't Helena."

"Our ancestors taught us that vengeance belongs only to God, Helena," Paul said to her in a changed voice, now filled with great compassion. "What was done to you is evil. But we were taught by our Lord not to answer evil with evil but with good. Christ is the only one who can transform this evil, who can bring good out of evil acts. I place you in his hands."

Helena lifted her head and her eyes – confused, doubtful – stared at him. He nodded in understanding and said, "May God bring you into the light, Helena, and may he give you the solace of his forgiveness," and he stretched out his hand. She bent her head and he placed his hand on the short hair and blessed her. They all saw that she was trembling. "I need to think on all this," she said, deeply moved.

Aquila returned to the workshop, and the friends talked together about the approaching departure for Kenchreaê. Helena listened and said to Phoebe as they were leaving, "You followers of your Christ—you think only of others, not of yourselves. Why should you be concerned with sailors and their families? It's a mystery." But she was smiling now, knowing that the people in that small shop had heard her and had loved her despite her past.

Chapter 12: De Profundis

Erastos had offered to accompany the two women on their journey to Kenchreaê, but first he had to fulfill two tasks: find out from Claudia if anyone had accused Helena of murder and recover the girl's possessions from the Roman household.

Phoebe had said to him: "She asks only for her father's scrolls and her musical instruments, but they may offer you other personal possessions; don't refuse them. She will need them later."

Erastos was thoughtful: "She's young and beautiful yet asks only for the things of the mind. Isn't this unusual for a woman? Have I been ignorant of modern women for too long, knowing only those who populate Sophokles and Euripides? Help me here, Phoebe."

Phoebe laughed. "No, you're quite right; Helena is most unusual. She has exquisite taste, but she seems indifferent to her looks. Aside from her father and Ares she has never been eager to impress anyone. It's the father who intrigues me: He taught her everything as he would have taught a son. This *is* most unusual indeed."

Erastos found the steward Alexandros alone in the villa. "The family is traveling, escaping their grief," he said with a straight face, but Erastos heard his irony. "The lady Claudia is escaping the gossips of Corinth's society," Alexandros added in his dry manner. "They are now in Rome. For the children's heritage. Never very fond of Rome, Claudia. She should have been born a Greek."

When Erastos asked him for Helena's belongings, Alexandros lost his detachment. "How is our beloved Helena?" he asked; then, without waiting for an answer, he gave instructions to two girl slaves to pack the necessary baskets.

While they waited, and aware that the household slaves must have gossiped about Helena, Erastos said to him, "I know you care deeply about Helena, so I want you to know that she's living with a good woman by the name of Phoebe, a most respectable weaver, well known in the city for her good works. And she has been with her since the night she threatened your master." Alexandros did not comment, but Erastos noticed a softening in his demeanor. It must have relieved the older man that the inevitable talk concerning Helena—that Erastos was keeping her—was untrue. Erastos asked, "What happened to Gaius' personal slave, the one called Demetrius?"

A wicked smile appeared on the narrow cracked lips. "We sold him. That very night. In Corinth, it was easy to do," and Erastos felt relief hearing it. He was finding the steward intriguing. He wanted to ask him, *What is your story?* But a young slave who was carrying two large baskets appeared, and the opportunity passed.

The boy with the baskets accompanied him to Phoebe's home. When Helena saw her musical instruments, she touched them, as if hearing their secret song, but it was the scrolls that brought tears to her eyes. She carried them to her room ignoring the basket with her clothes. Soon they heard her tuning the *kithara*, and then a melody strummed on it reached everyone standing in the atrium and in the workshops; they stopped what they were doing to listen, entranced, and Erastos joined them.

Helena's music continued to fill the house during her last few days in Corinth, Phoebe told him later, and they thought her content.

————— ✺ —————

They started out on a lovely, sunny Corinthian morning, Phoebe and Helena accompanied by Erastos and a slave who led two loaded mules. They had refused Erastos' offers to ride. Flanked by fields of red poppies, olive trees, and tall slender cypresses they savored the open air of the countryside and talked of history. The ancient, gnarled olive trees enchanted Helena, filled as they were with myths, the secret caves of their trunks reminding her of childhood and mystery. She whispered these memories to Phoebe, and she, not wishing to leave Erastos out of the conversation, asked him about the Roman milestones and road building, the statues that flanked the road, and together they speculated on how the land must have looked when it was Greek, not Roman. They avoided personal references.

As they trudged along they grew quiet and Helena stopped discussing history with Phoebe. She walked on faster than the others, and soon she was ahead of them, lost in her thoughts and memories.

She felt the old sorrow descend upon her. The sea appeared in the distance, before any signs of the port city became visible. This is the gift of Greece to her inhabitants: the startling indigo blue in the horizon, the suddenness of its appearance, the blending of mountains, sky, and sea in the horizon. *I'd like to keep on walking, to be absorbed by the blueness, to be lost as Ares and Father are lost. But what is beyond that? What memories remain? Is everything forgotten and erased as though*

*it had never been? What was it that Paul was saying one day—
something about not dying, about one day knowing and seeing
clearly, not—she remembered his exact words—"through a glass
darkly?"*

She walked on accompanied by her longing and by
Paul's words of which she had total recall. *These people know
something I cannot even begin to guess. Paul and Prisca are filled
with knowing. Phoebe knows because her heart is good; the rest
probably are only guessing. And I?*

———— ✣ ————

They arrived in Kenchreaê by late afternoon and were
welcomed by Junia, the captain's wife, and her household. The
house was even more modest than Phoebe's, its atrium large
and filled with light. The breeze brought with it the smell of the
sea. Erastos was reluctant to leave, but after unloading the time
came to take his slave and remove to a local inn for the night.
Soon after dark, Junia's household was asleep.

But Helena remained awake, listening for Phoebe's quiet
breathing, waiting for her to slip into that realm where even
the sense of hearing is lost. Then Helena finalized her plans.
She waited for darkness and stillness to engulf the house. There
were no slaves here to run back and forth doing household
chores by night, and Helena was sure no one would notice
her intended absence. She dressed carefully and waited for the
break of dawn. The time had come. She threw a long dark cloak
over her tunic and let herself out in the deep quiet of the shore.
Those who had been up most of the night were now sleeping
off the drink. She avoided the warehouses by the bay but
already knew her way to the Bath of Eleni so well that she
needed no light to guide her. She ran, listening to the gentle lapping of the water on her left, thankful for the stars and
the young moon that provided enough light for her feet. She
almost loved the sea at that moment and thought of Xenophon

and his people crying out, *"Thálatta, thálatta!"* at the sight of the familiar, beloved blue. In her hands she carried a vial of oil mixed with wine. "It's the best I can do, Ares," she whispered to his shade.

She could see well enough in the eerie light that played on the waters of the Saronic Gulf as she made her silent way past the southern jetty to the Bath of Eleni. No cargo ships docked here. She knew this port because she had come with her father and other young athletes to swim and to train for endurance. There was a long stretch of sand beyond the warehouses with only a few empty fishing skiffs in the sea. The Bath of Eleni, near the shores of the Saronic Gulf, was a favorite warm spring from the years of her happiness. She dropped her cloak on the sand and entered this sea of her love and hate. She waded into the cold waters of the night, flinching until she reached the Bath's current of warmth that tempered it. When the water reached her waistline she stopped and lifted the vial high, ceremoniously. She poured the libation drop by drop over the calm waters. The offering splashed, rippled in ever widening circles, and disappeared leaving only a trace of oil on the surface. "Oh, Ares, my love," she cried, "accept this offering of grief and farewell. The bitter sea has taken your young body. The fish have made a meal of your black eyes, and I am left bereft. Oh, Ares, if you had only stayed. We could have forgotten together. If I had the courage, I would follow you, my love. What must I do? Can you send me a sign? Is it as sad and desperate where you are as Odysseus found it in the under-world? Or are my new friends right? Do they have the truth that escaped even our beloved Homer? Do you remember, Ares? Do you remember how Father read to us from Homer and you called out, 'Eleni, Eleni, come back, don't go to Troy?' How we laughed those days. Who would have thought that Ares and Helena would never fulfill the vows of their childhood!"

She stood, half submerged, and wept aloud, crying out to

the heavens and the sea. The vial was now empty, but her arm remained upraised as if in farewell. And then, *de profundis,* a voice startled her and she almost went under. "Helena?" The sound slid over the waters. "Are you Helena, the daughter of Demosthenes?" Shivering, she looked around. Was she hearing voices? There was no one, no shadows on the shore. "Helena? Is this the betrothed of Ares the Corinthian?" She heard again the gruff male voice.

"Who's there?" she called out, frantic now. All the superstitions she had avoided came knocking, shaking her. "Who's there? Where *are* you?"

"Here, here!" the voice responded, and Helena looked toward the deeper waters. There was a small fishing vessel tied on a mooring just ahead of her, and it rocked dangerously as someone moved within it. A head, covered by wild long hair was peeping above the stern. The sun, just rising above the horizon, painted him red and gold. She made out the man's bleary face and sleepy eyes. "Who are you?" she asked and heard the chattering of her teeth, the hysteria in her voice. "How do you know my name?"

The man's torso now appeared above the stern; she heard a huge splash as he jumped in the water and swam the few meters to her, but she was frozen, growing heavy, rooted to the bottom of the sea, immobile. "This is the end, Ares," Helena whispered. "I'll be joining you soon."

"Don't be afraid," the man said as he reached her. His accent told her he was not a Greek of the mainland. He raised his massive body above the water, and she averted her eyes because he was scantily clothed. Incongruously, she remembered Odysseus and Nausikäa.

"How do you know my name?" she asked again, feeling a little less afraid.

The man laughed. "Even if I hadn't heard your name before, I would have learned it from your own lips. You were addressing Ares and you said your name is Helena. Your voice carries over the water. I did not mean to eavesdrop."

Helena was filled with embarrassment. "You were in that boat asleep and I woke you?"

"It was a lovely voice to wake up to," the man answered, a smile in his voice. "My name is Dionysos of Alexandria," and he made an awkward little bow over the calm waters.

"I wouldn't have been surprised if you had said your name is Odysseus of Ithaca," she quipped, and he laughed. She saw this scene as from the outside, the ridiculousness of her position. Here she was, fully clothed, unaccompanied, halfway submerged in the waters of the Saronic Gulf, conversing with a nearly naked stranger.

Then it hit her. She forgot shame, propriety, everything she had been taught. She faced him. "How did you know about Ares?" she cried. "How did you know he was my betrothed?"

"Because, my sad young woman, I lived with your Ares all these months, and he called your name out again and again, the way you were calling out his name a minute ago."

At that, she heard a pitiful sound—was it hers?—and she let the waters cover her. When she opened her eyes a little later, she was lying on the sand and Erastos was bending over her.

———— ⌘ ————

Erastos had started missing Helena even before they left Corinth for Kenchreaê. A year before, after that first delightful glimpse of her in a public place touched him to the core, he had given up all hope of knowing her, when Claudia had crushed him with the news that Helena was betrothed to another. But that first sighting of her had been another Helena, happy and secure in her father's and Ares' love. This sad, lost Helena he had come to know had become a part of his life; now he was about to lose her also.

His initial protectiveness toward her persisted, but now it

was filled with longing. After her move to Kenchreaê, Erastos knew he wouldn't have the many opportunities to see her as he had when Helena lived in Corinth with Phoebe.

He saw the two women safe at Junia's, in her large but simple house near the sea, and then he left with his slave to get comfortable in the inn; but sleep would not come during the long fitful night. The inns of the Roman world with their noise, dirt, and bugs were far from his favorite places, so he rose in the dark, walked to the sea, took a quick night swim to cleanse his body and then, wrapping himself in his wool cloak, he lay in a secluded spot to dream of Helena.

In the early morning, aware of the proximity of her quarters, restless and miserable, he splashed water on his face and strolled toward Junia's house. Hearing no sounds of life from within, he moved to the shore and then along the beach to the Bath of Eleni. The name appealed to him. *Eleni*, he thought, savoring the Greek form of her name. *She never leaves me.* He looked around him, saw fishing skiffs anchored in the water but no fishermen yet. With no one else about he was glad of the solitude and quiet.

He was startled from peace into a waking nightmare when, on a shoal south of the jetty, he saw a man with a woman in his arms in the act of depositing her on the sand. Because Helena had never left his thoughts, he was filled with the unexplained fear that she was the victim. He ran and fell on his knees next to her. "What have you done to her?" Before Erastos could rise from his knees, the man had run to the sea and was now swimming away with long powerful strokes. Helena opened her eyes.

"Erastos? What are *you* doing here? Where is he? Where is the man Dionysos?"

Erastos was shocked. "You know that man?"

Helena jumped up and looked to the sea. "Come back, Dionysos," she cried out with a strength that forced Erastos to stay quiet. "Come back and tell me about Ares!"

The man was already climbing onto a skiff. Helena turned to Erastos with fury. "What have you done?" she demanded, and for the first time in his adult life he felt like crying. "Why did you have to interfere? Go, tell him to come back. He must tell me his story."

For a long, troubled moment Erastos looked at her without comprehension, then he shook his head and waded in the water. When he got close enough he called out, "Stranger, I don't know what happened between you two, but she wants you to come back, to finish a story you obviously had begun."

Erastos heard the man laughing and then his head appeared above the side. "You two come here," he said. "I cannot afford to be seen on the shore now that the port is waking up."

Erastos returned to Helena who stood waiting, barefoot, and clad only in her short wet tunic. "Can you swim?" he asked her and she almost laughed. She ran to the water's edge, waded on the shallow part and then swam toward the boat. The stranger lowered his powerful arm to pull her up and Erastos, swimming behind her, saw her disappear into the boat. The man then offered Erastos his hand and he followed in confusion; he had no other choice. There they sat, the three of them, crowded in that flimsy little skiff that smelled of fish—Dionysos with an amused expression, Helena pale, and Erastos furious.

Her eyes were on the rough stranger's face as if it held the answers to the world's questions. "Tell me," she pleaded, and behind her determination Erastos heard a trembling that dissolved his anger. Any minute now she will shatter, he thought with pity. The man turned to Erastos. "Who are you?" he asked.

"Only a friend. I accompanied her and another woman friend to Kenchreaê just yesterday. But she is under my protection. You must speak to Helena in my presence."

Helena said impatiently. "You can speak in front of Erastos.

My *prostates,* Phoebe, trusts him."

He felt it like a blow between the brows, her lack of trust in him, and vowed to himself, *After this, I will leave. I will forget her.*

In a voice that now sang with hope, Helena asked, "Is Ares alive then? I must know before you say anything else, is he alive?"

Dionysos said, "When I left him about a month ago he was very much alive. It has taken me this long to make my way here."

Erastos was choking with unasked questions but Helena kept repeating the words, "He lives, he lives, he lives!" Then she lowered her head on her knees, and they saw her shoulders shaking with silent sobs. Dionysos said kindly, "You must have thought we drowned together with the ship." A strangled sound escaped her and he said in a monotone that barely hid despair: "We very nearly died, Helena; we were taken by thieves, runaway slaves. Our rescuers were kidnappers, and thugs." Erastos was now imagining he was in a play. He could not believe that this conversation was taking place in the everyday reality of his life. Being an actor had been much easier. *I'm a fool to be obsessed by this troubled girl and her mythical problems.*

She didn't seem able to move. Her head was hidden in her arms, but her sobs had abated. Dionysos looked to Erastos. "Who are you really?" he asked, and the answer came in a sad voice, "Only a friend who happened to be present on the most dangerous night of her life." And then he remembered another responsibility and stood up suddenly causing the boat to rock on the still waters. "Phoebe!" he cried. "Helena, does Phoebe know where you are?"

The girl whispered, "No, I left while it was still dark."

"Then we must go to her at once. She'll be out of her mind with worry." He turned to Dionysos. "Will you help? Will you come with us to our friend's and tell us your story there?"

Dionysos opened his arms. "Look at me," he said. "I'm not fit to be presented to respectable women in their home. I was once a prosperous physician. Now I have to live like a thief in order to survive. My practice and all my goods are in Alexandria, and I don't know if the kidnappers have agents here. Seaports are notorious for harboring thieves and criminals. These thugs will kill me, because I can identify them."

Erastos dismissed his worry. "I doubt they are here. This is a legitimate port and soon it will be broad daylight. Come, my cloak is on the shore. You can cover yourself with it, and then we must take Helena to her hosts. We cannot leave them in ignorance. It's dangerous for her and for you."

So Dionysos agreed. Swimming and wading they made it to the shore where they found Helena's cloak, and Erastos wrapped her in it. Then he covered Dionysos' head and shoulders with his own cloak. "I know a secret way," Helena said. "No one will see us." And she led them, two men of the world who seemed insecure that morning, behind the warehouses, to the neighboring beach, and from there to her hosts.

The captain's house was in commotion. Phoebe, fully dressed, was emerging from the front door with the rest of the women behind her, but when they saw the soggy trio they let out a joyous cry and Phoebe ran to Helena. Putting an arm around her she propelled her toward the house while the rest rushed to find towels and dry clothes. Erastos approached Phoebe. "Something very strange has happened. This traveler has some news for Helena; is it possible for him to come in and tell us his story?"

Phoebe and Junia conferred quietly. "As long as you are present for propriety's sake, Erastos, yes. But first we must offer hospitality to our guest. Do show him in." He led Dionysos to the back of the house while the women heated water and brought dry clothes. Since the captain had left his own tunics behind, they were able to clothe both men.

While the stranger washed and dressed himself in private and Helena was being rubbed down by the women servants, Erastos tried telling Phoebe what he had experienced on the shore. "I think I'm dreaming when I'm with her," he confessed. "There's an unreality about her and all her problems. When you've heard the stranger's story, you too might wonder, what kind of coincidence is this? The man has news of Ares. But how could she possibly meet up with a man who knew her betrothed? Are we dealing with magic?"

Phoebe shook her head. "We don't believe in magic. We believe in the workings of the Holy Spirit. Someone is looking after this orphaned girl, Erastos. You feature in her story as much as I do. And now, this preposterous visitor. What do we know of this man?"

"Nothing, except that he didn't harm Helena before I arrived; he claims to have been a physician in Alexandria, and Helena is convinced that he has some astounding news for her."

They waited in silence. Small tables were now covered with vials of warmed, honeyed wine, with freshly baked bread and cheeses, salted fish, fruit, and the dark olives of the Peloponnesos. "The stranger must be hungry," Junia said and then she left.

Helena emerged and ran to Phoebe. "I'm not to be forgiven for leaving the protection of your house so early this morning," she cried, "but, Phoebe, I was embarrassed to ask you to go with me to offer libations to the sea. I know you don't hold with such rituals. I needed to make a final offering to Ares' spirit, you see, to say farewell, since this is the port that saw him last. I was very careful to go where there were no people, to a secluded shoal I remembered at the Bath of Eleni from years past. I was safe, Phoebe, I was in the sea, calling out my farewell to Ares when I heard the voice of this stranger. He called me by my name, the 'daughter of Demosthenes,' he said, the 'betrothed of Ares the Corinthian.' I thought I had caused this with the intensity of my desire to see Ares again, but then I saw the man's face above the boat's rim. He said he knows Ares. Oh, Phoebe, he says Ares is alive!" Her voice broke and Erastos saw Phoebe's eyes filling up with tears. Helena, looking a bit ashamed, added quickly: "I don't know where Erastos came from."

"I couldn't sleep," he explained. "I seem to appear when you are in danger, Helena, for we still don't know with any certainty who this man is," and at that moment Dionysos emerged from the back rooms. He was clean and almost tidy, but what struck them was his bearing; the stormed-tossed adventurer was now a respectable man of the world. He held himself straight, the clean clothes hung on him with a surprising elegance, and he had managed to put some order to his wild long curls by pulling his hair back and tying it with a string. His face was ruddy and weather-bitten, with the stamp of long exposure to sea and sun, his skin baked into thousands of wrinkles that showed white when it was in repose.

He made a deep bow before Phoebe. "Dionysos of Alexandria," he said to her, "deeply grateful for your hospitality."

She accepted graciously, giving all the credit to her hostess Junia who had removed herself from the gathering. "Friend Dionysos," she said with her customary kindness, "you must eat and drink first and then tell us you story."

He looked at the citron and pomegranates and sighed. "It's been a long time since I have tasted freshness." Phoebe offered him a juicy sliced pomegranate and he sucked on the luscious fruit, his eyes closed. They all joined in the eating, not wanting him to feel alone. He took a long draft of watered wine and then looked at Helena whose face was pale, her eyes huge.

"I'm a physician still," he said studying her. "You need to eat more than you are eating, and you need rest. You're too young to look so pale and wan."

Phoebe patted Helena's hand. "I look after her," she said. "This morning's excitement has removed her natural, healthy color. And now we are ready to hear more from you."

Chapter 13: Dionysos' Story

Dionysos heaved a sigh that arose from his depths. He seemed to know that Helena could not wait another minute. But first, he owed an explanation to his hosts.

He smiled, and they saw that this was a man who once appreciated the ironies of life. "It wasn't a *deus ex machina* that brought me to Helena," he said. "I arrived from the north yesterday and started talking to a couple of fishermen, trying to find work. I knew I had to walk to Corinth to find Helena, but you saw my state. How could I walk to the city without being taken for a thief? One of the fishermen said I could sleep in his boat and he would give me work today. So I agreed. I had nowhere else to go. And then, this dawn, I heard a lovely voice calling out to the gods. If she was surprised, imagine what I thought. I had been feeling like Odysseus, and now, suddenly, here was my Nausikaä." He smiled, and they saw what an attractive man he must have been in his youth.

Helena said impatiently. "Please, we can talk about this later. Tell us about yourself."

His story started with some difficulty but soon his past

took shape and through recounting the painful memories the man emerged fully grown and worth knowing.

Dionysos had been a successful doctor in Alexandria, the rich, fashionable city on the northern shores of Egypt, a city populated with Greeks from the time of Alexander. He had become prosperous, married to a young woman he loved; he had three children with her and two more who felt like sons, trained by him to assist in his practice. Money and able assistants afforded him the leisure to travel, to expand his knowledge of the healing arts. He had visited Kos, the birthplace of Hippocrates, worshiped there as at a shrine, grateful for the ancient physician's wisdom and high ethical standards. Then he started visiting the mainland of Greece, especially Epidauros and the Asklepeion to learn of the practices of the divine doctor Asklepeios and his follow-ers first hand. Of mixed parentage, as were most residents of Alexandria, Dionysos felt a deep affection for Greece; he himself was born of a Greek mother, and for him Greece held both the mystery and the key to the mysteries.

It was after such a pilgrimage that Dionysos found himself in Kenchreaê where he sought a ship to take him back to Alexandria. Word had reached him that one of his assistants had disappeared, and the other had taken over the practice, announcing to the clients that Dionysos was dead. Dionysos' wife and children, he had heard, too, were no longer in their home. Fearful of what had happened to his family he decided to sail back immediately, even though it was late in the season and the winds were dangerous in the fall of the year. He found the Eirēnē, a large vessel that was already laden with the famous Corinthian brass ornaments and the votive lamps that were all the rage in Alexandria and Rome that year. The Eirēnē would return to the mainland filled with wheat in its large belly; in the spring and summer, the wheat would eventually reach Rome. The captain of Eirēnē was an independent Greek, an excellent sailor, unlike the Romans, a man stubborn and unwilling to be stopped by omens. He laughed when he heard from the Roman captains who tried to prevent him from sailing that the flight of birds should determine his chances. Superstitions didn't deter him. He wanted to make money, and he was sure both of his vessel and his expertise. The rich cargo of lamps, black amphorae, and Corinthian bronze would bring much profit. He was eager for it, and his income increased when a number of Greeks, for various reasons, paid him handsomely in their desire to come aboard and reach Alexandria before the winter set in.

The journey started out well. Soon the few passengers became acquainted with one another and Dionysos singled out the handsome young Greek who seemed exceptionally alone and quiet. Finding that they both loved the poets, they spent the long days talking about the Athenians of that glorious time that followed the Persian wars. At night, they would move north in their discussions, analyzing the battles of Alexander on his inexorable move to the east. It was heady conversation for both of them.

"You remind me of Demosthenes," Ares told the older man and Dionysos laughed aloud.

"That old Athenian windbag who hated Alexandros, the Makedonian king?"

Ares joined in the laughter. "No, not that orator. I am speaking of my mentor and adopted father, Demosthenes of Korinthia." So it was that Dionysos learned about Helena and her father and of Ares' love for her. Ares told him of his own sojourn to Olympia and his rediscovery of Helena as a desirable young woman when he returned to Corinth.

"So how could you leave her?" Dionysos asked. "What are you doing sailing to Alexandria at this time of year?" Ares shrugged, but by the fifth day he had come to trust Dionysos and revealed to him his need to make money in order to rescue

Helena from the rich Roman patron.

"But you're running away!" Dionysos said. "You could have waited; why didn't you?" Ares could not answer. Dionysos observed the accusation of running away seemed to sting the boy. He thought of his own youth and first love and hoped that before the journey was finished he could devise ways to help the two young people who had lost their Demosthenes and needed an older man to guide them.

The weather started worrying the captain that same night. They had made a stop at Naxos and one at Paros to deliver and pick up provisions and they were making for Crete when everything changed. Despite the weight of the huge, big-bellied vessel, by day seven it was being tossed like a halved nutshell, as the Greek saying went. That night the ship, tossed to the rocks of a small island, cracked; amphorae and lamps were sucked by the whirlpool; screams, yells, curses, and prayers mixed and rose to match the fury of the elements.

Dionysos' immediate concern was for Ares. In the bright flare of lightning he saw the boy sitting immobile on the deck, having given up hope. Ares cried out, "Farewell, Helena," and Dionysos heard it as a final goodbye. Dionysos stumbled to him and grabbed him by the arm. At that moment, the secondary mast broke and fell next to them; it barely missed crushing them. *The gods must want us alive,* Dionysos thought. He cried out to Ares to help him. Together they rolled the mast overboard and jumped after it. Holding on, they kicked powerfully to move away from the suction of the sea as the ship started breaking up and sinking. Dionysos, with his *zona,* tied one of Ares' hands on the mast by the wrist and then he managed to secure one of his own wrists. After a few agonizing hours of darkness they saw the first light of day and thanked all the gods they knew by name. Dionysos started talking to Ares, trying to keep him awake, struggling to see that he did not give in to despair and the force of the waters.

By morning a calm had descended on the surface of the sea, and they could see floating detritus and other pitiful signs of the dreadful night, together with bodies of the drowned. Holding on to the mast, their lifesaver, they endured the indifferent sun of that first day and the cold of the waters, and took turns sleeping; tied to the mast as they were they would not drift into a drowning end when exhaustion overtook them They kept each other alert by telling stories, until their throats dried out.

Here Dionysos stopped his remembered tale and reached for a beaker of water. He had lost his easy manner and his eyes had turned dark. Helena looked as if her life were hanging from his words. She shivered when he stopped to look at her. "Helena, are you with me?" he asked gently.

"Don't stop," she whispered, "please continue."

"We survived," the big man said flatly and then hurried on, as if that really was not the important part of the story. "On the afternoon of that day a ship spotted us and made its way toward us. We were overjoyed. Strange to behold, she was a *trirēmē* and did not look like a merchant vessel, so in a way we thought we were hallucinating. Who would have thought a *trirēmē* of old would still be traveling by using rowers instead of sails? Unable to speak, we looked at each other. We were dreaming of reaching port within days, since everyone knows the Aegean is dotted with islands.

"But we didn't know what awaited us. Had we known, we might have wished we hadn't survived the water's cold. The ship was a *trirēmē*, yes, a remnant of the fighting ships of old, but as soon as they hauled us on board it was obvious that slaves had already died tied to its oars. The stink that met us was unbearable.

"They gave us water and a little food, just to keep us alive; they tossed out two bodies, made sure our strength had barely returned, and then tied us to the oars."

At that memory, Dionysos stopped his easy recounting. He looked troubled. He rubbed his forehead and his eyes. Phoebe reached out a hand. "You don't have to talk any longer. Rest, my friend."

He looked at her, then at Helena. "I need to finish this," he said. "I'll abbreviate the horror. Like most people in this part of the world I thought that Rome had cleaned the Aegean and the other seas of piracy back in the days of Pompey. I was not prepared for such barbarity. I thought I was hallucinating, but soon I faced the harsh new day and admitted to myself that by the look and sound of our captors we must be in the hands of escaped slaves led by a few rich, ruthless freedmen. They had found an old vessel, had repaired it, and were now roaming the seas looking for wrecks, loot, and victims like us, preferring the treacherous winter months when fewer ships sailed and they were not as likely to be discovered by other vessels. So far their plan had succeeded. They needed many hands to man the oars, to carry the stolen cargo—and all of them expendable. Those they had helped to escape drowning made the perfect slaves for the brutal work of rowing.

"With no possessions, no documentation on us to show that we were Roman citizens of the provinces, we were easy prey. So it was that escaped slaves made slaves of *us*—free men—and used us for the hardest labor. They were heading for Troas, the other prisoners told us, but we had no way of confirming that it was so. I only hoped against all hope that our ordeal would not imitate that of Odysseus on his way back from Troas. On the way north, the thieves stopped often for provisions, but they did so only at night, on deserted coves, so no one could see us below deck, and we had no way of alerting anyone on shore that we were not slaves. Shouting would have brought more abuse on our bleeding backs and shoulders. It was obvious to me that these kidnappers had collaborators in the ports where they stopped and where the slave trade was brisk—an organized network of thieves.

"I was much more concerned for Ares than for myself, because by now he felt like my son, and I was deeply worried about him. He was such a handsome lad! In order to protect him from abuse I announced that he was my son and anyone laying a hand on him would have to deal with me." Dionysos lowered his head and whispered, "It helped, but not always." Only Phoebe heard the last phrase. Dionysos continued: "Ares seemed to have given up all efforts to survive. 'Think of Helena,' I would mouth at him whenever I was close. His eyes had grown enormous on his gaunt face and I kept hoping that because he had been an athlete, he would survive."

Dionysos couldn't share with her the horror he felt when he saw the reaction of the rapacious men of that crew at first seeing the beautiful Ares. He did all in his power to convince them that Ares was indeed his son, and that as a rich man himself he would reward them when he was freed. He couldn't tell her of the humiliation and degradation he felt, of his unending worry for Ares' safety.

It was Phoebe who sensed all this, and she reached out her hand in a gesture of compassion.

"Oh, you sad man," she said, "your memories must be unbearable," and now her tears ran freely. This gave Dionysos time to compose himself.

"Yes," he continued, "my fears for Ares were a particular torment, but as a physician I had other responsibilities. I could not endure seeing men dying in filth and with gangrene. What supplies they had for injuries were meager. They freed me from shackles for a couple of hours each day to treat the sick, but it was nearly hopeless. When we reached the large island of Lesvos I demanded to get off the ship for medicinal supplies—I assured them I would return because of Ares—but they laughed at me. So I changed tactics. I persuaded them to release Ares from his chains so that with his help in treating the sick I could double my effectiveness. To this they agreed. Yet as the days passed, we despaired that everyone who had heard of the *Eirēnē* must now know us as dead."

He looked at Helena who was so still she seemed not to be breathing, but when she didn't say anything, he continued: "The thieves threw us out before they reached their destination, whatever that was. I imagine they knew that if we found an opportunity when in a city we would seek out the authorities, who would go after them, to find them. But whatever their thinking, they had apparently finished with us as slaves and, having no further use for us, they dumped us on a deserted shore and left us with no provisions, sure that we would die before we met another soul. Even I lost hope then, because I didn't have anything with which to help Ares. I didn't know where we were and he could not walk. It was night when they abandoned us. In the morning I managed to lift him, and I climbed away from the shore in hope of finding help, inland. We were in desperate need of drinking water."

Now a smile appeared in his eyes and he lifted his head to look at Phoebe. "This is where the story turns peculiar," he quipped, and his audience stirred. Erastos poured more water for all of them and they drank thirstily.

"I found a path that climbed away from the sea, but I couldn't see anything made by man." The physician's voice now was stronger, his eyes no longer filled with the terrible images in his head. A dark weight had been lifted, releasing him. "The terrain, covered with short pines, climbed higher, then sloped and dropped, then another low hill rose—the usual features of Greek land. I was guessing that we must be somewhere in eastern Makedonia, near Neapolis or even on the island of Thasos. If I was right, there was hope for us. I stretched next to Ares, under the pines, to rest.

"After what seemed like a long while I heard distant singing, and I said, 'Hold on, my boy, help's on the way.' I stood up. I hid him behind a bitter laurel bush and waited. The singing drew closer. Then I saw an otherworldly procession climbing from the low hill closest to us; a line of heads appeared above the crest and soon, in the brilliant Greek light, as in a dream, the heads became attached to bodies that floated toward us. They were dressed in white, men and women—probably twenty of them—their tunics long and unbelted. They looked and sounded utterly peaceful, a shock to my system after the violence of the ship. I cried out, 'Friends, we are shipwrecked and in great need.' They stopped, formed a circle and seemed to be conferring. Then one of them stepped forward and said, 'Show yourself, friend.'

"I answered: 'Ask the women to turn their faces away, for we are a miserable sight.'

"They did as I asked and I stepped out, my arms held in supplication. I heard their indrawn breath, but two of the men approached me. 'I've a young person with me,' I said; 'he's gravely ill.'

"The apparent leader looked at me with pity. 'Philemon is my name,' he said, 'do not be afraid.' And I heard his name of friendship as a good omen. He came with me, while the second man ran back for water and returned with two beakers full. Philemon bent over Ares who now lay still and nearly unconscious. He dripped water into his mouth while I had my fill from the second beaker. He said to me, 'We have a woman among us who has the gift of healing. I will fetch Lydia.' And he ran back to his group.

Phoebe caught her breath. "Lydia," she murmured. "Could it be Paul's Lydia?"

"He returned with a woman of strong features and serene appearance. She carried bread and wine in her hands, handed them to Philemon and then bent down to examine Ares. 'He's in need of immediate attention. First, let's see if he will take some nourishment; then we will carry him to one of our homes to bathe him and look at his wounds.'

"I found it remarkable that she didn't cover her nose or show any distaste at the sight of us. So I said, 'I'm a physician, even though I look like a galley slave. If we can carry him to a bathhouse, I will treat his wounds myself.'

"Lydia and Philemon looked at each other. He said, 'We were on our way to the sea to baptize our new brothers and sisters. But your need takes precedence. We will look after both of you.'

"Just as simple as that. They had not asked us anything about ourselves, and they showed no fear. They took one of those white garments they were carrying, made a stretcher out of it and then two of the men lifted Ares and placed him on it. Meanwhile Lydia was speaking to the women who were waiting patiently. The group split in two. Some, led by Philemon, continued toward the water while the rest, with Lydia in charge, came with us. We walked in silence. When the first houses appeared she said, "We're approaching Neapolis and Philemon's home, which is nearby; you will soon rest.'

"We stopped at a clean whitewashed house, its brilliant red roof reminiscent of Corinth. After that sight, no shelter will ever look as good to me, as long as I live. Very gently they placed Ares on a rug on the tiles of the atrium and the women rushed to heat water. One of the men took me to a makeshift washhouse in the back and offered to help me bathe. 'All I need is a *strigil*—oil and water,' I said, but when he returned with all my needs he scrubbed my back gently and then left me alone. I have never been as grateful for the gift of sweet water and of cleanliness.

"When I returned to the atrium I saw that Ares had been washed and dressed in a clean tunic, looking almost comfortable as he slept on a couch. I examined all his wounds carefully and then Lydia showed me her store of herbs and unguents. We were afraid of gangrene where the chains had cut into his wounds, so both Lydia and I worked intensely for a couple of hours. Whenever we stopped to rest, one of the girls fed Ares from a bowl of broth, gently, as if he were a child.

"Then Lydia knelt by his couch and took hold of one of his hands. She closed her eyes and remained silent for a long while. Little by little I could understand words escaping her lips and I realized that she was praying to a God I did not recognize. She prayed for Ares' healing—that I understood. She was so intent that she seemed gone from us, in another realm. At last I couldn't keep myself from asking, 'Who are you?' and she answered, without opening her eyes, 'We are followers of the Lord Yeesous Christós.'"

At that Phoebe smiled and Helena made a noise, something that sounded like laughter, and exchanged glances with Phoebe. "You fell among people of The Way!" Helena said to Dionysos. "Just as I did on the worst night of my life, you too fell among the followers of Christ!" She laughed aloud and then, turning to Erastos, she gave him a radiant smile which he accepted like thanksgiving.

"You too are called Christ-followers?" Dionysos asked. "By Zeus, I should have guessed!" and now they all spoke together, with great excitement. Phoebe said, "Some call us by that name in derision, to mock Yeesous Christós and his death on a cross, but we carry it with honor." Neither Helena nor Erastos contradicted her. They turned their faces to Dionysos, waiting for the rest of his story. He rubbed his forehead and shook his great head.

"The amazing thing," he said with a wry smile, "was that even though I asked the question of them they never asked it of me, of us. They had cleaned and fed us and carried one of us for an hour and prayed over us, but they did not demand to know who we were. I volunteered the information so that they would know we had been respectable in our former lives. Finding myself among civilized people I wanted to reassure them and then take my leave as soon as possible to return to Alexandria, to find my family." He placed his elbows on his knees and lowered his head.

They waited. Without looking at them he continued, "I fear that I may have no family or practice left. If that is so, the only thing that matters to me is healing people. The other concern of my life had been to make money. The terrible adventure with the ship and the thieves deprived me of all I held dear. I need to return home but I'm afraid to trust the news of my survival in a letter. I don't know what dark forces await me in Alexandria and who, if any, among my associates has remained faithful to me. I have confidence that when my influential patients see me in the flesh I'll regain my livelihood among the Alexandrians. So I wanted to leave Lydia and her ministrations as soon as possible, but I could not abandon Ares who through the ordeal had become my son."

Now Helena, to everyone's surprise, reached out and placed her thin fingers on the man's rough hand and caressed it. Dionysos put his other large hand on top of hers and held on. "Forgive me for leaving him behind," he said to her. "He's in better hands than mine."

"You saved his life," Helena told him in a grateful voice. "There's nothing to forgive. But please tell me how you left him. Why couldn't he travel with you?"

Dionysos seemed now to speak only to her. "I'm a physician and a skeptic, Helena. In my life, I've come across charlatans and false and greedy priests. There are many stories of healing connected with the god Asklepeios. But what happened in Neapolis still puzzles me. The woman Lydia laid her hands on Ares and prayed to her strange God. His wounds started healing from that moment on. They no longer stank with the evil suspicion of gangrene, but he remains very weak. He has lost much weight and blood and he seems to lie in a deep melancholia. When I left, they were taking him to Philippi where Lydia lives, and they were working on healing his spirit. At least, that's what the formidable woman told me."

Dionysos shook his head and looked at Phoebe as if seeking her help. "You remind me of her," he told her. "What is it about you, People of the Way? Or do you prefer the word Christians? In the north they are using the appellation more and more. But I had thought this was a sect for slaves and for fools."

"It is," she said, "it is." She inclined her head with that self-deprecating smile that was her characteristic.

But Erastos had noticed Helena's silent tears. "How long ago did you leave him?" he demanded.

Dionysos shrugged and seemed to have lost a sense of time. "I stayed with him for a week," he said. "Then I volunteered to work as crew on one of the ships leaving Neapolis for Kenchreaê. I was planning to make myself presentable, walk to Corinth, and seek you out, Helena, to tell you his news. That is all he asked of me."

Her eyes were full of questions. He answered her without being asked: "He didn't want to write. The young are a mystery to people of my age, Helena. He wanted me to see you face to face, to tell you he's alive. His last letter to you was a mistake, he said, and it brought disaster upon him. He doesn't want to make another mistake. I'm to write to him immediately after seeing you to report your news, to see if you are safe. But he begged me to do all in my power to take you away from the house of a Gaius Marius Sylvanus."

A big question mark hung over his last sentence but, when the others remained silent, he addressed only Phoebe. "Ares is learning about your faith. He doesn't know if Helena will acknowledge him now that he's attracted to 'this new great love,' as they refer to your cult in Philippi. Ares carries a great guilt concerning Helena and he told me that he will return only when he's sure of her forgiveness."

Phoebe put an arm around Helena. She said with tender affection: "This is something only Helena can answer." The girl stood up. "I must write a letter," and she disappeared into the house.

They watched her go and Phoebe said, "All this has been too much for her young spirit. She has suffered enough. This new happiness of his survival can be as traumatic as the bad news that has pursued her for months, but I think she will do what she must."

Erastos turned to Dionysos, "You still have not answered my question. How long ago did you leave young Ares?"

"It must have been a month since. The ship I crewed on made several stops at islands on the way. I worked to make money for my passage to Alexandria but I barely made it here, so now I must find something else to do."

Erastos didn't even hesitate. "I would like to advance you the money for your passage," he offered. "A man of your profession should take better care of his hands."

Dionysos looked at his calloused palms; then he turned them over and they saw that several knuckles looked as if they had been broken. He shook his head. "Lydia also offered to give me the money for the journey, but I wouldn't take it. I told her to use it on Ares who is not able to work. I can't accept charity from anyone."

Phoebe now smiled at Dionysos. "My good, kind friend," she said in that low, warm voice that made people sit still and listen. "You yourself have been giving nothing but charity, and that in its purest form. Don't you realize this? It's a great gift you gave to Ares—you saved his life, you protected him. It's a gift also to accept Erastos' offer to you. He can well afford it, and he's making it out of *philia*. Do accept his gift."

Erastos felt such affection for this exceptional woman who always saw good in people that he repeated his offer to the surprised traveler who now looked deeply moved. "If it makes it any easier, you can call it a loan," Erastos insisted. "You may repay me after you regain your lucrative practice." They stood up and laid a hand on each other's shoulder. Dionysos couldn't speak. Erastos added, "You must stay here and rest. I'm off to the port to find out which ships are sailing, and then I will book your passage. I also think that as an official of Corinth I must alert the authorities at the port of the existence of these thieves who almost killed you and your young friend." And he left for the shore.

After Erastos walked out, Dionysos did not move, his face hidden from Phoebe. She gave him time to compose his features. She was drawn to this stranger, to his immense compassion and his strength. After a while he asked her, "Who *is* this man Erastos? He has the bearing and speech of an aristocrat. What's his relationship to you and to Helena?"

"It's a long story, and for Erastos it's a sad one, I'm afraid. He's the son of a good friend of mine. For many years he was Corinth's most famous actor. You see, of course, that he loves Helena."

"Oh, that's painfully obvious," the man responded, "but doesn't she realize?"

"No, she's too absorbed in her own love and sorrow right now."

She studied him for a while and decided that it was easy to trust him. "Friend Dionysos, the Roman Gaius Marius Sylvanus is dead. I don't know what Ares told you, but Helena suffered much in that household because of that Roman. One night, after receiving the news that Ares was lost in the sea, Helena was summoned to play her *kithara* and to sing at her patron's banquet. Erastos happened to be present. Helena threatened the host with death in front of everyone there. Then she hid in her room and waited. When all were asleep Helena left her room and walked to the Roman's chamber intending to kill him—so she has told us since. But Erastos, who had remained behind, followed her and witnessed the whole event. He's sure now that she was sleepwalking. When she reached the patron's chamber she discovered that he was already dead. All this was witnessed by Erastos who whisked her away from there and brought her to me that same night. She's been with me ever since."

Dionysos tried to absorb the tale. "Who killed the Roman?" he asked.

"They termed it a suicide. Erastos thinks it was probably at the wife's urging that someone stabbed him. No one has blamed her and no one has brought charges, so it remains a suicide."

"An astounding story," he said. "Both Ares and Helena are such appealing youngsters. It's impossible not to care what happens to them."

Phoebe agreed, though she had not yet met Ares.

———— ❧ ————

In her room, Helena was writing furiously. Maybe, in the process, the fact that Ares is alive will register, she whispered to herself:

"Ares, my one and only friend since childhood: How does one write to him who was dead for three long months? How does one dead write to another? How can I explain that I too died with you when the news of the sinking reached me? The people I live with, people of The Way, claim that their god returned from the realm of death to life. Married to logos as I am, thanks to my father, I couldn't bring myself to believe it. Now, because of you, because of the good man Dionysos' story, I can believe this claim, for you are returned from the dead also. Ah, Ares, hope arrived in the person of a big, rough-looking Alexandrian at a moment when there was no hope left in my heart. I was ready to follow you in your wet grave. I was standing in the waters in the

port of Kenchreaê from where you departed that fateful day in February. I was offering a libation, knowing that you were gone forever from me and from the earth. I felt the strong temptation to let go of myself, to forget how to swim, to walk into the deeper waters and to keep walking until nothing of pain was left in my heart. And then I heard a voice calling me. I thought it was Kharon come to claim me also. Instead the head of Dionysos, like that of a modern Odysseus, appeared above a fishing boat's rim and I knew that it was not Hades who had called my name. I wanted to live so I could hear your name and learn of your last hours. I did not believe that you were alive, but I did hope that there was one at least who had seen you those last days before the ship sank. Oh, to hear another person speak your name again, my dear friend, that's what I wanted—to know that you were real to someone else besides me. And for you to know, Ares, that when I met Dionysos I had already been whisked away from the terrible household of Gaius Marius Sylvanus. You need to know this immediately. A stranger rescued me and brought me home to a good woman who has become in unexpected ways like the mother I had never known. Can you imagine such good fortune? I was engulfed by goodness but could not respond in kind. After Father's ugly death, and after you left me, I had nothing to live for. No, I do not blame you for leaving. There's nothing to forgive, Ares. We were both victims of Moira. Let us go on from here. But you must know that our beloved Demosthenes was most certainly killed by Gaius Marius Sylvanus. I know now that Father and Claudia were in love, and Gaius punished them as he punished me for loving you. That evil man lives no longer. Someone killed him but, to my regret, it wasn't I. And now I must talk of other things. Dionysos says that you are in Philippi, in the home of a woman named Lydia, as I am at home with Phoebe, and they are both followers of The Way. Isn't this Moira's irony? People we had nothing to do with have become our saviors. I still don't understand what this means. I don't know if you plan to return to Corinth to fulfill the promise of our betrothal vows, or whether I should travel to Philippi. But I must tell you of a man I met in Corinth. His name is Paul. He is the most compelling person I have ever come across and that includes my own remarkable father. This Paul seems to be the leader of the ekklesia here. He has traveled extensively since he left Cilicia, his home—to Judea, to Arabia, and other lands unknown to me. Before coming here he first landed in Makedonia, I hear, and now I wonder if he met your formidable Lydia. Will you ask her? Paul is the kind of man who does not live for himself. This is my immediate impression. Although he is eloquent and proud and full of knowledge, he seems to me to be burning with a fire from within. He lives to talk about, to love, to worship, to serve the one Christians call their Christós. Do you find this true among the people who surround you these days? What strange people they are. And yet, how attracted I am to them. I am longing to learn more. But what will this mean for you and for me? I thought I knew my own mind, but I find myself confused. I wonder about your love for me. Do we resume our interrupted lives? I await your response. If I had the necessary funds I would rush to your side. You must write and tell me your wishes, but do not fret about your last letter. All of that belongs to another life. This is written by the hand of your betrothed, Helena, who loves you."

———— ✺ ————

Helena read the letter again, and then another time as well. Then she emerged from the room quite late to find Phoebe talking quietly with Dionysos. She said, "It's done. I let him know that there's nothing to forgive. You may read it, Phoebe," and she handed the scroll to Phoebe. Afterwards, the older woman was touched to see the brilliance of Helena's smile, how it transformed that sad face into something radiant and beautiful. She heard Dionysos sigh when he saw the young beauty. Erastos, walking in at that moment, caught sight of Helena's glowing face and seemed transfixed. *Poor, lovesick man,* Phoebe thought and suspected that Dionysos agreed.

It took a minute for Erastos to recover. "All is ready for you, Dionysos," he announced. "A ship sails for Alexandria on the day after tomorrow. Your passage on it is booked."

Helena turned from one man to the other. "What's all this about?"

Dionysos said to her, "Your kind friend here has arranged for me to return to my home. I owe him a great deal." And then he spoke solemnly to Erastos, "Thank you. I will not forget the generosity of a man I did not know yesterday. I hope one day you will journey to Alexandria for I would like to return your hospitality and show you my city."

Erastos replied, "That day may come sooner than you think," and Phoebe heard in that answer the first hint that he might go away from Helena, maybe even his dreams of her. He said to Phoebe: "Is that Helena's letter? Would you like for me to see that it reaches Philippi? The ships are faster than the land post."

Wordless, she handed him her rolled papyrus, but Dionysos asked for permission to add his own note before it was sealed.

And now came a time of waiting. Dionysos, eager as he was to resume his trip to Alexandria after the dreadful interlude of the storm and kidnapping, had to wait for his journey's end and a new beginning. Helena was waiting for Ares to respond, and Erastos decided it was time to stop waiting. All hope that Helena would eventually turn to him for comfort and love seemed extinguished. He told Phoebe he would be returning to Corinth as soon as Dionysos departed.

Chapter 14: Philippi

Inside Lydia's house, Ares was exercising his recovering body. Whenever he stopped to rest he jotted down his thoughts:

"The days pass. I'm feeling stronger. Every day I increase the length of my walks around Philippi. I look at the splendid art and architecture of the public places, always comparing them to those of Corinth. Two Provinces of Rome on Greek soil. We Greeks have long memories. I think of Thessaloniki, the place of my birth, sad not to remember anything of that city. I must find a way to it. The desire to see my birthplace means I have survived. The danger of my immediate death has passed for now.

"Why miss Thessaloniki instead of Corinth? What about Helena? She seems so far away, in space and in time. How long ago was Helena? Did I dream her?

"My memories are filled with guilt. How could I have abandoned her in her greatest need? The shame chokes me. She was the victim of an evil man. She turned to me for help. Like a coward, I ran away."

Back in the house later, he wrote: *"I've confessed everything to Lydia. She didn't pass judgment. She prayed for the healing of my soul. She says the healing of my body is now almost complete.*"

Ares stopped writing. He heard her footfalls. She was coming.

Lydia's step on the marble floor was unmistakable—hard-working, self-contained Lydia. *That description,* he thought, *failed to capture the essence of the woman.* She was confident, an artist who was also shrewd in business matters, a believer who forgave others their doubts, yet a woman who did not have patience with foolish notions. He had asked why she had never married. Her answer had been a shock to his system: "Paul is convinced that Christ will return soon to take us to himself. (*Whatever that means,* Ares had thought.) So there is much work to be done. I have no time for marriage."

Now she entered her atrium, a strong, commanding presence, and Ares, interrupted in his musings, asked her without preamble. "How can I be forgiven, Lydia? I've been trying to follow your advice to write down my thoughts, but this question keeps troubling me."

Lydia laid the folded cloths she was carrying on a stool and motioned for him to sit. Although she acted as if she had nothing else to do, Ares felt selfish in invading her privacy and work hours. But Lydia, as was her habit since his recovery, answered in one of her storytelling parables.

"Once, they brought to Yeesous a man who was paralyzed," she began, as if resuming an ongoing conversation between them. "The neighbors were so sure that Yeesous could heal this paralytic that they tore through a roof. Then they lowered the man and his makeshift bed in front of the healer who was teaching inside the house. You see, Yeesous was so popular in those days that the crowds overflowed and then surrounded the place, blocking the door. Yeesous took one look at the man on the pallet and said to him, 'Stand up, your sins are forgiven.'"

Ares interrupted. "What does it mean—'your sins are forgiven?'"

"It means that the effect of them—the heavy memories as you call them, the guilt—is lifted and thrown away. The man in the story needed to have his sins forgiven more than he needed to have his body made whole. After Yeesous talked to him the man was able to stand and walk on his own."

Ares didn't yet understand the connection she was making, but he was hungry for more.

"Lydia, it was you who healed me. I saw you, day after day. I witnessed your ministrations. I felt them. You know more about medicine than Dionysos does. Yet, you give all the credit to the one you call the Christ."

Lydia paused to think. "Let's take your arguments in order. First, I know very little by comparison to our eminent physician, Dionysos. The city of Alexandria should be grateful to have him when he returns. We both did what we could for you, but it was Christ who made you whole. What I did that Dionysos could not do at the time was to pray and ask Christ to visit and heal you. And God answered my prayers."

It's all a mystery Ares thought, but having been taught by the tough-minded Demosthenes he was not satisfied with mystery; he longed also to understand with *logos*. So Lydia told him another story. "To you, Ares, Yeesous is an attractive character who lived and died not long ago. To us, he is the *living* Christ. You see, he appeared to many of his friends *after* his death. He even appeared to one who was his avowed enemy."

She proceeded to tell Ares of the most important day in her life, the day she met Paul. "Come." She led the way as together she and Ares walked a distance to a shady part of the river Ganghitis, where the trees bent over the water, and the two shores seemed so close that people standing on opposite shores might touch hands. The dappled shadows played on the grass, the water sounded like a song, and Ares was enchanted. But Lydia was matter-of-fact.

"Like you, I was filled with longing for God, Ares. I wanted to know the one I both feared and worshiped. I had the desire but not the knowledge. And then Paul appeared, here, on this river bank and told me that God had made himself known in a very intimate, a physical way. In the person of Yeesous of Nazareth. Paul had been a devout Jew who practiced his ancient religion *to the letter of the law*. When he heard the followers of Yeesous claim that he, Yeesous, was the human face of God, Paul was furious. For him it was blasphemy. It was idolatry. There is no belief more important to the Jews than this: God is One. So, those who proclaimed that Christ was God's Son were committing idolatry. Faithful to the letter of the law, as he told me, he started persecuting the ones who talked about this Yeesous as the Son of God, their Savior. One by one or in groups, he dragged them before the religious authorities. Many were killed by the abhorrent practice of stoning. Then, one day, the glorified Christ, God's anointed, appeared to Paul and called him by name. He called him by name, Ares, and he claimed him for his own. Paul was convinced by this living presence. Utterly. From that moment Paul was transformed from an enemy of Yeesous to the most passionate of his followers. And now he offers this gift to others. He offered it to me. Everything changed after that day."

"Is that what started you on this path, this new way?"

"Yes, that was the day for me. Many more heard Paul during his time in Philippi, and for them, too, a new day dawned. The light of Christ entered our lives and has not been extinguished."

"All those people we met in Neapolis—they learned of Yeesous through Paul, then?"

"Yes. Some heard Paul and others have followed The Way because of them. Our lives are continuously transformed through our contact with one another."

"Where is this remarkable Paul now?"

"In Corinth. It's possible that your friends there have already come in contact with him."

"In Corinth?" Ares was alert. He'd been wondering how Helena would react to Lydia and her people. Something was nagging at him, but he couldn't quite grasp it. He thought at first that it was his guilt over abandoning Helena, but he had let go of that by confessing it to Lydia. So what was it that troubled him? He couldn't find the answer. *Can I never be free?* he wondered to himself.

------ ✂ ------

One morning, before the heat of summer engulfed the city, when the days were cool in the early hours and the marble gleamed, Ares climbed to the acropolis, testing the strength of his body, the wholeness of his legs that only weeks before were locked in chains as he rowed on the ship. As he climbed, he smelled the piercing tang of the pines, touched the rough sticky bark of the trees, and inhaled the resin aroma he had always loved. He remembered Helena with compassion and recalled how when they were little they used to run in the woods pretending to reenact the myth of Atalanta. Swift-footed Atalanta captured by Hippomenes who loved her, who threw the golden apples in her path to cause her to lose a second, to be defeated by love. *Maybe we'll run again*, Ares thought, and it was at that moment that he was assaulted by something from another realm. Assaulted was the right word. It hit him between the brows, like a blow, this memory that made him cry out loud. He remembered a promise he had made in that stinking ship of death, a promise he had revealed to no one else. During the worst hour of his life, when he was convinced he was dying, he had made a vow he now recalled with the immediacy of trauma. *"Oh, divine one, whichever of the gods is listening to me, save me from this horror, and I shall dedicate my life to you."*

At that moment, surrounded by the trees that led to the acropolis, he knew who it was who answered his prayer. *It was, it is, the God of Lydia, and this is a God who cannot be ignored or fooled. The Christ of the unknown Paul and Lydia.* He started running downhill, to Lydia's house. *But what about Helena?* To that question, there was no ready answer.

"Lydia, help me!" he cried when he finally caught sight of her near her house.

"Have you not yet learned to pray to God and not to me?" she asked him.

He felt surrounded by presences he could not identify. He heard the chirping of birds in the courtyard and was keenly aware of the smell of the flowers. All his senses were alert as never before. He felt the peace of Lydia's silence and gradually his panic diminished. "Something very strange has happened," he told her and even he could hear how his voice sounded different from his own. "It's a matter of life and death."

"Everything that has to do with the Lord Yeesous," she said, "is a matter of *life*, not death. *Don't be afraid.*"

"Of course! That's it. In this house, I've been aware of life, not death. I have spent too much time with death. Help me find this life."

"First, tell me exactly what happened to you this morning."

He started pacing, words pouring from his mouth. "Walking in the woods, thinking of Helena, of your words on healing the body and the soul—forgiveness. Shame and sorrow stalking me. Remembering. Remembering how we first knew we loved each other. The games we played. The vows our childish mouths had uttered. Suddenly assaulted by a more recent memory. Where was it until this morning? A vow, Lydia. A vow that shook me. The words engraved in my brain were uncovered by something, someone. In that ship of death I think I cried it out: *Oh, divine one, whichever of the gods is listening to me, save me from this horror, and I shall dedicate my life to you.'*

"I promised my whole life to the god who would deliver me, Lydia. I know now who this God is. A God who cannot be mocked. I must serve him."

Lydia was very still. "You think I'm mad, don't you?" he asked her.

"No, no. I'm thinking that only Paul can help you now. I've done all that's within my power."

They heard feet running through the courtyard and a young messenger appeared before them. He pulled a scroll from his pouch and handed it to Lydia. "It looks like a letter, Ares," she told him, "for you." She withdrew to let him read it.

His hands were trembling like those of an old man, but he managed to break the seal. A short note on a scrap of papyrus written by Dionysos dropped at his feet but on the longer scroll he recognized Helena's handwriting and his eyes started blurring. He tried reading Dionysos' note first while he waited for his vision to clear:

"*You were right all along,*" Dionysos began in his familiar teasing manner. "*She's a beauty. Too bad I'm too old for her; otherwise I'd fight you for her. Helena will tell you how we met. A strange fate pursues us, my young friend. I meet you on the rough sea, and I meet your beloved in her calmer waters. She has been sheltered by Lydia-like persons. These strange Christians. You and I were rescued by them. Is this someone's myth or a divine joke? I trust your health is improving. With the formidable Lydia by your side, I can't imagine anything going wrong. Only good can come from such a presence. There's a similar woman here, a softer version of Lydia. Her name is Phoebe, now a mother to your Helena. Whatever decision you make, do not rush, do not feel guilty, do not make a mistake this time. Your faithful friend and fellow traveler, Dionysos.*"

Ares placed the note inside his tunic and stared at the longer letter. He took deep breaths to calm the thudding of his heart. "*Ares, my one and only friend since childhood,*" he read. *My only friend,* he repeated aloud. He remembered her terrible sorrow when Demosthenes died. They had shared their previous lives, but Helena would never understand what happened to him in that ship of slavery and humiliation. He bent over the *impluvium*, splashed water on his face and finished reading the letter.

"Someone has brought us to you—may I call you Christians?—and then bound us with Paul," he told Lydia when she came to find him later in the day. "If Helena had not written about Paul I don't know how I would have responded to her. I'd probably be on the first ship to Kenchreaê forgetting vows and resolutions. But now that she knows him, she'll understand why I must serve him."

Lydia looked doubtful but didn't say anything. Ares withdrew to write to Helena:

"Lovely Helena, my childhood and ever friend. Your letter brought me consolation. You are well and away from the Roman's hated home. I rejoice. I rejoice that you met my good Dionysos. He has praised your loveliness. Above all I rejoice that you are also with the ones called Christians. What joy that the man Paul has touched your soul. I don't know him but his story has altered my soul. All this, through a woman named Lydia. And now I'm facing a dilemma. I want to keep my promise to you. But I need to fulfill a vow: I must dedicate myself to the Lord of these loving people, to Christós himself, to serve him through Paul. It was Christós who saved me from the ship of death and I had made a vow to serve the god who would deliver me from it. Now I know who this God is. The ordeal made me unfit for marriage but fit for service. Receive this letter with love, a constant since childhood. I will continue to love you, Helena. You must marry. I will never marry. You are released from the betrothal vows. My life is destined for something greater than human love. Forgive me for abandoning you. Your devoted friend, Ares."

He cringed when he read it aloud at its choppiness, its lack of elegance. What would Demosthenes say? What would *she* say? What kinds of excuses was he giving her? Maybe the truth lay somewhere else: that he did not want to marry; that Eros no longer interested him, not after his ordeal on the ship of death. He needed to talk to men who were wise, as Demosthenes had been, as Paul obviously was. A true brotherly affection for Helena filled his heart, but desire had abandoned him, at least for now. And if he had to travel as Paul did, what would happen to his family if he married? The questions and excuses persisted.

Finally he sealed his missive suspecting that it was as unkind as the letter he had sent her from Kenchreaê months before. He sealed it knowing that Helena would not want to see him again, and at that he felt despair. But his decision stood firm. He now focused all his energy toward waiting for an answer to the letter he would write to Paul.

──── ❧ ────

With the weather now perfect for sailing, a letter from Philippi to Kenchreaê did not take long to arrive. The house of Julius, the Captain, and Junia, his wife, was well known, and the messenger went there first to ask for Helena. He learned that together with Phoebe the Weaver she had moved to a house on the outskirts of the city, near the Bath of Eleni, and he was led to them without difficulty.

All the members of Phoebe's household were now at home in Kenchreaê. Alexandra and Evniki, together with the devoted steward, Aristos, had arrived from Corinth, bringing with them beautiful dyes for the cloth orders they had promised to fulfill for their Corinthian customers. On this lovely late spring day, Helena and Phoebe had been experimenting with the expensive Alexandrian blue and laughing with excitement at the results. "It looks like the Aegean blue when the sun is just rising," Helena said and burst into a song about the sea, having exhausted their stock of hymns. She had learned them the first time she heard them.

When Evniki brought the letter to Helena, the women

gathered to congratulate her and then they left her alone to read it. They watched her from a distance. She broke the seal with trembling fingers. She read it quickly, and then she stood rigid for a long time. It looked to Phoebe that the girl was gripped by an intense anger. After a long while, she seemed to shake off the paralysis of fury and marched to her room. When she emerged not long afterwards she was holding a basket filled with possessions. Phoebe saw her hurrying towards her, the basket on her arm, and she had a sharp recollection of the lost girl she had first seen the morning after Helena's arrival at her home in Corinth. The smiling, singing Helena she had come to love had changed again into that lonely and withdrawn girl of months before. Phoebe heard Helena's voice—altered, poignant—as she called her name. With great sorrow, Phoebe moved to join her.

Helena said, "I must leave, Phoebe. I'm retuning to Corinth. I need to be alone, to forget about the people of The Way. And Ares."

Phoebe stared at her in astonishment, opened her mouth to say something but then immediately thought better of it. She reached her hand to touch Helena but the girl pulled away. Phoebe, however, had learned patience in dealing with people who were troubled. She waited. Confronted with Phoebe's quiet, steadfast love, Helena dropped her basket and, putting her face in her hands, cried through her sobs. "I thought this was all about a new love. But Ares' new love has killed the old." Phoebe, her own eyes filled with tears, said gently: "Love doesn't die, Helena. It does evolve however, sometimes in directions we do not expect, or even like."

After a while, Helena whispered, "I must go." Phoebe did not argue. She opened the box with her coins. "You will need money," she said. "This payment belongs to you. You have worked with skill and imagination, and these are wages you have refused to accept up to now. Please take these *denarii* and

I will ask Aristos to arrange for your transport."

She handed a purse to Helena who took it after an initial hesitation; she said in the same stilted voice, "I plan to return this to you as soon as possible. You owe me nothing, but I thank you for the temporary loan. I'll wait in the atrium."

Phoebe wiped her tears and went to look for Aristos. She instructed him quickly: "Please, take care of her and see that she returns to Corinth safely. Find out where she is going and then let our friend Erastos know the situation before you return to Kenchreaê."

Aristos made the necessary arrangements and within an hour Helena, without further goodbyes, left with him. Alexandra and Evniki were hurt, even scandalized at what felt like rudeness and rejection.

"Really," Alexandra voiced her own disillusionment, "after all you've done for her! Not even a thank you and farewell. What possessed her?" Evniki, always more sensitive, wiped a tear.

"It was the letter," Phoebe said, her eyes now spilling the tears she had held back. "The poor girl has been hurt so much. She was not ready for more bad news. I don't know what Ares wrote to her, but I'm suspecting the worst. All we can do is pray for her and wait for her return. Be certain of this—she *will* come back to us. Helena will return one day, when she finally knows her own heart and mind. Now I must be alone." And she shut herself in her room while the girls sighed and murmured about Phoebe, who never saw ill in anybody.

Chapter 15: Gallio in Corinth

Two weeks before Helena made her abrupt decision to leave Phoebe, a disheartened Erastos had returned to Corinth. After a refreshing visit to the baths, he walked to Aquila's shop longing to see Paul, to hold on to what was solid and unchanging—Paul's faith and the love he shared with his hosts and coworkers. Erastos always felt rejuvenated after a visit with them. The leatherworkers' *stoa* was busy as usual but as he approached the familiar shop he saw that it was empty of customers and friends. Only Prisca was sitting at the counter and that was most unusual. She was bent over two square pieces of soft leather, struggling to pass a large needle through the many matching holes she had pierced on their edges. As she drew the yellow thin cord sewing them into a pillow, she sighed deeply. Erastos, troubled, ran up the steps to the *stoa's* platform.

"Oh, Erastos, you have returned," she cried out, and he saw that her eyes were red.

"What is it, Priscilla?" he asked, using the diminutive form of her name, for he had great affection for the good woman. "Has something happened to Paul?"

She shook her head and motioned for him to sit near her. "Did you just return from Kenchreaê?" she asked. "Let me bring you some water," and made to stand but Erastos stopped her.

"No, Priscilla. Something is troubling you and you must tell me immediately what it is."

She bent her head, silent, gathering her thoughts. She put aside her work. "Erastos, my dear friend. You came to us from another world, the Greek world of your glorious theater, you accepted us as friends, and we have delighted in your friendship and your support. We were pleased to have you with us whenever Paul preached in Phoebe's home in the months before she left for Kenchreaê. But you are a Greek, not a Jew, and you did not attend the synagogue with us. You, therefore, may not know how things stand among our people."

Erastos nodded. He was aware that Paul preached every Saturday in the synagogue but he hesitated to attend; since his former profession was frowned upon by the Jews he felt it was not proper for him to worship among them. Not yet.

"What you don't know is that quite a bit of dissension has arisen between the people of the synagogue and Paul," she continued with regret.

"But why? Even I can see that Paul loves his own people."

"Yes, he does. But they do not return the feeling. A few of them, even Crispus, the official of the synagogue, have accepted Paul's message that the cross has the power to save, to bring us to God. Paul says that most of the Jews regard the shame of death on the cross as a stumbling block, while the gentiles consider the cross a foolishness. I think that they do not like to think of a weak god, one who died willingly. Paul's preaching, you see, centers on the crucified and resurrected Yeesous, and that approach is a scandal for the Jews."

"I don't pretend to understand fully what you and Paul mean but I can see that this does not bode well for Paul's future in the synagogue."

Prisca said, "They are being very cruel to him now. He has been sad and troubled because he believes that God sent him here to preach to his own people, but now that they are rejecting him, as those from Thessaloniki and Berea previously did, I'm afraid he will have to leave Corinth also."

Before Erastos could reply they heard Paul and Aquila climbing the steps. Paul's face lit up when he saw Erastos, who stood up immediately to embrace him. "I want you to know that I am ready to offer you my help," he said before Paul had a chance to speak. "I will not stand by and let them push you out of Corinth."

Paul smiled at his friend's passion. "All is well," he announced. "I had a visit," and looked at Prisca as if that explained everything. "Your good Aquila led me to one of the green spaces of your city," and here he nodded toward Erastos with a smile. "There he left me to absorb the warmth of the sun and to pray. And the Lord's messenger came to me and said, 'Do not be afraid, but speak and do not be silent, for I am with you. There are many in this city who are my people.' That convinces me, my dear friends, that from now on, if my people, the Jews, continue to reject the cross, I will preach only to the gentiles. I will not return to the synagogue and I have no intention of leaving Corinth."

Erastos looked at Prisca and saw that her sadness had lifted. The four friends sat together and talked until darkness fell and Erastos decided it was time to see his mother. But as the week progressed he observed that more and more problems were surfacing between the Jews of the synagogue and Paul's new converts. What troubled Erastos even more was that their community, their *ekklesia*, was facing its own problems. He sensed the converts' loss of peace. The conversations with Prisca and Aquila continued while he tried to make sense of the emerging conflict.

Erastos understood that the *ekklesia* had started within the synagogue, where Christianized Jews were soon followed by non-Jews who also were attracted to the New Way. Many of them were Greeks, like Phoebe and Erastos, others were Romans who lived and worked in the city, and quite a few claimed nationalities from neighboring provinces, but Paul called them all Hellenes—Greeks. The Jews of the city, prosperous and comfortable, were thoroughly Hellenized. They spoke Greek and they mingled with the ones they called gentiles with no difficulty, while retaining their own customs and their dietary distinctions. The Jews who now belonged to the *ekklesia* tended to retain many of the old restrictions and habits. "Our ancestors gave us the Law," they would argue. "We will never abandon the Law." But the converted pagans laughed at some of the Jewish practices. They had not grown up hearing about Abraham and the Law of Moses; the names of these patriarchs meant nothing to them.

Yet, Erastos learned, their understanding of the Law and the prophets was used by the synagogue Jews as a weapon against Paul. "We have seen no sign of Messiah," a man named Sosthenes explained to him when Erastos asked him for details. "Messiah is expected to come with signs in the sky, but this Paul is preaching that Messiah has already come in the person of Yeesous of Nazareth. But Yeesous was put to death, crucified! How can our God allow Messiah to be crucified? Preposterous! Paul blasphemes." *No wonder Paul has left the synagogue,* Erastos decided. He said to Sosthenes. "Our city has been hospitable to the Jews up to now. I urge you not to stir up trouble, for your sake as well as the sake of Paul's followers. Paul will not trouble you again. He will not preach in the synagogue. Will this satisfy you?"

Sosthenes nodded agreement, but Erastos was not fully convinced. As he moved around the markets he sensed a certain discontent among the merchants and artisans. "These people of a new sect called The Way are not helping our city," they murmured. "They don't buy animals and birds for sacrifice, they don't buy idols and ornaments for their homes, their women dress without silks and jewels. Suppose they increase in numbers; it will hurt our commerce."

Erastos suspected that the arguments were spurious, spread by instigators who were circulating among the merchants. If trouble comes between Jews and Paul, he thought, the gentiles will side with the Jews for the sake of their money. He made an effort to warn Paul who looked at him with sorrow. "It is probably as difficult for you to comprehend why the Jews fear me as it is for me to fathom the hold your Olympians have had on the Greeks all these centuries," and he withdrew into deep thought for a while. When he lifted his head, Erastos was disturbed to see Paul's eyes shining with tears. "We are children of one God," he said to his friend, his voice alive with a conviction that made his listeners believe that Paul had a direct connection with the Divine. "It is love that binds us together, not the Law. Once you come into the light of God's grace, nothing but nothing can entice you back into the darkness of mere legalism. The freedom Christ gives us does away with enslavement by customs, regulations, and tradition. *For freedom Christ has set us free!* False teachers have tried to destroy my churches in Galatia, Erastos. I will not allow them to do so in Corinth. How I grieve for my *ekklesiae*. How I grieve for my people, for my Jewish brothers and sisters."

Erastos was moved by his words. "It would be good if your kind of love proved more powerful than the love of money that dominates Corinthian life," he said. "If the Jews who are against you persuade the merchants of the city that the presence of a new sect means less money for them, there will be trouble; this is what we must forestall."

"I must leave it to you then, Erastos," Paul said. "You understand about markets and money. As for me, I must tend to my flock here in Corinth. For I am convinced that this is a very important center for God's mission. I had troubles in Philippi, in Thessaloniki, and in Berea, but I am not ready to leave Corinth. There is much that needs to be done here, so I ask for your help."

Erastos knew that this was the kind of help he was able to give to his friends and he started by going directly to Claudia's. He knew how influential she was. At the gate, the man he called Tiresias greeted him with surprise. "It's been a long absence, gentle Erastos," he said. "You don't visit us anymore. We miss your Excellency, your fine voice. You used to be her frequent guest." Erastos merely nodded. "Is the lady Claudia *in situ*?"

"Not only that," the gatekeeper replied, "but she's not alone. We're famous these days. The new proconsul, Gallio, is staying here."

"Ah. So Corinth is to have a new governor at last."

Soon Alexandros appeared to lead him to his mistress who welcomed Erastos with warmth and good humor. He responded in kind.

"My dear Claudia, you've been absent from Corinth for too long. How was the Roman sojourn?"

"Interesting for a week, but then a bore. I tell my friends in Rome that I find the provinces more exciting, and that sends shock waves through them. They find me insulting. But I've always preferred the learning of the Greeks. I chose to educate my children by Greeks without the noise and infighting of Rome. But now tell me your news."

Erastos recounted his quick trip to Kenchreaê but did not elaborate. He let her assume that it had been a business affair and quickly changed the subject. "I hear that you have an important guest?"

"Ha! My servants are as gossipy as ever. Yes, the noble Gallio is residing here until he finds suitable quarters of his own. I find his appointment as proconsul rather amusing. He will be good for the arts, but he doesn't seem forceful enough to be governor. I think the emperor appointed him as a favor to his brother Seneca—have you heard of him? He's the Stoic philosopher who's becoming famous in Rome. He seems to be in vogue these days, though Rome and Stoicism seem so far apart in my mind. The current Empress, Agrippina, has entrusted Seneca with the education of her precious son, an odious youngster by the name of Nero."

Erastos looked around him with alarm, but she said, "Don't worry. The palace spies are not to be found in this villa. One of the main reasons I despise Rome—the gossip, the treachery, the infernal jealousies, and all the murders in the palace circles. They kill even their own, Erastos! However, even though the emperor Claudius has shown him favor, I don't think Gallio is too thrilled to be in Corinth. He's a sweet-natured man, but you'll find him a snob. He gives the impression that nothing interests him, but I do think that in a family of hypochondriacs he's truly the sickly one and thoroughly spoiled by his mother. You, Erastos, must stay and meet him. I want him to see that there *is* high culture in Corinth and of a better quality than in Rome."

Erastos laughed and readily accepted her invitation. Claudia left her *tablinum* to give her new orders to Alexandros. When she returned to Erastos, she changed the subject.

"Where is Helena?" she asked him. "You may think me indifferent, but I worry about my ward."

"No need for that. Helena is staying and working with a very successful weaver, a friend of my mother's," he said. "They are currently setting up a new workshop in Kenchreaê. And she's very well, I think."

"An artisan? She's now a weaver? Her father would be appalled." Claudia could not hide her condescension, but some memory seemed to distract her and she changed tactics once again. "Are you betrothed to her yet?"

"No, she barely acknowledges my existence. But, Claudia, there *is* surprising news. Young Ares is alive. At least, we heard from a reliable source that he's alive and well in Philippi, after a harrowing shipwreck and other adventures. He's in good hands now, receiving excellent care, we understand."

Claudia stared at him in disbelief as he summarized Dionysos' story of slavery and rescue. He said nothing about his own feelings and avoided talking about his friends and their devotion to a mystical new love. When he finished, Claudia asked, "But who are these people who are sheltering Ares? There's something you're not telling me, Erastos."

He made a decision. This is what he had come to do and now was the time. "Claudia, have you heard of a Jewish sect and its adherents? It's called The Way, and in some circles its followers are known as Christians."

She made a noise of distaste, "Oh, no, you're not mixed up with *them*. It's beneath you."

He raised his powerful actor's voice, startling her. "Really, Claudia, among your finer qualities I've always admired your curiosity and your intelligence. But in this case, you are jumping to conclusions—unjustified ones, at that. I can say with authority that *I* am not up to the level of the Christians I know. In my mind I call them 'the people of a New Love.' If you would only meet them you would be convinced of their decency. They truly care for one another."

"Well, well," she muttered in astonishment. "You do have an interesting way of reprimanding me. You're right; I haven't met a single one of these new friends of yours. I did hear whispers about them in Rome, however. They were saying that they follow the teachings of a certain Galilean? I'm always interested in new things. Do tell me what you know."

"The truth is that this is why I've come to you, Claudia, to ask for your help. And now I see that the time may be more propitious than I had imagined. It's possible that your noble guest may be able to offer much needed assistance in this matter."

Claudia, whom he knew to be proud of her reputation as a leader in the arts and the affairs of the city, listened carefully as Erastos explained to her the critical situation: the hostility shown to Paul by his fellow Jews and the danger he ran of being chased out of the city.

When he finished she stood up and said. "You've aroused more than my curiosity. I must look into this. Maybe you will bring the remarkable Paul to see me? Meanwhile, let's prepare to dine; it's important for you to meet Gallio and his retinue."

A slave was sent to assist Erastos with his attire while Claudia inspected the *triclinium*. During dinner, Erastos felt strangely detached. He looked again at the exquisite, familiar mosaics of the *triclinium*—the god Dionysos playing his flute, more beatific than wild—and at the vivid bucolic images on the wall behind the seat of honor painted on a background of deep cinnabar red that proclaimed the wealth of the household. How much money had Claudia spent on those rare colors? His mind was wandering. He recalled the last time he had dined in this particular space, Helena's troubled face, Gaius' madness and drunkenness, Claudia's fear, his own awareness that he must save Helena at all costs. All that seemed so long ago. The places where he used to feel at home were now becoming alien to him. Tonight he was acutely conscious of Gallio's Roman arrogance, his air of indolence and superiority, his indifference to the conversation Claudia attempted and her diffidence before her guest. He looked critically at Gallio. Here was a rather frail man, about his own age but looking much older despite his well-chosen *chiton* that was embroidered with gold thread. Gallio was sharing anecdotes of life in Rome, especially the palace intrigues, and Erastos listened not just with indifference but distaste. He made no effort to exchange witty remarks. His mind drifted to a sunny courtyard in Kenchreaê; he heard again Dionysos' deep voice and recalled Helena's pale, rapt face as she listened to him and, above all, Phoebe's serene, loving presence. *The people of a New Love who are despised by these Romans are really the most challenging people I have met. I continue to learn from them. They certainly are not bores; these Romans are the bores.*

He felt Claudia's subtle kick and was startled out of his musings. "Noble Gallio," she said in a voice that sounded a bit too bright to Erastos. "Our friend Erastos has offered to act as your honor's personal guide to our vibrant city. Erastos, I expect you to ensure that Junius Annaeus Gallio will feel at home here as soon as possible."

Gallio made a sound that suggested such a hope was improbable and not particularly welcome, but Erastos found himself making plans to guide him through the public places within a week.

Later, as Alexandros the steward was escorting him to the gate, Erastos asked him, "And is Claudia going to marry the proconsul, Alexandros?"

The steward smiled enigmatically. "You're asking this of a slave?"

"A slave who's obviously like a father to her," Erastos replied. "I'm quite sure you know her better than anyone else—perhaps even more than she knows her own mind."

"He's an attractive man," the slave said of Gallio, "well connected. But he does not like the provinces. Marrying him would mean leaving Corinth, and Claudia will not leave."

Out of curiosity, because the intelligent slave intrigued him, Erastos asked, "Do you, by any chance, know anything about a new sect, the so-called Christians in the city?"

"Should I?

"I think so. Nothing seems to escape your notice and I'm thinking you'd find them worth knowing."

Alexandros, bemused, shook his head. "Maybe so," he said cryptically. "And now, *my* question: How is our lovely Helena?"

"She's well and safe," Erastos responded readily, knowing the old man's affection for the girl. "I am sure you remember her betrothed, Ares? I have it from a reliable authority that the young man has resurfaced, alive, and also well."

Alexandros, usually so unflappable, seemed nonplussed. Then the old slave sighed deeply, nodded his farewell, and returned to the interior of the villa. Erastos departed, unaware that Helena would soon be entering through the same gate.

———— ∞∞∞ ————

It was with great surprise that the day after Erastos' visit to Claudia, the steward saw Helena—emotions tightly controlled, proud and angry—appear at the villa after months of absence along with Phoebe's steward Aristos. Alexandros had imagined Helena safe in Kenchreaê, reassured by Erastos that she was in good hands. He supposed she looked healthy enough, but even to her old friend her initial greeting was guarded. Alexandros hastened to reassure Aristos that he would take care of her, and led her to Claudia's quarters.

She looked startled to see Helena without warning, although Claudia was glad the girl seemed no longer lost in the unrelieved sorrow that had engulfed her before her disappearance. Yet she thought that Helena appeared unusually cold, impatient, and demanding. As soon as Alexandros presented her to Claudia, Helena went straight to the point. "I came to see the children and to find out what you have decided to do about the legacy you had promised to my father."

Claudia moved as if to touch her, but Helena backed off. "No need for hypocritical gestures, Claudia. Ours is now a business arrangement."

Claudia opened her mouth but bit back a harsh response. Alexandros could read her thoughts: *No matter what has happened, Helena is still Demosthenes' dear child.* "Welcome, Helena," she said aloud in her most formal voice. "I promised your father to do right by you, and I keep my promises. I will act immediately to give you the dowry you deserve."

"Don't call it a dowry," Helena retorted bitterly. "I've no intention of getting married. Let's call it a debt you owe to my father."

"But, Helena, I hear that your beloved Ares is back from the drowned and the dead. Is this not true?"

"It's true that he's alive, but he's not my 'beloved,' as you called him. There was only one man I loved, Demosthenes, and he's dead." And at that Helena's voice broke and she struggled to recapture the anger she was wrapping around herself to stave off her grief.

The reference to Demosthenes broke through Claudia's defenses. She took Helena by the hand. "I too loved your father," she whispered, human now, her rare warmth pulsating through the words as finally Claudia confessed the long-consuming passion that had bound her to Demosthenes. "Oh, Helena, how I loved him. It feels good to simply say it aloud. I loved your father as I have never loved anyone else."

And now they wept together. "He was," Claudia sobbed, "the most beautiful man I have ever known." Such genuine grief finally thawed Helena.

"But why didn't my father tell me about your love for each other?" she asked in a little girl's pitiful voice.

"Ah, but that isn't an easy thing to share with one's child, Helena. You were devoted to one another, but he was still your father, and he was always worrying about you and your future. He didn't want you to know he was having an affair with a married woman. He was a man of the highest ethics, Helena. He was tortured by 'the betrayal of Gaius,' as he called it, something that stunned me because my husband had never been faithful to me. Demosthenes wanted to live in a way that would make your life easier and better than his own. It's a good thing I had signed the papers for your legacy before he and I fell in love, when I first invited him to teach my children; otherwise, he would never have accepted it."

"Your friend Erastos is convinced that Gaius killed my father. I think he's right. Why did you tell me that my father did away with himself?" Helena's anger was returning and she pulled away from Claudia.

"For one reason only, Helena. Your safety in this house. I didn't want you to know what Alexandros and I suspected, because we feared that the knowledge would put you in mortal danger. We were even more concerned about Ares' reaction to the truth. Ares, after all, considered Demosthenes his father also. Drink and greed had changed my husband from a man of military dignity into someone mean and vindictive. A man who kills once may kill again."

Helena stopped to think about this and seemed to decide not to argue any longer. Alexandros could see that her grief for her father would always be with her, but as he knew from personal experience, acute pain diminishes eventually into a dull, inescapable presence. Now that she knew that Demosthenes had not abandoned her by killing himself, the ache would be a bit easier to bear.

Soon Helena moved to the other burning question they anticipated. Her gray eyes stared at him and then at Claudia. "Who killed Gaius Marius Sylvanus? I know now that I didn't do it. Your friend Erastos saw me that night, and he assured me that Gaius was already dead when I entered his chamber intending to kill him."

"I believe he fell on his own dagger," Claudia said with only a shadow of a doubt in her voice. "I persuaded him that it was his only way out after the crime he committed against you. He was drunk that night, really drunk. And that made him belligerent but also maudlin. At heart he was a coward. I threatened him with going to the authorities—I told him that I had proof he had killed Demosthenes, and that I had many witnesses who would testify that he had violated you like a slave. He was slobbering and saying he was sorry, but this time I was adamant. I left his room and ordered all the slaves away from his quarters. I waited until morning before allowing Alexandros to check on him. He found him dead."

"But what did you do with that slimy Demetrius? How is it that since that night he's not caused trouble for you and for me?"

Claudia turned to Alexandros. "Tell her," she said simply. So the old slave explained: "That same night, I took him to someone I knew, a slave trader, and I sold him on the spot. The trader promised me that Demetrius would be out of the city by the next day. We haven't heard from him since."

Helena tried to take it all in. She recognized now how easily the blame for the death of Gaius could have been placed on her own shoulders after her outburst at the banquet. She said to both of them, "I must thank you then. You saved my life."

"No," Claudia confessed. "I didn't think of you that night, Helena; I was thinking only of myself, of avenging my beloved Demosthenes' death. Someone else saved you." She waited, but Helena did not elaborate or express further curiosity. So Claudia continued, "What's happened to Ares? I thought you two were destined for one another. How happy you must have been to hear of his survival."

"Yes, oh, yes. It seemed like a happy myth at first, this *deus ex machina* rescue from the sea. But although he's alive, now he's dead to me. Once more I'm mourning the dead. He wants to serve the god of a new sect in the city—you may have heard of them. The people of The Way? Therefore, no marriage for us." Her voice fell to a whisper. "So I would like not to talk of him again." She paused and then continued in normal tones. "Now I'd like to see the children."

Alexandros reflected, as the children were brought in and with glad cries hugged and kissed Helena, that compassion was not one of Claudia's virtues, but he could see that she was feeling sorry for the young woman who was her ward. He wondered suddenly: *What is there about these people of The Way that two of the most engaging young people we know are attracted by them? I must find out.* But for now he pushed the thought away.

———— ❧ ————

That same afternoon Aristos, who had long been a faithful member of the *ekklesia,* approached Aquila's shop, intent on delivering another message from Phoebe.

Prisca welcomed him into the house, asking immediately about Phoebe's welfare. "She is well," Aristos explained to Paul, Prisca, and Aquila who were there along with Erastos, "but something rather unexpected has brought me here."

They offered him hospitality and urged him to rest before telling them his story. Reassured of Phoebe's good health, Paul and Aquila returned to their work at the shop, but Erastos and Prisca were eager to learn what had brought Aristos to Corinth. Aristos broke the news that Helena had abruptly left Phoebe and returned to Corinth. "But why?" Prisca and Erastos asked at the same time. Aristos shook his head. "It seems that she received a letter with news that upset her."

"Letter, what letter?" whispered Prisca, but Erastos spoke louder. "Where is she?" Aristos, seeing his face flush with rising anger, said carefully:

"She asked me to accompany her to Claudia's villa. An older slave by the name of Alexandros welcomed her, reassured me that she was in good hands, and then bade me farewell. I came to tell you the news, as instructed by Phoebe."

But before any of them could say more, Paul reappeared from the next room holding a scroll in his hand. "A letter from Lydia has arrived," he announced, "a most intriguing development. It seems that young Ares—isn't he Helena's young friend? This Ares has fallen under the spell of a group of our brothers and sisters in Philippi, namely our beloved Lydia who was used by God to heal the boy, so now he has decided to join us, to work with me."

"But he doesn't know you or us!" Prisca exclaimed.

Paul smiled. "That may be true, but I'm not at all surprised. The only unexpected detail is that I thought my new helper would be from Thessaloniki." He addressed himself to Erastos who seemed unable to utter a word. "You see, all this has been revealed to me in a dream. I've been asking for a worker for Makedonia, someone to assist our sister Lydia. This Ares may be the answer to my prayer. However, I shall do nothing before I speak to Helena. I think the two young people must meet again before I make a decision."

Erastos stood up abruptly and said, "I must leave. I will see to it that Helena receives your message." And he departed, fuming. He was angry at Helena for leaving Phoebe and returning to the villa but irritated with Paul, too. What was this communication Paul received in dreams? Why didn't God send him a vision to help him out of the mess that was developing in the communities of the synagogue and the *ekklesia*? He had no answers. At home late that night he wrote a note and sent it with one of his mother's slaves to Claudia's villa.

Early the next morning Alexandros saw the gatekeeper rushing toward him and wondered what the important message was. "This came for Helena," he said, "delivered by one of Erastos' slaves".

Alexandros took it to Helena who motioned for him to

stay. "*Helena,*" she read aloud, "*I will not even begin to ask you why you left Phoebe's so abruptly. She has not complained to me and, knowing her character, I'm sure she has forgiven everything. Her servant Aristos told me of your departure. This is to inform you that Paul has received a message from your Ares through a friend in Philippi, a woman by the name of Lydia. The message is urgent but Paul will not respond without consulting you. He asks that you come to Prisca and Aquila's place to confer with him. I'll come tomorrow to escort you to their house. Be ready. Erastos.*"

Helena paled at the sharp rebuke but asked Alexandros to accompany her to Claudia who was supervising the arrangement of flowers in the *triclinium*. "It's getting more and more interesting," Claudia said after hearing of the summons. "Of course you must go, Helena. This man Paul sounds like a fascinating specimen. I'm tempted to come with you. What do you think?"

Helena shook her head. "Oh, Claudia, I can see us now, in your fancy litter, approaching the leatherworkers' quarters— the Roman aristocrat among the poor Jews and others! No matter how hurt I feel about Ares choosing these people of The Way over me, none of them—Phoebe, Prisca and her husband, and especially Paul—have intentionally caused me pain. They have their own dignity, and I will not humiliate them in any way. I'll go by myself before Erastos gets here. He sounds furious, and I don't want to deal with his self-righteousness."

Claudia laughed. "Do as you please, but don't be so hard on Erastos. He's my friend, after all." She looked sharply at Helena whose face was unreadable. The girl asked, "May I take Alexandros with me?" Claudia nodded and so within the hour Helena and the steward made their way into the city.

———— ᘓᗢᘖ ————

They had passed the Theater and were still some distance from the *stoas* with their shops. Although Alexandros tried to keep her away from the more congested streets Helena looked at the growing crowds with curiosity. "I hear the Agora is in a turmoil," he explained. "So let's cut west of Octavia's Temple and then circle south to find your friends' place."

"No," Helena protested, "let's go on the Lechaeon Road and then right through the Agora. I have had so few chances to see the city at work during the day. Since you're with me, I'm not frightened." As they walked on she told him of her resentment that women and girls were still as carefully controlled outside their homes as in ancient times. "Only slaves, workers, and *hetaerae* can move in the Agora without fear of being misunderstood," she complained. The smells and sounds that assaulted their senses seemed to be giving her a thrill, and Alexandros mused at the difference between them. He was so used to these everyday scenes that he didn't pay attention to them, but Helena noticed everything.

"Come then," he told her. "We'll go toward the Old Temple and through the heart of the city, then on to the southern *stoas* and the leatherworkers' quarter."

When they reached it, Helena talked about the Greek's Old Temple, the great one dedicated to Apollo, the one structure that had resisted Mummius' destruction of the ancient city. She told Alexandros how she had admired its massive Doric elegance when as a child of six her father had taken her by the hand to lead her through the city and her long history. "I miss Father's presence," she said as she touched one of the ancient columns, and the slave, who had never had a child, longed for her to trust him enough to share her loss with him. But she seemed afraid of her own emotions. She stopped to gaze at the green of the precinct of Athena Chalinitis, then suddenly she turned, skirting the wall, and entered the peaceful enclave. She stopped before the statue and he waited patiently while she stared at the austere goddess. Athena, looking straight ahead, held the reins of an invisible horse in her hands, hence her name, Chalinitis. Helena, solemn now, said, "Alexandros, do you ever feel this way? Do you ever feel that someone is holding your life in her hands, directing you and leading you and occasionally whipping you, but you have no way of escaping?" When he didn't answer she continued, "Ever since my father died I've felt Moira holding the reins of my life and I cannot escape, I cannot. I wanted to avenge Father, I wanted to avenge Ares, and now even that has been taken from me. I don't know what I'm living for."

Alexandros tried to hide his worry from her. "Come, Helena, listen to this old man. First things first, that's what I tell myself. You've something to do this morning—and that's visiting your friend Paul. Forget about your fate, and do the task of the moment. And then another task will be given you. Do that one and wait again for the next. When you act, then you don't feel so helpless. The time will come when you will not feel that an Athena Chalinitis is holding your life in her hands. You will take the reins yourself. Trust me, Helena. I've lived a long life and have survived much."

He wasn't used to giving long speeches, and Helena was deeply moved. She said kindly, "You must be right. But I do wonder how many people I'll hurt on the way." He didn't say anything, so they continued on toward the southern *stoas* of the city in friendly silence.

But neither was prepared for what met them when they approached the leatherworkers' *stoa*. They couldn't get close enough to enter the street, much less to see the shop. A large crowd was milling in the narrow way and spilling onto the *stoa* of the leatherworkers' shops. The mob was yelling and pushing, so Alexandros took hold of Helena's arm to pull her back. "This doesn't look good. Maybe we should return another day."

"No," Helena was frightened but insistent. "No, we must find out what's happened to them."

"I can't push you through these crowds," he said, knowing the ways of mobs. "You don't know the strength of them; they respect no one when they are in this state." Frantic, Helena looked around her. "There," she cried, "that shop is empty with only a child to guard it. Let me hide in its shadows and you go find out what has happened to Paul and to Prisca. Go, Alexandros, please go."

He gave a coin to the little boy who grabbed it gratefully and made room for Helena just inside the door. She stood there trembling and said, "Phoebe warned me about this danger, and now it has arrived."

It seemed a long wait. The noise was hurting her ears and nausea was rising in her throat. She remembered Phoebe with a pang and guilt filled her for abandoning the good woman with such indifference. "What have I done? I'm no better than this mob." She must have said it aloud because the young boy asked rudely, "Talking to me, lady?"

Helena tried to distinguish faces among the yelling crowd, to recognize someone from the *ekklesia*, and for just a moment she thought she saw Stephanas, a friend of Paul's, running to escape the mob. Where was Erastos? Where was Aquila? What had they done to Paul? She knew then that she would never again be indifferent to the fate of these people, but she couldn't decide if this was a good thing. When she finally saw Alexandros approaching she ran from her hiding place to meet him. He looked angry. "Come," he said. "We must see Claudia and ask her to intervene with Gallio." As they were rushing north of the city she begged for details. "Is Paul alive? Is he safe?"

Alexandros' pace did not slow even as he shared his news: "Some of the troublemakers among the Jews came and grabbed him and dragged him to their gathering place. I learned they call it a synagogue. He was perfectly willing to go in peace, but still they dragged him. They said something about stoning. That's what I understand from your friend Prisca who, by the way, sends regards. They're accusing Paul of all sorts of religious misconduct, details I don't understand. We need help from Claudia's friends. The quarrels of these Jews are too difficult for me to follow."

Helena, too, could run and talk. "They would probably say the same thing about the Athenians of old who put Sokrates to death."

He smiled thinly. "You *are* your father's daughter."

Chapter 16: Before the Tribunal

Their return to the villa did not take long, for Alexandros knew every shortcut in the city. As they entered the vestibule, both of them breathless, he told her in a voice that reminded her of her father's teachings: "Go wash and rest for a few minutes, Helena. Then put on one of your finer gowns; you need to make an excellent impression on Gallio. Few men can refuse a request from a beautiful and earnest maiden. Today, you're the best advocate your friend Paul has. So, for once, take advantage of your beauty. Meanwhile, I'll speak to Claudia, and I think she'll invite you to sup with Gallio." He gave her an encouraging smile before he left her.

With the help of a young slave who had been devoted to her when she lived in the villa, Helena washed and then donned a pristine white *chiton* with long sleeves. She favored the dress of her ancestors, without regard to current fashion, so over it she added a short blue *peplos* embroidered with gold thread; and then the girl tied blue ribbons through the curls that had finally grown long enough to frame her face and cover her neck. Around her tall forehead she wrapped a wider ribbon like a garland. And then the slave pronounced her lovely, "like an Aphrodite," but the girl stopped when she saw Helena's tears. *What good,* Helena thought, *has my beauty ever done for me?* She determined to think like a musician, but then a tremor went through her when she remembered what she had done with her *kithara* in this household on that last fateful night. She was still looking at it, afraid to touch it, when Alexandros appeared at the door. Without a word he picked the instrument up and then motioned for her to follow him. His only words to Helena were: "Don't hesitate to look Gallio in the eye. There are times when a beautiful woman must face a man with courage." Mystified at his worldly instructions, she promised to follow his advice.

Claudia and Gallio received her in the *triclinium,* and Helena was relieved to find no one else there. Claudia looked at the *kithara* and, taking in Helena's elegant attire, improvised with her quick mind. "Noble Gallio, may I present to you my ward, Helena, who has been a teacher and companion to my children, sharing her fine musical talents with them. Her father was a philosopher and a cherished friend. I asked her to play for you and she consented."

Gallio, reclining on one of the couches, a shawl over the expensive, gold-rimmed tunic covering his thin body, raised a limpid hand, heavy with ornate rings. "A lovely apparition," he said, studying her. "Be glad, my dear child, that you are not in the emperor's court." And with that cryptic comment he motioned for her to begin. She had not performed in public since that fright-filled night months before. Now her fingers ran lovingly over the strings, tuning them, plucking them without the *plektron.* She dared to risk a haunting melody with a particular meaning. One of the *ekklesia's* sweet hymns of thankfulness rose to her lips and she sang of one who died and rose again to bestow mercy on those who love him. The plaintive but triumphant lyrics touched even Claudia who nonetheless looked at first alarmed but then, seeing the rapt look on Gallio's face, allowed herself to enjoy the performance.

When Helena stopped singing, Gallio opened his eyes and spoke to no one in particular. "What a strange hymn," he said, "for it is a hymn to a god, isn't it?"

His perception gave Helena courage. *I owe you this, Phoebe.* She took the plunge. "At a very critical time in my life I was rescued by people who call themselves followers of Christós. They taught me this hymn."

Gallio raised himself on his elbow and looked directly at her. "Lovely Helena," he said, "you are full of surprises. I repeat that you are fortunate to be living here and not in Rome. The emperor's household is full of men who devour young beauties like you. These followers of *Christós* are probably safer."

As Claudia remained quiet, looking at him with narrowed eyes, he continued: "Since she is your ward, Claudia, I'm assuming you must have been in Rome when she consorted with these…*persons.*" But when neither of the women responded to his implied question, once again Gallio turned to Helena. "These followers…these people—I seem to have heard that they are troublemakers. You say they treated you well and taught you songs?"

The girl took another chance. "They treated me with what I can call *agapē*—a kindness that asks for nothing in turn." She felt the threat of tears rising, and she knew a profound regret for having abandoned her friends, running away as she had from Phoebe. She placed her *kithara* on a table and approached the proconsul's couch. "Noble Gallio," she began, "I have come to ask a great favor of you."

He looked at Claudia who shrugged and smiled. "I know nothing of this," she assured him. "Helena never fails to surprise me. If she asks a favor, you must know that this is very rare for her. She must see something very fine and exceptional in your noble self."

He seemed touched by the flattery. He kept his eyes on Claudia for a while and then turned to Helena who had remained close to him, her head slightly bent in respect, her heart beating so furiously that she was sure they too couldn't fail to hear its throbbing. Gallio made a permissive gesture. "Proceed, Helena. It will be a pleasure for me to respond to such loveliness combined with honesty. You seem a remarkably straightforward young woman."

"It concerns a good man named Paul," and now Helena's voice was steady. "He has been in the city for a few months preaching about the god whose hymn I just sang for you, noble Gallio. He's of the Jewish race, but many of his fellow Jews of Corinth have turned against him. Something about religious and legalistic differences I don't understand, but I can testify to this: I have heard Paul's *kerygma* repeatedly and he has never said anything that would be construed as disrespectful to Rome or to the emperor." As she spoke the words she wondered if she was being truthful: *What do I understand of Paul's words, after all?* But now she had no choice but to continue. "My friend Paul loves the one who inspired him with a passion rarely seen among men; he calls him the Lord Yeesous, but he is not of this world. This is what I understand. There is nothing unkind or rebellious in the man Paul. His differences with those of the Hebrew synagogue are esoteric, since he is one of them after all. These arguments have nothing to do with Rome, nor with her power over the provinces. Your brother Seneca would find him a kindred spirit since Paul sounds more like a Stoic than a revolutionary." She ran out of breath and stopped.

Gallio smiled at the reference to his brother. "What has this to do with me?" he asked her.

"A few zealot Jews captured Paul this morning and have taken him prisoner inside their synagogue. They dragged him there by force, even though for months he has been having peaceful discussions with them in that same place. No Roman has interfered, since the local officials think all this has to do with questions of Jewish worship and is not their problem. But I saw the mob today and I was afraid of them; I'm terrified of what they might do to Paul. If they bring him before your tribunal, sir, I ask that you show mercy by allowing him to speak in defense of himself." She knew that she was trembling from head to toe.

Gallio said in a voice that may have contained excitement; with him, it was difficult to tell. "They have no right to arrest anyone. It's too late in the day to do anything now, but I am scheduled to hold court tomorrow. When this Paul of yours appears before the Bēma, I will remember your words." Helena bowed, thanked him and followed Alexandros out of the *triclinium*.

She was still trembling, and he had to support her as they walked back to her room. "Your performance was admirable. I've never heard you talk this much," he said, and that coaxed a smile to Helena's lips. "I was scared," she confessed, "but I didn't know it until it was over. Go with me tomorrow," she pleaded. "I must attend the tribunal."

He started to protest but he knew it wouldn't do any good. "Yes," he finally agreed, "and now I'm very curious to meet and hear this Paul."

———— ∽∂∾ ————

All through that tense overnight, Paul's supporters— including Prisca and Aquila—stood watch across from the synagogue. Despite the denials of his Jewish captors who were now guarding their house of worship, no one doubted that Paul was held inside. Next door was the house of the rich Titius Crispus where the ekklesia now met regularly. On this day it was full of women and children who took turns sleeping and praying for Paul's safety. It was an agonizing night for all those who loved him.

In the morning, a large Jewish mob gathered in front of the synagogue where, urged by a vocal few, they broke inside, and, pushing Paul's friends away, formed a thick cordon around Paul as they propelled him to the Agora.

"They have stripped him of all dignity!" Erastos cried but Prisca was fierce. "No, Erastos, no. His dignity is from within. No one, but no one, can take that from him."

"But we must do something," Erastos insisted. "I shall appeal to Gallio myself as soon as I can get near him. I returned to Claudia's late last night, but the servants had strict orders that Gallio should not be disturbed. It seems that his health is poor and he needs much rest. However, I have every intention of approaching him later this morning."

The Agora was teeming with people. The Bēma, massive and impressive, rose in its center; the handsome Propylaea faced the Bēma, together with the columns of the beautifully appointed Northwest *stoa*. The Julian basilica in the east and the graceful temples and monuments in the west enclosed an elegant space that passionate Corinthians never tired of extolling. Statues, painted marbles, and even representations of golden chariots glistened and winked under the Greek sun. Amidst the commotion ordinary life continued: the shops of jewelers and bankers on the Agora's periphery were open. Women carrying empty urns disappeared down the steps of the ornate Peirene Fountain to emerge later chattering, water spilling from the filled *hydriae;* men entered and exited bankers' stalls, while priests with their acolytes performed their duties in the temples. In front of the Bēma, an altar to Aphrodite and a statue of the goddess stood as anathema to the Jews of the city.

The open spaces of the Agora were heaving with the idle and the determined. The Jews were noisy, but the gentiles, especially those involved with the commerce of the city, were responding in kind. They were furious that their shops were empty, bitter with the crowds that showed interest only in what was going on around the Bēma and not in their wares. They needed a scapegoat for their fury.

The followers of The Way, Erastos among them, for he could no longer pretend that he was not one of them, stayed close together, near the south *stoa*; the Agora was on a higher elevation on their side than on the one facing the Bēma, so they tried desperately to see what was going on below.

It was impossible to distinguish Paul's small frame among so many furious men. Prisca feared that he would be injured by the pressure of the crowd. *Not again,* she prayed, *not again.* Aloud she said, "Erastos, I didn't want you to know this before, but he has been flogged repeatedly in the cities he has visited in the past. His back is a pitiful sight to behold."

He felt a sympathetic twinge run through his muscles and gritted his teeth. "We must not allow it to happen this time."

Suddenly a hush blew and moved like a southern wind through the crowds. A way was opening in the throng on the south side of the Bēma as a procession of dignitaries approached from the South Stoa and the Fountain House. Seeing them in the distance, all of Paul's friends moved forward to get a clearer view. Stephanas nudged Erastos: "Look, look, isn't that our Helena?" He felt the impact of her name and immediately spotted her slender form. From that point on she became for him the only visible focus in the procession. Stephanas persisted, "There's another woman with Gallio. Do you know her?"

"Yes." Erastos forced his glance away from Helena's white and blue loveliness to the elegant Claudia who was adorned in green. At that moment they were climbing the steps of the Bēma and he wondered what all this meant, whether they were there as friends or enemies. "That's Helena's legal guardian," he explained to Stephanas, "a Roman matron named Claudia. I have mentioned Paul to her." The aristocratic members of the procession, attended by their slaves, were now arranging themselves on the platform behind the tribunal's throne. Paul's friends pushed through to the open part of the Agora and took a collective breath. Where was Paul?

Gallio, a frail figure despite his fine toga and obvious Roman prestige, took his place on the throne of the tribunal; lawyers and sycophants grouped close by him, and the court proceedings began. The crowds returned to their noise and indifference hushing only when a person who interested them was being tried, one by one. And then a large and rowdy group in the middle of the Agora plowed through the bystanders, their force opening a trajectory toward the Bēma. "What's all this?" Gallio asked, and even those far away must have recognized his words and tone, for there was a pause, like a breath taken in the course of singing, and the noise of the mob abated. Then voices started babbling all together again. Gallio nodded to his guard who moved quickly from the foot of the Bēma toward the crowd, and for at least a moment their menacing thrust toward them quieted the throng.

Watching those close to Gallio, Erastos spotted Helena once again; *she's trying to be inconspicuous*, he thought, as she stood almost hidden behind Claudia and—yes, that was Alexandros just there, near them, as close as space and decorum allowed. Erastos wondered, *What is she thinking? More to the point, what is Helena doing there?*

———— ❧ ————

Helena was riveted by what she saw beneath the Bēma— Paul's balding head that had blistered in the sun, and then his eyes on her, eyes without accusation, filled with love. She was trembling as if freezing despite the heat of the Corinthian sun and wished desperately for a way to let Paul know that all would be well, but she saw no worry on his face. She heard Gallio ask, "Who speaks for the Jews?" Paul, though alert, didn't appear particularly intent on the proceedings, yet Helena was quite sure that nothing escaped his notice.

A man approached the Bēma and said in a loud voice, "My name is Sosthenes, leader of the synagogue. Your honor, the great Roman emperors have always protected our right to worship. But now this man, this Paul of Tarsus,"—and at this the mob pushed Paul roughly to the front—"is persuading people to worship God in ways that are contrary to the Law."

Gallio turned and glanced at Helena as if to say, "Is this the great Paul?" But her eyes saw only Paul's face. He looked serene. *If the word peace had a face,* she caught herself thinking, *it would be that of Paul's.*

Gallio's ironic eyes were now on the man Sosthenes. "Whose law is he abusing?" he asked.

"Our Law," Sosthenes answered but one could hear his courage diminishing. "The Law of Moses. That is, of *our* God."

"And you call that a crime?" Gallio asked scathingly. "In a city where there are thousands of cults, you disturb the peace of a Roman province by complaining about a harmless man who also worships *your* god?"

A nasty-sounding protest rose from many throats in bitter disagreement with the Roman proconsul. "You don't understand!" "The Law is what sustains us!" "He betrays the Law!" were a few of the phrases Helena's ear caught and still she could not take her eyes away from Paul's irenic face. "Speak," she mouthed to him. "Defend yourself," but Paul only smiled. Gallio lifted his limpid hand.

"Is he a criminal?" he asked the man Sosthenes, and the other made to answer but gulped. Gallio persisted. "Is he a villain?"

The other Jews yelled at Sosthenes to answer, to say yes, but Sosthenes repeated his earlier charge. "This, this man is persuading people to worship God in ways contrary to our Law," he said, but his voice was no longer steady. "He proclaims one whom Rome crucified."

At the terrible word, *crucified*, Gallio turned to look at Helena who cried, "Don't listen to them, listen to Paul!" and then Claudia bent to whisper something to Gallio. He closed his eyes for a moment and then addressed Sosthenes. "You, Judeans," he said, and contempt dripped from his Roman lips. "I sit here in the name of Rome. We Romans have our laws also. And our laws say that a man must be a villain and a criminal in order to be arrested and punished. You have not said anything that makes me convinced that this man has broken any Roman laws or offended against the emperor."

A high-pitched protest rose from the Jews, and then the gentiles turned against them, yelling in matching volume. Gallio made another motion to his guards who stepped forcefully against the crowd, their javelins visible. There was a small break in the noise and loud curses, and then Gallio's voice, dripping with contempt, continued. "You argue," he told Sosthenes, "you Jews always argue about things that don't matter—names, and words, and your own laws, and your own god—what has this to do with Rome?"

Gallio looked again at Paul as if debating whether to let him speak, but he seemed weary of the heat and intense light of the Corinthian sun, and he apparently did not find Paul worthy of any more effort. He made a dismissive gesture. "See to it yourselves; this does not concern me. I do not wish to be a judge on these matters," and he stood up.

Frantic now, Helena spoke to Claudia. "Please, for my father's sake, listen to me. That mob will tear Paul apart. Send him some help." Claudia motioned to Alexandros who quickly moved with slaves under Gallio's command to rescue Paul. By then, too, Erastos, together with Stephanas, had managed to open a way through the crowd, and his partisans tried to keep Paul from being trampled underfoot. But one of the mob managed to tear Paul's tunic from the shoulder, suddenly exposing his back. The mob was ready for blood. Alexandros and Erastos, assisted now by Gallio's guard, moved to cover Paul, so the mob turned on Sosthenes, who had let them down. "You fool!" they screamed. "Could you not tell the Roman that this man is a criminal?" And they started beating the leader of the synagogue.

But Helena didn't care about that. She had seen Paul's back, the terrible scars from the whip, the welts and redness, the purple swelling and, without meaning to, she cried out in dismay. Claudia turned to her, irritated. "What now, Helena? Gallio did what was proper. Your friend is safe."

For a moment Helena did not respond, but she knew now that her heart was with Paul's and Phoebe's people. She had to remain for now, however, with Gallio and Claudia, and the proper thing for her to do was offer thanks to the proconsul. At least Paul's life had been spared, and she was grateful that Alexandros was now in place to protect him.

As they made to leave Helena noticed that Paul had turned toward her. Without a word spoken, she knew that she was being blessed. With her eyes on the face of the courageous man who had not lost his inward peace when in grave and immediate danger, she followed the procession away from the Bema.

———— ✁ ————

In the open heart of the Agora, as the crowd seemed intent on taking its revenge on poor Sosthenes, Paul finally opened his mouth. "Erastos," he cried, "where are you, my friend?" Erastos motioned to Alexandros to let him get nearer to Paul who said, "My dear Erastos, see to it that something is done for my brother, Sosthenes. Ask the power of Rome to intervene if necessary. They are beating him, a man who was used by God today to keep me from harm. Ask these soldiers to rescue him and take him to a safe place."

Erastos looked confused, but at that point he would have

given his life for Paul had he been asked. He quickly conferred with the Roman guard who moved among the blood-thirsty mob. One of the guards pointed his spear while the other reached in with his long arm and plucked Sosthenes from their midst. The crowd made way. Erastos said to the bleeding man: "Paul, the one you accused, your prisoner of last night, has asked me to rescue you. Follow us, and we will look after your wounds." And an unlikely group of Romans, free Greeks, assorted slaves, freedmen, and Jews reached Aquila's place about the same time Alexandros arrived with Paul and the guards loaned to them by Gallio. Having deposited their charges safely, the guards left. All the sympathizers stayed.

The shop was entirely too small for so many people, and Paul suggested that they all proceed to Titius Justus' much larger place. When the disciples who had waited there saw Paul, they ran with cries and laughter to embrace him. But then they noticed his torn and bloody tunic and their laughter turned to weeping. Paul raised his arms. "Peace, my friends," he said. "I'm well and safe. I'm not injured. We must minister to this poor brother first." And he led Sosthenes forward. "I want those of you who have the gift of healing to wash his wounds and then let us all gather together to offer thanks to our God and Savior."

Everyone who was not identified as a member of the *ekklesia* had already left, except for Erastos and Alexandros; curious and not a little surprised, Alexandros was riveted by Paul. *What kind of man is he, really? Why is he concerned about someone who had wanted to do him harm?* Paul's friends, after some argument, led Sosthenes to the interior of the house. Alexandros recognized Prisca who approached and tried to minister to Paul's scarred back, so he moved in to assist her. The experienced slave blanched. In the course of his long life he had seen slaves beaten and whipped, but he had never seen a back quite like Paul's. *What has this man done to bring such hatred and punishment upon himself?* Without a word,

Alexandros stretched his hand to Prisca, who thrust in it a jar filled with salve and then left in search of a clean tunic. Alexandros washed Paul's old wounds and spread on them the cooling balm of yarrow and oil that Prisca had given him. Paul submitted to his ministrations, then turned and focused his burning eyes on him. Alexandros was shaken.

But at that moment Sosthenes emerged from the interior, his face now clean and his wounds no longer bleeding. He was wearing a borrowed tunic, a bandage around the head, and he moved like a man stunned into deafness. Aquila also approached and wrapped a clean *himation* on Paul's back. The apostle gave Alexandros another piercing look and then turned to Sosthenes, embraced him, and offered his accuser the kiss of peace. Sosthenes drew back. "What're you doing?" he croaked. "I had you imprisoned and almost stoned. What're you doing?"

"Only what Yeesous Christós asks of me," Paul answered. "To owe you nothing but love." And he led Sosthenes to the side, speaking to him quietly but earnestly.

To owe you nothing but love! Alexandros stopped and stared at Paul. He had heard words from the wise and the foolish of this world, but nothing had ever struck him with the force of Paul's last statement. After a few minutes of stunned silence, he approached Erastos and said, "You asked me recently if I had heard of these people, these Christ-followers. Now I have, and I like what I hear and see." And with that, knowing that all was well with Helena's friends for a while, he left to report to Claudia. He learned later that by the end of that day Sosthenes had joined his life to those who belonged to the *ekklesia* and thus lost his position as the leader of the synagogue.

When Helena saw Alexandros enter the atrium of the villa, she ran to him. He made a downward, calming motion with his open palms to reassure her that all was well. His taciturn self was in full control again. But before looking for Claudia, he said to Helena, "You remember your words in front of

Athena Chalinitis?"

"Of course."

"I've been thinking about them, Helena, and your desire to avenge your father and the loss of Ares. I understood that desire. But your friend Paul taught me something else today: *You don't owe revenge to anyone.* He said that all we need owe one another is love. Can you begin to understand what this means? These are words that make revolutions happen. These are words that would make *me* join the revolution." And he walked on, while, astonished, Helena remained staring at him.

Chapter 17: Return to Kenchreaê

In the peaceful days that followed Helena spent as much time as she could with Prisca, asking her questions and listening to her stories about the man Yeesous who lived and died in the province of Judea. Prisca spoke with the authority of an eyewitness, since her stories originated from those who had known the Galilean. Riveted by what she heard, Helena longed to know more about the short public life of one who inspired so much love. She was surprised, however, that almost everyone else wanted to talk to her about the "risen Christ," not the man Yeesous. She only vaguely understood that they made a distinction between the man Yeesous of Nazareth and Christós, God's anointed, who they believed still lived among them—though invisible.

"Not invisible to all," Prisca corrected her one day when Helena had shared her perplexity. "Paul saw him and heard him. Yeesous and Christós are one and the same. No one knows this better than Paul. You see, after his encounter with the glorified, resurrected Christós, Paul was changed forever."

Helena considered this information intriguing and longed to ask Paul about his encounter, but it was now increasingly difficult to find him with any free time. All his people were clamoring for his attention, he was teaching during his wakeful hours, and she did not want to add to his burdens.

One morning, thinking about the man Yeesous and the stories that attracted her so powerfully, Helena said to Prisca: "Don't you feel the need to write these stories so they will not be lost?"

Prisca considered the question as if this had never occurred to her. "The words of Yeesous' stories are engraved on our hearts," she said. "How could we ever lose them or forget them?"

"But how are the rest of us going to hear them?" Helena asked her.

Prisca hesitated before answering. "You see, Helena, we believe that Christós is returning, soon. Paul thinks that this will happen within our lifetime, but he is not certain of the date of his return. So the need to write the stories has not become urgent for us." Helena stared at her. How was it that she had missed this important bit of information? There was so much she needed to learn. For a moment she wondered: *If this Christós returns, will I meet him?* But then she saw that Prisca was becoming pensive so Helena moved from future probability to immediate concern.

"Listen, Prisca, you and Paul are very dear to me. Please tell Paul that if he needs Ares, who I believe truly longs to serve him, I will not stand in the way. Tell him, 'Helena pleads with you: Do not hesitate to take Ares on my account.'" And Prisca, relieved, promised to deliver the message.

Surrounded by the kindness of Paul's people, Helena was grateful that none of them asked her exactly why she had left Phoebe's household. Prisca's willingness to share stories of her

Judean life with her convinced Helena that her new friends had forgiven her.

———— ❧ ————

One morning a note from Paul to Alexandros arrived at Claudia's villa. He read it, passed the tablet on to Helena and then withdrew. *"Friend, Alexandros,"* it said. *"It was good of you to minister to my back. I ask you to offer the thanks of the ekklesia to Helena. Written by my hand, Paul."*

Helena read it and then allowed herself to feel the total forgiveness of the people she had in a way rejected when she stalked away from Phoebe. Then she decided to act on what she knew her heart longed for, and she ran to find the steward who was her oldest friend. "Alexandros!" she called before she reached him, "We're leaving for Kenchreaê!"

"By the 'we,' you mean…?

"You and me, of course," Helena said and laughed at his surprise. "Do you think Claudia will object to my taking you away?"

"The mistress is too busy organizing the proconsul's affairs," Alexandros reassured her. "There are enough slaves in this villa to look after her own affairs. I'll tell her I deserve a few days away from Corinth."

Helena went close to him and studied his face. "I don't know why you are on my side, but I'm glad you are. I miss my father so desperately." Alexandros regarded her with affection: *Is that a tear I see?* Helena wondered but took care to respect his privacy. *Of all slaves in the world, Alexandros deserves his dignity, I'm sure of this.* "I'll leave it to you then," she added briskly, afraid to reveal more of her own emotions. "Let's depart as soon as possible. Tell Claudia that I left all my belongings at Phoebe's and I need to retrieve them. I'll send our news to Paul and Prisca immediately."

Having made her decision, she felt free for the first time in months. A darkness had been dissolved, a burden lifted. "I'm going back to Phoebe," she sang, and it felt like a promised return to her loving mother. Two days later they were on their way to Kenchreaê.

———— ✿ ————

They walked together, Alexandros carrying a small bundle with a change of clothes for himself; Helena carried only her *kithara*. She still had sufficient clothes and other necessary possessions at Phoebe's and so didn't need to carry more with her. She felt an increasing closeness to Alexandros who seemed changed since Paul's day before Gallio. Helena decided that the time for truth telling had come.

"Why did Claudia marry him?" she asked the dignified slave, breaking the companionable silence of their walk. "Why did she marry that brute?"

"Who knows the mysteries of the human heart?" Alexandros was in a talkative mood. "Gaius was a handsome young man before wine and debauchery changed his countenance. In Makedonia, he was one of her father's officers. When Claudia noticed him he had already received his orders to Achaia, so she made an impulsive decision. She was very adventurous, even as a young girl, and thought life with him would be interesting—I remember her using that word—*interesting*. He didn't have money, only his looks and his army salary and position, but Claudia was very rich and her father indulgent. Her large dowry may have been her husband's undoing. In Corinth he didn't have serious army duties and he became lazy. He lost interest in promotions, started playing dangerous games with her money, and she, embarrassed, not wanting her father to know her mistake, kept quiet and continued to give him what he asked."

Still sick at the mention of Gaius Marius Sylvanus' name, Helena moved away from the subject of the hateful man

Claudia had married. She asked, "But you, Alexandros, what's your relationship to Claudia? I've wondered for a long time." She didn't think he would answer, but he surprised her, speaking in his laconic, rather dry manner that hid so much depth.

"You do deserve to know something about me, Helena. Like you, I was orphaned early. My mother also died at childbirth, but, unlike yours, mine was a slave. My father was Claudia's paternal grandfather. She's the daughter of my half-brother. But he was the child of the legitimate Roman wife and I was the child of a Greek slave."

She turned her indignant face to him, furious at the injustice, but he motioned for her not to say anything. "It happens, Helena, you know that. We grew up together, my brother and I, we were friends, he was good to me. He wouldn't study unless I studied with him, so I too received a good education. He treated me fairly even after our father died. When Claudia married she begged her father to let me go with her, and he agreed, eager to see that she was cared for. I gave him my word that I would look after her. I've done so, although, to my regret, I had no influence over Gaius, and she suffered as a result."

Helena tried to imagine his tragic fate, for what can be more terrible than slavery? But Alexandros had trusted her with his story and she had to accept it as he told it. So she returned to the other questions that had troubled her for months.

"Who killed him, Alexandros? Who killed that terrible man, her husband?"

"He killed himself," Alexandros answered quietly, but she could read neither truth nor evasion in his voice. He showed no inclination to continue. After a while he announced, "We are now changing the subject. Tell me what you know about these followers of Christós."

"Her name is Phoebe, and this isn't a non sequitur," she answered readily. "Phoebe is the only Christ-follower I know well, and there's nothing about her I don't like. She took me in, though she knew nothing about me. She never pressured me and never forced her ideas on me. When I asked questions, she told me stories about the man Yeesous, the one they call Christ or Lord. She treats her servants with respect and kindness and never calls them slaves. I think she has manumitted them, but since they don't discuss it, I don't know their status. She's always thinking of others. Phoebe treated me with love, and I'm ashamed now that I ran away from her as I did. She deserved more from me." They walked on. He said quietly, "If Phoebe is the person you describe, she probably understands your abrupt departure as the confusion of a young girl in love."

"A young girl in love," she repeated. "Maybe so." Then she shook her head. "Don't excuse me so readily, Alexandros."

"I agree that the young should also be held accountable for their actions. But how do these Christ-followers deal with that which is inexcusable?"

"With their favorite word—forgiveness."

"Wouldn't that be a shock to the shade of Gaius Marius Sylvanus!" Alexandros laughed, and she joined him.

At noon they stopped under the shade of olive trees and Alexandros, after spreading a cloth on the ground, served the bread, cheese, and olives. Helena handed him a cup filled with wine mixed with water and waited for him to drink. He took one sip to please her and then continued, "Now tell me about the others. What do you know about the man Paul?"

"Only that he's a good man and a total mystery."

"A mystery, yes. Explain this mystery, Helena."

She had the answer ready, because Paul had occupied her mind a great deal. "He's highly educated, obviously a man of extreme intelligence. Yet he has chosen to follow an obscure cult of an obscure Galilean. When he speaks, one is mesmerized not so much by the words as by his passion. The words are also a mystery, because I don't know much about Judaism. He could have been the leader of a fine philosophical school but he chooses to work with his hands, cutting and tooling the leather used in tents. And this man of intellect and passion has suffered severe punishments. Oh, Alexandros, did you see his back?"

"Prisca allowed me to rub some salve on his old wounds. There were hundreds of scars, welts and grooves that I have seen only on the backs of slaves."

Helena felt sadness creeping up on her again, but Alexandros hadn't finished. "What did they tell you about his punishments?"

"Prisca told me once: 'He suffers for the truth.' Can you imagine that? Such pain for the truth." She looked up and saw Alexandros' eyes on her face. Fire and longing were in them for something she could not yet grasp, and now she felt lost. "You admire him also, don't you?" Helena asked him and he did not deny it.

Soon they were back on the road. "What will you do in Kenchreaê?" Alexandros asked after a long silence.

"I've not thought about it," she confessed. "I only know I must see Phoebe before I can go on with my life. And then, maybe, see Ares once more. I don't know what will happen when we see each other again. The thought frightens and excites me at the same time."

They stopped to drink water from a marble cistern next to an extensive olive grove. Flocks of sheep grazed further on, the buzzing from insects was dizzying, and the cicadas raised a constant mass celebration, an accompaniment to every step they had taken but only now seemed to notice. The beloved aroma of dry thyme filled her nostrils. A swallow swooped over her head, and she was hit with a sudden shaft of joy that almost disoriented her. She turned to Alexandros to see if he had felt it also, and he smiled. "Helena, I haven't seen you happy like this since before your dear Demosthenes died." Her smile was wiped off before he continued with remorse, "I'm sorry, child, forgive me."

"No, no, don't apologize. I know you were fond of my father. I'm glad to hear people who liked him mention his name. My difficulty is that when I remember him I'm so sad now. I did not grieve him properly because of the evil of Gaius Marius Sylvanus, and then all the sadness over Ares..." She pondered the next question, wanting to ask it but afraid of the answer. "Do you know how my father died, Alexandros? Do you know? I didn't have the heart to ask Claudia."

"It seems that he was poisoned," Alexandros answered, and she heard his deep regret. "Poisoning would have been easy to prove, so Gaius had his slave stab Demosthenes with your father's own dagger after he was already dead in order to mislead us. At least this is what we surmised. Then they turned him over so that it would look like suicide and Gaius concocted a story about a loan your father could not repay; hence, the suicide. Claudia was immediately suspicious of that claim. She knew your father so well and could never believe that he had borrowed money from a man he despised. But by that time the body had been burned and we had no evidence. I remembered that there had been no blood on the wound, and when we put it all together, we became convinced that poison must have been involved. By then it was too late to bring charges of murder. Besides, Claudia, in her usual single-mindedness, decided that her own revenge would be more fitting than the state's punishment. She doesn't have much faith in the justice of the Corinthian courts."

Alexandros recalled all this as casually as he was able, but she sensed his regret and even guilt at the deception and her eyes filled with tears. Alexandros saw them and was moved.

"You were young and in love with Ares," he told her. "We decided it would be easier for you if we didn't tell you the truth as we suspected it. And Claudia was afraid of what you and Ares would do if you found out how your father died. She worried about your courage and devotion to your father, but she was more afraid of Gaius' meanness." He sighed. "We probably made many mistakes covering everything up. But during that time I had another concern: protecting Claudia. I've known her since she was born, you see. I am in fact her uncle. She could have been my own child had circumstance been different ..." His voice trailed off.

Helena touched his hand. "I know, Alexandros. All our griefs are personal, all our sorrows are unique."

Already the smell of the sea was meeting their senses, greeting them. Memories and longing pierced her. She remembered that strange dawn when she stood in the waters near the Bath of Eleni, the voice coming out of the deep, her first sight of Dionysos mingled with the memory of Odysseus, the knowledge that this remarkable encounter between a young girl and a stormed-tossed man had happened before, in her beloved Homeric myth, and she was reliving it. And then the good news, the astounding news of Ares' return from the dead. What happiness, what awe had filled her that morning!

Now the anticipation that had propelled her from the moment she had made the decision to return to Phoebe was turning to anxiety. What would she find in Kenchreaê?

They turned southeast, away from the commercial port, then along the shore, heading for the few houses that were springing up on the way to the famous Bath of Eleni, her heart beating fast. This road was unpaved, a dusty path parallel to the shoreline, and at this sleepy hour, when activity slowed down considerably after the midday meal, empty of wheeled traffic and pedestrians. Helena took off her sandals, handed them to Alexandros and let herself run. She knew that Alexandros could still see her, so she ran freely, unafraid. *Oh, to run again,* she thought. *To run with the salt sea air in my nostrils, the wet sand under my toes, the breeze that smells of faraway lands in my hair. Oh, to be free, to be alive, to be returning to someone I love.* How strange that other Helena seemed to her this minute, the Helena who had left a month before, a bitter, angry girl who had felt betrayed.

She could already see the house Phoebe had rented. There were no windows facing the road, but suddenly the front door opened and a woman came out and looked toward her. And then she too started running, not as fast as Helena, but in a hurry nonetheless. They met in the middle of the street and, breathless, they embraced, laughing and crying. "Forgive me, Phoebe, forgive me," Helena kept saying as Phoebe rocked her in her arms. "Oh, my beloved child, my beautiful *korē*. I knew you would return to me, I knew it." And now they held each other at arm's length and searched the wet faces, looking for signs, for what? "How did you know I was coming?" Helena asked. "You emerged from the door as if you were expecting someone. How did you know?"

"I sensed your coming," Phoebe said, "I *felt* your coming. How good God is."

And Helena, feeling at home, said, "I have news, about our dear Paul."

"Did you bring letters?" Phoebe asked and the girl exclaimed, "Oh, here I am, being a fool again. I was so anxious to come to see you, I forgot to offer to bring any."

And then they heard Alexandros' dry cough behind them and a simple, "I do have letters." They turned to look at him and Helena laughed.

"Phoebe, this is my friend Alexandros, Claudia's steward and administrator of her household. He has met both Paul and Prisca; he's always been a true friend to me."

Phoebe extended her hand. "Welcome, Alexandros," she said in her warm, inviting voice. "I thank you for your care of Helena, and I thank you for accompanying her here. Come and refresh yourselves, and I will look at the letters."

And they entered Phoebe's world together.

Bathed in the gold light of a departing sun Aristos was

grilling a freshly-caught fish on the hot coals of the brazier. The travelers sat, washed and refreshed, under the serene gaze of Phoebe who could not stop smiling. The atmosphere smelled of the sea, and the fish sizzled when Aristos poured olive oil on it. Helena sighed, content. "It's so good to be here and to be hungry."

Phoebe insisted that Alexandros sup with them, but he refused; then Helena announced that she would not eat a morsel unless he complied. That persuaded him. They raised their cups of wine and looked at each other. "To the reunion and the meeting of new friends," Phoebe said and they took the first sips.

Phoebe asked them no questions until they had finished eating. Then, at Helena's urging, Alexandros described Paul's ordeal and his appearance before Gallio. "Glory and thanks be to God," Phoebe kept saying as the story unfolded. She turned to Helena. "Alexandros mentioned Erastos and his efforts on Paul's behalf. How's my good friend?"

Helena shrugged. "I'm hesitant to tell you that I've not seen him at all. I was afraid he would scold me for leaving you—I was so ashamed, you see."

Phoebe glanced at Alexandros, but said to Helena, "And now, tell me what new adventure in your life persuaded you to return to me."

"It had nothing to do with me, but everything to do with Paul, I think. I remembered where my allegiance lies. The letter I received the day I left you was from Ares, Phoebe; I'm sure you guessed that. But his answer was not at all what I had expected. I took it as a final rejection when he said that he was giving me up to follow your Christ."

"How extraordinary!" Phoebe exclaimed. "Who would have ever thought it? But you must know, Helena, that one allegiance does not necessarily exclude the other."

"It seems more complicated than this for Ares who is

indeed a uniquely single-minded person," Helena reflected quietly. "Don't you agree, Alexandros?" The old man nodded and Helena continued with some difficulty. "Ares had made a vow during his slavery on that ship of thieves, something that apparently he never told his friend Dionysos. He vowed that he would serve forever the god who would rescue him. When Lydia helped him recognize that this God is the one you worship, Ares decided that he had to give me up and be like Paul."

"And be like Paul," Phoebe repeated, mystified. "Does he know Paul?"

Helena shook her head and said softly, "He's under his spell, nonetheless. The power of your stories leaves even me breathless at times."

"And what has Paul said about all this?"

"I understand that he wants us to meet one more time before he will accept Ares' decision. Paul says that Ares must see me once more to know his own mind. And I suddenly thought, Phoebe—no, I hoped—that we could meet here, in Kenchreaê."

"Ah." And Phoebe smiled. "That sounds reasonable enough."

Alexandros pulled out a tablet and handed it to her. "Perhaps Prisca explains it more thoroughly," he suggested and Phoebe read it eagerly.

"*Beloved sister in Christ,*" Prisca had written, "*reading this means that you've already welcomed Helena and Alexandros in your home. We pray daily for you, that you are in good health and that you are well settled. Paul is anxious to receive a full report on the work of the Lord in Kenchreaê, which report you may send back with Alexandros. Use your loving judgment concerning Helena. The two young people must see each other again before Paul can be certain of Ares' desire to follow him as a worker in the vineyard. He must not enter into a commitment with Paul that he will not be willing to keep and to fulfill. You know how much the beloved apostle dislikes a half-hearted allegiance to our blessed Lord. We will trust you on this. May blessings cover you and follow you and illumine your way. In Christ's love. Prisca, writing also for our brother Paul."*

Phoebe looked at her guests and smiled. "There's some news also directly written by Paul, but it concerns the work of the church here." She placed the letter on the table. "The light is fading. But it's *so* good to receive his encouragement." She beamed at Helena. "And now, my dear *korē*, let's see how we can notify Ares to come meet you here."

Again they heard that dry throat-clearing from Alexandros who had kept so quiet that they almost forgot his presence. "Helena, I didn't tell you. As soon as I heard that you wanted to see Ares and were retuning here to Phoebe, I sent a message to our young friend in Philippi urging that he come to Kenchreaê on the first ship available. Sea voyage is frequent and relatively safe this season. I believe you shall be seeing him soon."

They stared at him and then, as if in agreement, laughed aloud. "I had suspected for some time that you are remarkable," Phoebe told him, "but I realize how limited my appreciation was until this moment. A man of forethought and action. Come, friend Alexandros, I want you to get to know my own steward, Aristos. He too is a man worth knowing."

Helena went to visit her favorite loom and see what had resulted from the pattern she had abandoned in its weft. She was shy with Alexandra and Evniki but they welcomed her and tried to put her at ease by showing her the lovely cloth they had woven from her own design. "I *am* truly sorry," Helena told them. "You were good friends, and I abandoned you."

"Welcome back," was all they said, and the three girls relaxed together.

———— ⌘ ————

Phoebe spent the next day in the writing of a long and detailed report to Paul. Alexandros walked around Kenchreaê with Aristos and, as Helena found out later, he asked him question after question about having been a slave and then a freedman in Phoebe's household. Left alone, Helena decided to write a letter to Dionysos:

"*Good friend Dionysos. My first thought of you prompts me to call you Odysseus, the prince of Ithaca, returned sea-tossed and briny to the land of the living. I always think of you this way. The story of Nausikaä and Odysseus came alive that morning in the gulf of Saronikos, near the Bath of Eleni. The ancients again, Dionysos, Homer and his stories, and all the sorrows of his people. Am I avoiding my own sorrows? Perhaps. I need to talk to a friend and, suddenly, you seem the only one I can speak to without fear of being ridiculed or misunderstood. Of course, I can hear you laughing and saying: Only because I'm not there, little one. And yes, Phoebe would understand, but there is much that went on between us that makes me hesitate to burden her further. First, a confession: When I received a letter from Ares in response to mine I was so shocked and hurt that I turned against the Christ-followers, abandoning Phoebe to return to Corinth and to my patroness, Claudia. I hear your exclamation of surprise and your disappointment in me. I know how much you admire and respect Phoebe. But my reaction had nothing to do with her. It had everything to do with me and my love for Ares, my resurrected love. (Do you know that the Christ-followers believe in a resurrected god? No, it's not at all like Osiris; this is about a real man who lived in a specific place.) Here's something else Ares didn't tell you, good Dionysos: When he thought he was dying on the ship that almost killed both of you, he vowed that whatever god delivered him would have him forever. And this forever, this vow, did not include marriage to Helena. Did he ever mention this to you? He wrote it to me coolly and rationally. He's decided to be like Paul, a spiritual leader of the Christ-followers. An unmarried leader. You don't know Paul and his ekklesia, so all this is probably meaningless to you. When I*

176

returned to Corinth vowing to myself never to see these people again, I found that I could not keep away from them. What irony, eh? After life with Phoebe, the Roman villa and its inhabitants seemed pretentious. The new proconsul, Gallio, sent by the Emperor Claudius, was staying at the villa when Paul was taken by the Jews of the city and held prisoner. I heard this and asked Gallio to intervene. But when Paul was brought before him, Gallio dismissed all the charges yet made no effort to hear Paul. So this powerful man missed hearing perhaps the most important speech of his life, all because Paul is a Jew and not an aristocratic Roman. What double irony. Now I wonder, Dionysos. Is it possible that something good is happening to me because of this one positive deed of mine on behalf of Paul? I have been strangely at peace ever since. I have asked Ares to come to see me one more time. The truth is that Paul asked him. Paul refuses to take him on as disciple until he sees how Ares feels about marrying me. Do you think the sight of me will change him? Are you most thoroughly confused by now? Why are you not here to help me? And how is it in Alexandria and your practice? Have you punished the man who tried to steal it from you? Ares will want answers to all these questions. When will you come to see us again? I greet you with gratitude for saving Ares. No matter that he is lost to me, I'm glad that he is alive. Your friend always, Nausikaä."

Helena grinned at her mythological signature and went in search of Aristos who promised to find someone sailing to Alexandria to deliver her letter to Dionysos.

On the following day, loaded with presents and letters, Alexandros left for Corinth. Yet before he left he had shared startling news with Helena. She watched him go, stunned by what he had told her. "Helena, dear daughter of Demosthenes, I must tell you that the Christ of Paul and of Phoebe is now the Lord of my life also." Then he threw back his head and laughed. "The Lord of my life who liberated me. Now I am free." She stared at him openmouthed but he kept smiling. His revelation lit up his sad eyes, taking away that familiar look of his—world-weary cynicism. Helena was shaken. "But how," she stammered, "why?"

He thought for a while and then said, "Remember our talk about the statue of Athena Chalinitis? I told you then that I knew how it felt to have someone holding my life's reins, because I was born a slave. Yet, even as a child, though a slave, I kept control of my inner life. Paul, and then your Phoebe, changed all that. For the first time in fifty years I don't want to be my own. I now belong to the Lord of life. After spending all of last night asking questions of Phoebe and Aristos, I now know who this Lord is."

Helena felt a sudden longing for that kind of assurance but suppressed it. Her heart had belonged to her father and to Ares and had been cracked in two. She didn't want that to happen again. They said good-bye, and Helena felt lonely without her old friend and protector. Aristos and Phoebe had tears in their eyes also, and yet they were radiant.

Later Helena mused aloud to Phoebe, "Alexandros of all people! He was a cynical man when first I knew him. I thought he possessed everybody's secrets in the villa and could use them without compunction when he needed to do so. I saw him as capable of employing any means to protect Claudia. But now, look at him—he smiles, he's more talkative, he is so kind—what has happened to him?"

"An encounter with Christ," Phoebe answered as if it that were the most natural thing in the world.

Chapter 18: Dangers and Sorrows

The days took on the easy rhythm of summer and the three young women of Phoebe's household spent more time outdoors. At the first light of dawn, together with the tittering of birds, Phoebe heard the sweet voices of the girls whispering and laughing as they awakened to their chores of the day. The sun dispelled the coolness of the night so rapidly that they had to work fast, before the intense heat enveloped the land. Phoebe smiled with affection as she saw Alexandra, Evniki, and Helena in the atrium, shaking the linen together and then folding it. Their movements looked like a dance. Evniki carried the folded sheets to their cupboard and then returned with baskets of rough wool. They spread it on the tiles of the atrium and then, taking turns, they held taut strings between them and with this bow they whipped the wool into fluffiness. Later, in the cool of the evening, all of them together would spin it into the thread used for weaving. She loved the rhythm of these days, the presence of youth and laughter, the briny smell of the sea reaching them like a blessing.

A week after Helena's return Phoebe said to her, "I'm so

glad to see you reacquainted with joy," and the younger woman smiled: *Is it really so?* Helena did feel much more interested in others, especially the two girls from Makedonia who were turning into good friends—the first women friends of her age.

On a hot summer day, the three of them decided to visit Junia's family before going on to market. Junia's husband, the sea captain, was due to return in a few days, but the waiting for that homecoming was nearly unbearable for the mother and her children. So the girls went to offer diversion and to play with the children who so enjoyed their visits. Afterwards, happy and carefree, with no premonition of what was to come, the three of them continued to the city center and their various shopping chores.

———— ❧❧ ————

The market is full and noisy, and the girls, caught up in its energy are laughing, exploring its stalls but staying close to each other. They fill one of their large baskets with bread and eggs, with leeks, parsley, and the aromatic figs and grapes of the region. Helena picks a purple fig, peels it slowly and eats it with obvious relish. She loves the fragrance of figs, the succulence and the rich seeds as they fill her mouth and tingle her tongue. *Life is good*, she thinks, for the first time in months, and the thought surprises her. *Phoebe is right; I'm happy again.*

Leisurely, they move to the elegant city spring, descend the tiled steps, and fill their two urns to overflowing. Helena is carrying one of them, Alexandra the other, and Evniki keeps hold of the loaded basket. They decide to return by walking on the sand, their feet lapped by the salty sea. The fish market is at the end of the jetty, close to the house, so they will pick the fish, wrap it in wide grape leaves to keep it fresh in the heat of the morning, until, back at home they prepare it for the feast. They are pleased to have promised Aristos an afternoon of rest not only from shopping but also from the daily chore of cooking. Helena's dark curls are now long enough to cushion the urn as she lifts it from her shoulder to the top of her head. She is trying to recapture her days of athletic balance. The blonde, strong Makedonian girls are teasing her. "You'll lose your balance, Helena, *oop, oop,* watch, you'll drop the *hydria.*" She laughs, extends her arms, and does a short dance, but the *hydria* stays put. They cheer her on. Then the two try pushing each other into the shallow sea and when they come close to Helena she nearly loses her balance.

This turns her around and she sees a ship docking at the bustling part of the port. "Look," she says to the girls. "Look at the crowd disembarking. So many people. I wonder…" She doesn't complete the thought lest she tempt fate. "I've never traveled by ship," she says instead. To herself she muses: *I wonder how long it will take Ares to arrive from Philippi? If he ever loved me, he will respond to Alexandros' summons.* But she shakes the thought to concentrate on the moment, clinging to her newfound peace. All three of them pause to gaze at the disembarking travelers who, from the distance, look like a colorful sail that is undulating in the breeze, and then the girls turn around to continue toward home.

After a while they tire, stop talking, and concentrate on feeling the delicious coolness of the water moving through their dusty toes; in the approaching noon quiet they listen to the lapping sounds of the gentle waves. Now at the fish market they select the fresh, still wriggling creatures carefully, wrap them in the palms of wide, moist grape leaves, and add the bundle to Evniki's basket. The seller knows them and she sends her greetings to Phoebe. Helena says, "It didn't take long for all of Kenchreaê to learn to love our wonderful Phoebe," and they agree happily. They move on. The noise of the port is getting fainter, the people are disappearing indoors for their noonday meal, escaping the heat, and the girls, concentrating on the water at their feet are oblivious to what awaits them.

And now the stillness is broken with a terrifying suddenness. From the hidden side of a red-painted vessel beached on their left, a man jumps and grabs Helena by the arm. Her water urn falls and bursts open. Her shock is so intense that she can't make a sound; the other girls scream and scream but Helena is frozen mute, back in Corinth again, on the night of her assault by the hated Roman. Alexandra yells to Evniki, "Run for help, I'm staying with her." Used to obeying, Evniki drops her basket and runs away as another man appears from behind the ominous boat. The attacker is now groping Helena's body in a manner that awakens her fury and jolts her out of the paralysis of fear. She struggles to free herself and at that moment she has a glimpse of his face. "You!" She spits at him, "Demetrius, you odious creature, you slave, you dragged me before Gaius once against my will, but you've no right to touch me now, you dog. Let go of me!"

The second man, who looks more like a sailor than a slave, is uttering crude encouraging noises to the slave. Demetrius yells, "She's a murderer, she killed my master. Let's bring her before the magistrate."

The other man snorts. "Or, we can keep her for ourselves and demand money from the widow. She has plenty of it, right?" A disgusting laugh escapes him.

Helena manages a well-aimed kick at the slave. "I did *not* kill Gaius, though I wish I had. You idiots, you don't know what you're doing. You there, are you taking the word of a slave against a free woman? If you don't let me go, Demetrius, you'll regret it. You can't assault a free woman and get away with it." She is turning from one to the other, yelling, her anger barely concealing her terror. She knows that if she gives in to fear it will paralyze her anew.

"I've *proof* you killed him," Demetrius, now confident, persists in his heavy Syrian accent. "I heard you that night with mah own ears, beaut'ful Helena." Alexandra screams with horror as the slave now bends his face to Helena's and, alerted by her scream Helena turns her head sharply to avoid him. She sees Alexandra lifting her urn to bring it down on the slave's head but the sailor grabs her arm, and stops her. She too is forced to drop her urn, but this one does not break. The sailor's hand covers her mouth but Alexandra manages to bite it drawing blood. The man curses and raises his arm to strike her, but something holds him back when she turns her severe eyes to look at him. She's a head taller than he is.

The two men are now dragging the girls toward the north side of the red-painted boat; it had been hidden from the girls' sight as, oblivious to danger, they walked on the beach only moments before.

Helena feels her fury rising and she prefers that to despair. In the lightning fast pace set by danger, questions rush through her mind: *How can this be happening to me now, when I've finally begun tasting peace? Where's the god of the Christians now, the god who loves orphans?*

In a second's silence she hears Alexandra's prayer in loud Greek and takes heart. "Save Helena, Lord Yeesous," she begs. "Save Helena."

They are now on the side of the boat hidden from the port. Someone from above has lowered a rope ladder, and the slave is struggling to lift Helena by pushing her from below. She has found her voice and screams and kicks at her assailant. *This could be the end,* she thinks. *I'd rather die than get on this boat,* and she refuses to climb. He gives her a hard push upward, and she clings to the ladder to free her legs. Just at that moment, she feels his hold on her thighs slacking. With both hands on the ropes, her legs now swinging free, she dares to look down, not knowing whether it's safe to jump, to escape. Demetrius utters a hoarse cry, his hand loses hold of Helena, and his body drops with a thud. She sees his cracked head bleeding, half-submerged in the shallow sea. She sees the hand of another man holding the large heavy shard of the broken water urn; the blow from the sharp edge of the pottery has been accurate and probably deadly. The man holding it now turns rapidly around to attack Alexandra's captor, but this one has already loosened his hold on her and is running away to the other side of the red ship. Helena slides down and looks at her savior's face as he pivots and turns toward her. She gazes at the lean bone structure, the fiery eyes, the black, close-cropped hair. "Oh, Ares, you came!" she cries and everything becomes dark as she loses consciousness.

———— ❧ ————

"Ares?" Alexandra's mouth dropped open. She had heard Helena talk often enough about her possibly lost love. Now he had appeared to save her just in the nick of time? "You, here?"

She stared at him. During the attack Alexandra had been praying frantically for Helena, totally oblivious of the danger to herself. Her eyes had been on her friend as the nasty Demetrius was pushing her, lifting her to climb the rope ladder to the dreaded ship. Alexandra had kept yelling for help, confident that Phoebe's Lord would not abandon them. *Surely she herself had not been set free by Phoebe in order to be enslaved again. No! Never!*

And then in a blur she had seen him, the young man running swiftly toward them followed by others in the distance. *They must be from the ship that was docking,* she had thought as he drew near. He had grabbed a large shard from the sand and, swinging it like an expert, smashed it against the slave's head and immediately turned toward Alexandra's captor.

As she continued to stare at their savior, wondering who he could be, the coward who had a grip on her arm had dropped it and run away. Then she heard Helena whisper, "Oh, Ares, you came," just before she fainted. Alexandra felt like laughing. *Ares, this was Ares....*

Their liberator looked so confused that Alexandra felt pity for him, as he stood immobile, the shard in his hand. The shallow water covered Helena's slim body so Alexandra bent down to lift her head as Ares finally emerged from his shock. He bent and scooped the unconscious girl into his arms. All color had drained from his face. His lips were pale as he whispered, "I thought nothing would ever surprise me again." More of the travelers had now arrived and they were gathering around. Two of them had caught the running sailor and were holding him between them.

"So *you're* the famous Ares," Alexandra was saying. "Oh, my *heavens*. You chose the perfect time, didn't you? I asked the Lord Yeesous to send help, but never thought he'd send *you*."

"I just came ashore," Ares said. "I didn't know who was crying for help. And here you are, whoever you are, uttering the name of Yeesous. You see that ship over there in the distance, just unloading?" he pointed. "We were coming down its plank and I was asking the locals how to find Phoebe's house. But then I heard screams and ran. It didn't matter who it was. I've been in danger myself and have sworn not to run away from anyone in distress—not ever again." The men who had traveled with him were nodding in agreement.

And then the shore seemed to fill with people. Phoebe was running to them together with Evniki, followed closely by Aristos. Roman *vigile*, sailors, and a few curious bystanders were approaching from the direction of the town, the *vigile* marching in their disciplined manner, the sailors running with much noise. Alexandra was thankful, comforted by their numbers. Ares was still holding Helena in his arms. The slave Demetrius was bleeding in the salt water.

Phoebe approached, fear contorting her face. She reached for Helena. "Is she…" she started but couldn't finish. "She's alive," Alexandra reassured her. "She saw Ares and fainted. She's had enough shocks for one day. Let her be."

Phoebe looked at the young man's face. "Are you Ares?" she whispered.

"I didn't know who she was," he answered, confused, almost stuttering. "I only knew that I wouldn't run away from a woman's distress again. But you must be Phoebe."

A loud groan from the bleeding man on the sand brought them back to the current predicament. Demetrius was regaining consciousness. Curious people were coming close, asking questions, adding to the confusion. One of the Romans, the officer of the *vigile*, blew a loud whistle.

"What's happened here?" he asked, but Demetrius spoke up from the ground in his heavily accented Latin. "This girl 'ere killed my owner, Gaius Marius Sylvanus of Corinth." He pointed to the unconscious girl.

"This is *not* true," Phoebe intervened and her beautiful voice made everyone hush and look in her direction. "The death was termed a suicide by the wife, Claudia, and by the Corinthian authorities. I can produce witnesses who can testify against this man's deliberate lie."

"He and his partner tried to abduct us," Alexandra said to the officer, her voice unnaturally loud, but then the reality of what had almost happened hit her and she started shaking, her teeth chattering. Phoebe wrapped her own shawl over Alexandra's shoulders and the girl managed to continue her accusations: "His partner is dressed like a sailor and ran off, he's probably hiding on this ship. Get him." The bystanders reassured her that they already had.

Phoebe said to the Roman. "I live close by. I need to take these distressed girls back to the house and summon a physician. We'll stay there and make ourselves available for your interrogation."

"Abduction is a serious charge," the official said to Alexandra. She agreed but added, "You must not forget to add assault. The slave was assaulting Helena, a free woman, the ward of a

Roman matron who is the widow of Gaius Marius Sylvanus; she's a person of great importance in Corinth. And his partner was trying to abduct me before this young man rescued us."

The officer of the *vigile* gave orders for the arrest of Demetrius and for his collaborator. Demetrius himself changed tactics and started blaming his new owner for the attempted kidnapping; he pointed to the red-painted vessel where his owner, its captain, was now being held. "I recognized this here Helena," he said. "I tell 'im how she threatened to kill mah master the night he died. My new owner, he ask me many questions. Then he orders me 'abduct her, demand ransom.' I'm just a slave, 'tis not my fault. I had to do it."

"Rome doesn't look kindly on slaves putting their hands on freeborn Roman women," the official barked at him. "You're scum. I'll deal with you later." And then he shouted at the crowd to disperse. He turned now to Ares. "And who are you?"

"I'm her friend, her brother," Ares answered, still holding Helena in his arms as if she weighed nothing. "I was just arriving from Neapolis in the north and was on my way to meet her when I heard screams and found her and her companion being forced aboard this vessel. At first I didn't know who they were, but it was obvious they didn't want to go with these men. I saw them being grabbed and pushed against their will, and yelling for help. To stop him from hurting Helena, I hit him, and it was then that I recognized her."

The Roman turned to Phoebe. "I'm obligated to follow through on the allegations against the young woman, even from a slave. We'll torture him to learn the truth."

Phoebe blanched. "Is torture necessary?" she asked. "I have an utterly reliable witness. I'll send a messenger to Corinth and have the witness, an honorable Roman citizen, return here. He will tell you the whole story as he saw it with his own eyes. You don't need to torture this man."

The official looked at her, shrugged, and ordered his men

to take the prisoners to the city. The two groups separated. Aristos offered to carry Helena home, but at that moment she opened her eyes. "Phoebe?" she asked and tried to stand on her feet clinging to Ares the whole time. "I'm so sorry to worry you again." She turned to Ares as if dreaming. "You are real? I didn't dream you? Then you must meet Phoebe, and Alexandra, and Evniki, and Aristos..." and then she burst into sobs, unable to continue. Phoebe looked at Ares who moved aside as she put her arms around Helena. "Come, my *korē*," she told her, her comforting voice betrayed by tears. "Come home and let us look after you."

And, very gently, she led her down the road, but Helena did not let go of Ares' hand.

Aristos had already rushed to town to summon a physician. Evniki had presence enough to recapture the basket, and Alexandra bent to pick up the remaining unbroken urn. They walked home without speaking.

As soon as they entered the house Phoebe uttered a loud thanksgiving and Evniki brought a basin of water to the atrium. She and Phoebe washed Helena and Alexandra, but Ares refused their ministrations and asked to be allowed to wash himself. In a bundle still tied to his back were his possessions together with a change of clothes. When he returned to them he was clean, all blood had been washed away, and he looked at each one of the women with undisguised curiosity.

The two girls, feeling polluted, had thrown away the tunics touched by the abductors and were now freshly dressed, their bruised arms covered by long sleeves.

"I've never before hit a man to kill him," Ares was telling Phoebe in an earnest voice. "I didn't even know it was Helena he was assaulting but I did try to kill him. What does this say about me? Where has all this violence been hiding?"

Phoebe considered this seriously. "Dionysos told us about your helplessness on the slave ship," she told him quietly. "You must have felt so humiliated—a free man treated like a slave—unable to defend yourself… No wonder you were angry when you saw the defenseless girls. Still, you didn't kill him, Ares. You tried to stop him, and you did."

Helena was gaping at him more in surprise than adoration. This was a person she had known like her own self, but now she stared as if she wanted to read him in the manner she reserved for her precious scrolls. But the other two girls were also riveted by him. He was so handsome, that it was like looking at a statue. But this statue had sad eyes that had seen too much. Helena said bitterly, "Know that if you had not stopped him, I would have found a way to kill myself. I would *never* have allowed him to violate me. Why is it that women have to suffer violence at the hands of men, *why?*"

Ares shuddered visibly, so Phoebe took another tack. "Now, my dear friends, we should agree to cooperate and answer all questions when the authorities come. And let's invite friend Erastos to come here to testify that Helena is indeed innocent of killing Gaius."

"Erastos?" Ares asked. "I'm not familiar with the name." He looked at Helena but she didn't offer an explanation.

"Erastos is my friend," Phoebe said. "He was our most distinguished actor in Corinth, don't you remember? On the night Helena came to me to find shelter, it was Erastos who brought her. She had threatened Gaius in public after she heard of your drowning. Erastos saw that it was not Helena who killed that man."

"Yet I went there with every intent of killing him," Helena said to Ares. "What does that say about *my* violence?"

"But you did *not* kill him," Phoebe said, emphatic now, "and Erastos was the one who rescued you, so we owe him much." She addressed the last to Ares. "We depend on him for Helena's continuing safety. Erastos is our most important witness."

"I can see that," Ares said. "Is he also one of the brothers?"

Phoebe understood what he was asking. "His heart is."

The physician's arrival interrupted the conversation. He found the girls shaken but whole. All of a sudden Helena showed signs of her extreme exhaustion and Phoebe urged both her and Alexandra to rest in her own bedroom. "He's a lovely young man, your Ares," she told Helena. "I can see why you missed him so desperately." Helena's eyes filled with tears. "Ah, but is he mine? I don't think he belongs to me."

"We all belong to God, Helena, my dear. And that sets us free. Remember this."

By the time Phoebe left the room Helena was already asleep, but Alexandra decided she was well enough to help with their guest and the authorities.

Junia meanwhile had heard of the attack and rushed to Phoebe's where, while Helena slept, the rest of them dealt with the official from the *vigile*. He asked Phoebe, "Why don't you want the jailer to torture the slave? After all, he was hurting your young friend. The law, as you must know, states that the only testimony Rome accepts from a slave is taken under torture."

Ares and Phoebe exchanged glances. They had already agreed that this was a stupid and unjust law but had decided not to be confrontational. Phoebe said carefully, "This is a household of peaceful ways. We don't practice and we don't approve of or even condone torture."

"Even for those who hurt you?"

"Even for those who hurt us. Our God forbids it."

The *vigilis* made it clear that he thought this very foolish and incomprehensible, but he didn't look like a man who questioned ideas. He took his leave with reluctance, and Alexandra suspected that this had to do with herself. He had not been able to take his eyes off her, and she wondered: *Why isn't such scrutiny making me uncomfortable?* To herself she smiled. *Maybe there are some decent Romans.* At the gate he told her he would return, but she said, "You must come only if you find people like us worth knowing. Even though I hate what the slave Demetrius did, I too would not have agreed to torture." The official looked thoroughly bemused when he left.

Aristos volunteered to go to Corinth to summon Erastos, and Phoebe urged him to invite Alexandros also. So once again, Aristos started on the road to the big city.

Chapter 19: Eros and Agapē

Cool-headed Prisca took charge when Aristos arrived in Corinth with the troubling news of Helena's assault and Demetrius' resurfacing. She summoned Erastos and asked him to go to the villa and see Alexandros: "Claudia must be informed that her former slave has threatened her ward."

He agreed and left for the villa. Apprehensive about the reappearance of both Demetrius and Ares, he walked rapidly, and the moment he reached the villa he asked for Alexandros. Their previous meeting had been a solemn occasion. Erastos had finally admitted publicly that he was indeed a follower of Christ and joined Alexandros in a joyful celebration within the *ekklesia*. Later, on a communal visit to the Corinthian Gulf, Paul had baptized both of them, something he rarely agreed to do in Corinth. But now even as they greeted each other warmly, Alexandros saw that Erastos was agitated.

"Something's wrong?"

"Yes. The slave Demetrius has resurfaced in Kenchreaê." And he related all that he had learned from Aristos.

"We must inform Claudia immediately," Alexandros said,

his face paler than usual. "Of course I'll accompany you to the port city, to give support to Helena. The poor girl doesn't need to be reminded of her shame."

"Her shame?" Erastos was angered by the word. "Why should Helena be ashamed? She threatened Gaius but did not kill him."

"It's the rape I want her to forget, not the threat," Alexandros retorted and then, seeing Erastos' face, he hit his forehand with his palm. "Ah, you did not know…"

Erastos sat heavily on the edge of the *impluvium* and splashed water on his face. He felt as if he had been hit. "What a fool I've been," he said. "This explains so much that has puzzled me. I have avoided considering it."

"It was a terrible thing, Erastos. Claudia never forgave her husband for what he did to Helena."

"I finally understand Helena's desire for revenge, and I can't say I blame her."

Alexandros sat next to him. "I blame myself for not protecting her, and for so much more," he began sadly. "In my effort to protect Claudia, I acted unjustly against many people. Only now do I recognize this in myself. Gaius was a bad man, but the disappearance of Demetrius was my responsibility. I took him away in the middle of the night, before his master's death was discovered."

Erastos' mind cleared as he realized the implications of what he had just heard. He grabbed Alexandros' arm. They stared at each other. Alexandros articulated slowly, "So if Demetrius wasn't here when the body was discovered, how could he know of his master's death? This changes everything."

They found Claudia in her *tablinum*. She knew immediately that they were not bringing good news, and she quickly dismissed her other visitors from her presence.

Alexandros told her of the slave's reappearance and his assault on Helena and then added, "He has accused her publicly of killing the master. My question is: How did he know of Gaius' death? Remember, we didn't find the body until the next morning. By that time I had already sold Demetrius, and he was gone."

Claudia looked from Alexandros to Erastos and then back again. "I've already told Erastos of my complicity. He knows that I did everything I could to persuade Gaius to kill himself. Yet, if you have any doubts of my veracity, Erastos, there's no way Alexandros would ever give me away."

Erastos ignored her efforts to justify herself. He said, "The question remains: How did Demetrius know? What hour of the night did you remove him from the villa?"

Alexandros said thoughtfully. "After Claudia had retired to her rooms, I saw that she was safe there and then confirmed that Helena was still closeted in her own room. I went immediately in search of Demetrius. I had put three slaves as guards at the entrance of the master's chamber because I didn't want him to wake up suddenly and go in search of Helena. Demetrius had disappeared. Nearly an hour passed before I found him in the kitchen wing drinking what wine was left over from the dinner. I took him away immediately. He didn't have a chance to return to his master."

Erastos leaned forward intently. "Was his tunic bloody?"

Alexandros considered the question. "There were stains all over it, but I thought they came from the wine and from the wound on the master's forehead when Helena hit him with her *kithara*. His tunic was brown, and the light in the kitchen was poor at that hour. I should have examined him more carefully. He was drunk and incoherent, so I had to force him to walk around the grounds in order to get him sober enough to travel through the city. But first I made him change clothes—I already had a clean tunic with me for that purpose—and took him away from the villa as quickly as possible. I told one of the kitchen girls to burn the dirty tunic. It must have been two hours after midnight by then. I've wondered since why Demetrius was so willing to leave Corinth immediately. He seemed grateful to me instead of angry when I sold him to someone else. Why did he want to leave Gaius Marius Sylvanus who preferred him above all the other slaves? But I didn't get beyond the questions."

They sat together thinking, trying to remember. Claudia said, "The slaves you had put as guards, Alexandros…I went to them and dismissed them. I had stayed with Gaius immediately following the banquet debacle, trying to persuade him that after all his crimes the only honorable way out was for him to fall on his own sword. The shame of a trial was more than I could bear. I tried to remind him of his honor as a former soldier, a knight. I thought, if Gaius were to do what I had urged, no slave should be nearby to hear him call for help; I knew he'd change his mind at the last minute…"

The men stared at her. The events of that night were unfolding before Erastos again. "Gaius must have been dead by the time you dismissed the slaves who guarded his quarters, or wounded…in which case, you could have saved him if you had called for help, Claudia."

She said without regret. "Nothing troubles me about what happened to him that night. Gaius deserved to die, and he did. Death for death. Stabbing for stabbing. He killed my beloved Demosthenes," and only at that name her voice cracked.

"I wonder," Alexandros mused, "if the master asked Demetrius to stab him." There was relief in his voice.

It was now Claudia's turn to stare. Then she started laughing. "So, my faithful Alexandros, all this time you thought that I had done the deed, didn't you? And you said nothing about your suspicions. As always you're willing to protect me, even from the accusation of murder. Thank you."

He looked at his feet. "I must confess, it was weighing heavily upon me. Especially now that I have thrown my allegiance to

Christós, this was something I found difficult to live with. My complicity in all this is not small."

She cried out, "What are you saying? You, a follower of this sect? I can't believe such nonsense."

"You might as well," Erastos said as kindly as he could, "for I count myself among them also."

She stood up and faced them. "What is this? A conspiracy of lunatics? Helena begging for a Jew named Paul, you, an aedilis of the city becoming a member of this cult, and now you, Alexandros, the most rational and cynical man I know, joining them? What's happening to my world?"

Alexandros reassured her. "It's all for the good. Don't upset yourself. I've no intention of leaving you or doing anything to displease you."

She sighed, suddenly deflated. "Oh, Alexandros. You are not a slave, so don't act like one. You've never been a slave, for your mind is free. Just an accident of fate and of war put you where you are. I've intended doing this for a long time now, and only perversity and the fear of Gaius kept me from it. You deserve your manumission, something my father should have done years ago. I'll sign the parchment to that effect immediately." And she went to her desk.

"It's the Lord's doing," Erastos whispered to Alexandros. "You'll be of greater help to the *ekklesia* as a free man. And you deserve this."

When she handed him the signed and sealed parchment, she kissed him on the cheek. Alexandros had tears in his eyes. "Thank you, uncle," she told him, "you have been faithful, but I don't know how I'll manage without you."

"I've no intention of leaving you, my brother's daughter," he said solemnly. "I wouldn't know what to do outside your home. I'll remain as administrator if you let me, but first allow me to have a few days in Kenchreaê to settle the problem of Demetrius."

"The days are now yours," she answered. "You can do as you please with them." She shook her head as if to throw away the emotion and said to Erastos, "What's happening with that willful girl?"

"We must go clear her name. We'll pull the truth out of Demetrius and see that the magistrate knows the whole story, and then the rest is up to God."

"Which God is this?" she asked bitterly.

"There is but one God," he said, but she only laughed.

———— ✿ ————

Back in Kenchreaê Helena—and Ares, too—were confronting a new world neither of them recognized clearly.

After a deep sleep in the middle of the day, she awakened, her heart beating fast, her breath shallow, yet forgetting the terror of the encounter by the sea, the threat of abduction, the panic of those unbearable moments of, *This then is the end, now I too must die.* Instead she woke up thinking, *Something good has finally happened. What is it?* And then the reality of Ares filled her, his presence in this house, the feel and security of his arms as he held her when she came to, the joy of his existence—his life, his life…. After having mourned him as dead during those heart-numbing months of thinking, *He is no more,* now she cried, *Ares is alive! Ares is here.* She sat up and held her knees to her chest, lowered her head, and was still, savoring the knowledge of his presence somewhere in Phoebe's house. She thought of his eyes, that dark fire in them, the rare but sweet smile on the finely chiseled face, the curly black hair that fell unruly on his forehead and over his ears, and then she came to. *But does he still love me?* She remembered that he no longer belonged only to her and she lost some of the joy. *Of course he loves me. I'm so filled with love, how can he not be?* Feeling refreshed she emerged from her room.

Phoebe and Ares were sitting together, in deep and

serious conversation. When they saw her, Phoebe smiled and Ares stood up. "Are you well, Helena? Have you rested enough?"

"Yes," she said, "yes, I'm well. What a terrible welcome I offered you. There I was, in trouble again. So sorry." Her musical voice pulsated.

He smiled. "Phoebe and I have been thanking God repeatedly for letting me come to your aid. I don't even want to think of what might have happened to you and Alexandra had I not arrived on time." He took her hands in his. "Let Phoebe be my witness that I confess my sin to you, the sin of abandoning you when you needed me the most, and I beg your forgiveness."

The solemnity of the moment touched her, but the old mirth stirred inside her and teased her. She smiled at him. "Well, you certainly made up for it today, Ares. Who would have thought you could wield a pottery shard like a sword? Achilles couldn't have done better." She laughed with the wonder of it. "You saved my life! There is nothing greater than this."

Phoebe was watching them. It was late afternoon. She suggested that the young people might like a stroll by the sea. Helena turned to thank her, but Ares hesitated. Phoebe urged them on, so they left quickly.

Helena said, "Come, I want to show you where I met Dionysos. I've written to invite him to come here to see you. Do you think he'll come?"

"I love Dionysos," Ares said with warmth. "I thought your father was the only one I could ever think of as my father, but Dionysos became brother and father and mother to me during those terrible months of rowing in that galley."

"Can you talk about it?" Helena asked, but he shook his head. "No, I can't bear it."

They walked slowly, savoring the cool breeze coming from the water, seeing the purples and blues playing on its surface. "Ares, is it true that you're a follower of Christós now?"

"It's the only certainty in my life, Helena." She felt sadness touch her like the breeze, but she refused to give in to it.

"But how did it happen? How can you be so sure? I've spent months with his followers, but I can't begin to call myself one of them."

"You must try to understand how it was with me when Dionysos and I were thrown out on the shore of Neapolis. I was very nearly dead. I couldn't even lift my hand. I was vaguely aware of the stink, the pain. I had lost the will to live. And afterwards, each time I opened my eyes, each time I regained consciousness, Lydia was there, nursing me like the mother I never knew. Even when I couldn't speak, I could hear her. I heard her prayers, Helena. I wondered: *How can she speak to a god with so much love and such assurance of being heard?* That kind of intimacy was what affected me first. Then her deep and unrelenting compassion. She would not let me die. Both she and Dionysos refused to let me die. He's the physician, but it was Lydia's touch that healed me. I'm sure of it. How else can I explain what happened to me? So, when I finally emerged from a rotting state to a state of wholeness, I wanted to discover the reason. It had to do with Lydia's prayers, her unwavering devotion. I was a stranger, Helena. And yet…That kind of *agapē* was a revelation. I wanted to be like her. It's as simple as that. And what she is comes from Christós. Do you understand?"

She couldn't speak. His passion silenced her. She closed her eyes for a moment, unwilling to yield to the power of Lydia's image. They had reached the Bath of Eleni where they found a shaded spot under a clump of pines and sat together on the sand to gaze at the deepening colors of the water. Helios, the favorite god of the Greeks, was in his golden, setting glory. His slanting rays kissed and caressed his beloved Greek sea with hues of red and gold, indigo, and deep purple. They were both aware of the sea's powerful beauty, its pull and its hidden horror of drowning in its depths. Beauty won. They remained quiet for a long while.

When they started to speak, their words tripped over each other's until Helena said, "No, Ares, you speak first. Once, we made a vow to each other; I want to know where we stand now. Remember how truthful we used to be? I don't think I can endure another moment of not knowing."

He lowered his head and then, without looking at her, his face turned to the sea, said, "You're speaking of vows, and I want to come to that. We grew up together, Helena, under the tutelage of a good man. He was a man of intellect, not passions. You father left an imprint on both of us, but did we ever feel loved?"

She thought about this and tears, unexpected, unwanted, filled and clouded her eyes. "And yet, he had a passion, Ares. He was in love with Claudia. How blind we were. He was in love with Claudia and we did not even suspect."

"No, we did not. We had turned to each other for affection because we had received none from parents. Yes, I do know that in our harsh world few children receive the degree of affection we all need, but I know now there are some fortunate ones who have mothers and fathers who are different—I saw them among the people of The Way in the north."

"And I have seen them in Junia's house," Helena said thoughtfully, "and in the household of Stephanas—they are Paul's friends."

"What was different, did you notice? Did you see how they were not afraid to touch each other, to say words of affection and encouragement?"

"I always received that from Father."

"I never saw him touch you, Helena. I think this is why we were so starved for each other's affection."

She turned to look into his eyes. "Is that all it was for you then? Ares, I've been filled with *eros* for you since I was sixteen. You must have known. I saw the same desire in you. Most of our compatriots are married at that age."

"And it was your good fortune that your father did not believe in such an early marriage. Look at what happens to the girls, Helena. They grow old before their time. You, my beautiful Helena, you would have had children by now had you married at fourteen or even sixteen. That is, only if you were lucky. Both our mothers died at childbirth. Instead, you are still alive, free, you are lovelier than ever, you can do what you like with your life now."

She said, tasting the bitterness, "Except have your love, is that what you are telling me? You are all I ever wanted, Ares; and for Father to be alive, to see us happy together, that's all. Is this too much to ask of your god?"

He turned to her now and saw her anger.

"Helena, you can't ask anything of a god in whom you don't believe. Your father taught you this much. He taught you about superstitions and false gods. No, please listen to me, Helena. I found out that there's something else. *Someone* else. When I cried out in my horror, 'O, God, if you exist, save me and I will serve you forever,' I was not pretending. Do you know what it means to me that we were rescued by these good people some call Christians? Do you know what it is to be convinced that Lydia's prayers saved me? When I came to, I knew my own prayer had been answered. I wanted to serve this God and to keep my vow. Something happened to me when I heard about your friend Paul. It felt like a compulsion. Please don't think me foolish, but it was as if someone told me: *this is the man.* Do you understand me at all?"

And now she saw that this mattered to him above all else. His eyes were glistening. She turned her face away and let her own tears drop on her chest.

"I understand that you don't love me any longer," she whispered, but he grabbed her hand.

"Oh, but I do love you, Helena. More than ever. That's why I will not marry you. Think about your friend Paul—his life,

Helena. Would you like to be married to someone like him? You'd always be alone. You'd worry about me. You'd come to hate me for abandoning you, again and again. You need someone who will be a father to your children, a loving, present father, not someone like me who is burning to serve the one who called me to Himself."

"And what if I want to go with you?" Helena asked, hating herself for begging like a little girl.

"I would not allow it. Lydia told me about Paul's suffering. Have you seen his back?"

Mute with ache she nodded, yes. "The most scarred back imaginable," she finally uttered. "A terrible sight…"

"Do you know what it is to be beaten like that?" he asked and his voice was dark. "Look, Helena." He turned his back to her and lowered his tunic from his shoulders down to his waist. She saw on his young back the purple marks of the whip, and she cried aloud as she had done over Paul's back. She bent her face to kiss each long dark stripe. He let her kiss him and it felt like a prayer; he lowered his head on his arms folded on his bent knees and he wept. She laid her own wet cheek on those wounds and let her head rest there, on his scarred back, and so she said goodbye to her dreams.

They remained in that position for a long while. Then, very gently, she raised her head and said, "I will always love you. There will never be another. If you can remain single, I can also."

He turned to her slowly, raised the sleeve of his tunic over his shoulder, and took her wet face between his hands. "No, Helena. You are born to be loved, to be a wife and mother. I see you teaching your children all that you learned from your father—his wonderful gifts of knowledge to you. Above all I pray for you to know the Lord Yeesous Christós and to find his peace. But don't deprive yourself, Helena. Don't let me carry any more guilt."

When he kissed her gently on the lips she thought, *Now I will finally die happy*, and she clung to him in desperation, grieving as if he had died anew. Finally, she let go.

Hand in hand they walked back to Phoebe's house and when she saw them she said to herself, "Oh, dear children. This is the end of *eros* but also the beginning of *agapē*." And the good woman ached for them.

Chapter 20:
Decisions and Departures

Erastos arrived in Kenchreaê accompanied by Alexandros and Aristos and entered Phoebe's house apprehensive— longing to see Helena, wary of meeting Ares. "May I present our brother Erastos," Aristos announced formally and the women expressed their delight, but the news of Alexandros' manumission brought even greater joy.

"How proud I am of you both," Phoebe told them and gave them the kiss of peace.

Helena was looking at them without smiling, her face calm but etched with grief. She kissed Alexandros. "She finally set you free legally," she commented quietly. "How long you have deserved this, Alexandros, and how glad I am for you."

He looked at her carefully, studied those sad eyes he knew so well, and his heart was touched by her renewed sorrow. Erastos, on his part, could not begin to understand why, after receiving her heart's desire, she was again so terribly sad. He heard Alexandros telling her softly, "It will pass away. You will laugh again, I promise."

She turned and stood next to Ares who was watching everyone with avid curiosity. Erastos wondered: *Should I go to her?* But he knew that she was hardly aware of his presence. He forced himself to speak. "Helena, all your friends in Corinth miss you. Prisca and Paul send their warm greetings."

She bent her head in acknowledgment. She said at last, "I hear that congratulations are in order, Erastos, on your re-election as *aedilis*. I hope Claudia did not rope you in this expensive honor for her own benefit and willfulness."

The others turned to her in surprise but Erastos smoothed over the moment by saying, "No, but she promised to help." *Something has happened to her again,* he thought. *I hoped to find her happy but she is slipping back into that bitter girl of months ago.* Then he addressed himself to Phoebe, a little less formally but still with the self-consciousness that afflicted him whenever Helena was present. "We've come to see the authorities and offer our testimony regarding Helena's innocence in the death of Gaius."

Helena felt heartsick, standing so close and yet so far away from Ares. Her mood was darkening by the moment. What cared she for sin and intention? All she had ever wanted was love. "Helena's innocence?" she repeated now. "Erastos, did you ever ask Paul what the difference is between one who commits a crime and one who *wishes* to commit that crime?"

The silence was broken by Ares. "The distinctive difference is that Christ forgives us and commands us to forgive. Helena, you are innocent of crime." She shrugged, relieved when they moved from reflection to action.

After the initial awkwardness of the encounter, things now progressed swiftly. Alexandros and Ares accompanied Erastos to the basilica while the women occupied themselves with laundry and, as sometimes during routine household chores, a heart-to-heart talk.

—————— ⌘ ——————

Phoebe and Helena were airing linen and spreading freshly laundered ones on couches when the older woman leaned and whispered to the younger one. "My dear girl, your face is troubled and your eyes sorrowful. Has it not helped to talk with Ares face to face?"

Helena bit her lip, then confided: "I don't know, Phoebe. It's the difference between *knowing* and *not knowing*. I had waited for this encounter for so long. I suppose I knew deep inside that it was hopeless from the moment I received his letter, but I guess I must have had the faint hope that when he saw me, his old love would be rekindled, and we would be as before. But he's firm in his conviction that his new life cannot include a wife. I'm left alone once more, and I don't know what to do with my thoughts, with my life. I see no future without him. We were used to each other from childhood on. It's as if he died for a second time, but this time only to me."

Phoebe moved around the couch, and putting her arms around the girl held her like a child. She said, "I promise you this, Helena. Out of death comes life. I have learned it from Christ and from Paul. One day you will learn this truth also."

Helena considered the beloved woman's words but remained silent as Phoebe enveloped her in a love that touched the girl with its healing power.

—————— ⌘ ——————

Erastos easily took charge of the proceedings at the basilica. As an *aedilis* of Corinth he held enough official weight to compel the cooperation he needed from the authorities in Kenchreaê, since the municipality served as the eastern port of the provincial capital. He introduced himself by saying: "I've been sent from Corinth to inspect the weights and measurements used on the goods that enter the port with

Corinth as their destination; we suspect that much is stolen before it reaches the city." He was an official in charge of the Corinthian markets, and that demanded respect, but what seemed to weigh in even more strongly with the local officials was his manner which was radically different from *aedile* in the past. He was straightforward and consistent, refusing to accept bribes. Erastos knew that he was a kinder man since his baptism; his new companions and his new faith had inspired him to trust in the power of mercy, not retribution. And so the officials decided to cooperate with him.

He announced to the local magistrate that he intended to clear the matter of Helena, a ward of Claudia of Corinth. Helena, Erastos said, has been falsely and publicly accused by a slave. A scribe wrote down his deposition concerning the last banquet given by Gaius Marius Sylvanus, and then Alexandros, the freedman, added his own recollection of the hours preceding the death. He admitted that he had sold Demetrius that very night and then described the discovery of the body at dawn. Ares, when his turn came, recounted his own timely arrival in Kenchreaê and the scene of the attempted abduction. He was most insistent on the complicity of Demetrius' current owner in assaulting the young women. But when they asked to see Demetrius, the official objected. "The slave must be tortured. There's no way you can get the truth out of him otherwise. This is the law."

But Erastos was determined and firm. "I have with me a signed statement by the slave's previous owner, the widow Claudia. She also would like for me to interrogate Demetrius without torture. The two young women who nearly became his victims insist that he not be tortured. You see, we are all convinced that we have a better way of securing the truth from him since we believe that torture, more often than not, forces a slave to lie in order to be spared."

The local Roman magistrate looked shocked at such

unorthodox assumptions, but at last he acceded to their request. A truculent, dirty Demetrius was brought in chains before them. "Well, well," he said to Claudia's steward with his usual insolence, "if it ain't Alexandros the Great."

Erastos raised his voice knowing that he could use it as a whip when the need arose. "You must know, slave, that you are now addressing a free man; control your tongue. Alexandros has intervened and asked that you escape torture. Don't press your good fortune and don't challenge his kindness."

Demetrius made to speak but, after seeing that his accusers were calm and that there was no torture equipment in the place, thought better of it; although still sullen, he kept his mouth shut.

Alexandros said kindly. "Demetrius, I regret that I sold you in such a hurry. I knew your life would be in danger if Gaius were no longer able to protect you. You remember he did not seem at all well those last days and you had earned the hatred of our other slaves. Did you know that the mistress was ready to have you arrested for the many crimes lodged against you? She could have brought them to the notice of the authorities, but she didn't."

When the slave didn't answer, Alexandros continued, "Now listen carefully, and for once, answer truthfully. How did you know that the master was dead? You announced to the *vigile* that Helena killed your master. How did you know he was dead? I had already sold you when we discovered that he was no longer alive."

Demetrius kicked at something invisible on the floor and grunted, but said nothing. Erastos intervened. "If you tell the truth, Demetrius, I'll use my authority to have you exiled but not tortured. However, you'll have to swear that you'll never come near Kenchreaê or Corinth again."

The slave ignored him by saying to Alexandros in his rough

accent, "Why care what 'appens to me? Nob'dy said a decent word t' me the whole time I was with master. All uv you hated me."

"Maybe it was because of the way you did all his dirty bidding against others. Think about this, Demetrius; and now tell me what happened between you and your master after the lady Claudia had left his quarters that night."

The slave shrugged but started his speech. "I'd hidd'n mahself there while she wuz in his chambers, waitin' for her to leave, and for his instructions to me. He bellowed after she left. She'd threatened 'im, told 'im she'd drag 'im to court. He tol' me he'd rather die. He din't want to appear in public as an accused man. He din't trust nobody's justice but his own, he used to tell me. I asked him, 'Master, how can you do away with yo'self? You always manages to get rid of others.' The master laughed at my question. Stinky drunk he was, but he still had a plan in that crafty mind of his. He says to me, he says, 'Hey, Demi, you an' me, we don't die so easy, eh? 'Fall on your sword like a soldier, like a knight,' she kept tellin' me. Let her think I tried. But you'll have to help me. You'll only wound me, and then you'll tell her I tried but failed. She'll forgive me once more. Ha! She always does. The money'll keep coming.'"

Demetrius paused, obviously trying to think of a way out for himself. He looked at each one of them, speculation in his eyes. Suddenly he focused on Ares, and for the first time seemed to recognize him. "Well, well, if it ain't the young lover," he mocked. "When did you come back from the dead? We thought you drowned, and good riddance."

"You leave Ares out of this," Erastos demanded, anger making his voice harsh. "If it hadn't been for Ares, there's no telling what crime you would have committed against Helena —and I can assure you that you'd be dead by now for such an act. I warn you to keep remembering what the Romans do to slaves who lay their hands on respectable free women, and I tell you again to focus on the issue at hand. *Did you help kill Gaius Marius Sylvanus?*"

"No," the slave said, sure now of what he must say—the actual truth, for once—to save himself. "He ordered me to 'old his long army dagger. Always the show-off, he wuz gonna to run into it with his shoulder, see, just a-touching the blade. Then, I wuz to put him on the bed—face down—and call for help. But he wuz drunk, and in 'is stupor he stumbled and fell on the dagger, but with his chest, not his shoulder. It went right through his heart. I kep' his weapons well sharpen'. The blade went deep 'cause he wuz a heavy man and fell with all that weight. I drug him to the bed, since that's what he'd wanted, but I knew it weren't just a wound. I'd seen dead men before. I wasn't about to call for help. Who'd believe a slave? Who'd believe mah story? I drew the drapes 'round his bed and run to the kitchens to find some wine and to think about what I wuz gonna say to this here Alexandros. But he come looking for me instead. He hadn' come to beat me nor drag me to the mistress. Wuz I surprised? You bet. It were dark in the kitchens and he din't see the blood splattered all over me. He ev'n give me a clean one to wear and tells me to follow him. I thought he's come to punish me, but 'stead he sold me away, to the sea, and I wuz glad, I tell you. Gaius Marius Sylvanus was crazy right there at the end. Even I wuz scared of him, and glad to get away."

The three men exchanged glances. Alexandros let out the breath he was holding. Erastos started writing; he said, "Whether you let the blade slip on purpose or not is something you have to live with. It would be easy to have them kill you as punishment. But I want you to put your mark on this paper, and I'll keep my word. You may not have killed Gaius. The magistrate cannot punish you for something you did not do. But you should be punished for accusing an innocent young woman and for threatening her life."

"Uh, we weren't planning no harm. The new master wanted a little fun with her, that's all."

At that Erastos drew back his arm and slapped him hard. Then they turned the slave over to his jailer, made arrangement for his exile, and Erastos, with Alexandros and Ares, returned to Phoebe's.

—————— ᴄᴀᴀ ——————

That night, her heart mourning the end of the love that had been hers for years, Helena had to make an effort to follow the rise and fall of the conversation around her. Ares, full of stories he had heard from Lydia, had the floor. But when he paused to ask her to sing for the group, she refused. "It's your turn," she said quietly. "I've been with them a long while. They long to know you now. Tell us about Lydia."

She would remember forever the tender story he told them then of Yeesous' birth, the sound of his voice while recounting it, and the desire that arose within her to know more and more stories about this Yeesous. *I'm falling in love with the stories as I had done once with Homer. Even Yeesous' birth was modest,* she thought. *What a strange god this is.*

Her attention drifted and when it returned to them they were talking about Thessaloniki. Because Evniki spoke so rarely Helena now paid close attention to her words. Her diffident, rather sad voice was saying to Ares, "Yes, I too was born in Thessaloniki, but I lived there longer than you did. Ever since Phoebe set me free I've dreamt of a return. I need to remember my mother, find out something about her."

Helena's impulse was instantaneous and so was her decision. With it, relief washed over her and she felt the tension relax as she announced in a strong voice: "You will go, Evniki, and I will go with you."

They all stopped eating to stare at her but she stood firm.

To dispel Phoebe's anxiety, Helena told her later, in the privacy of her room, that thanks to her father's legacy from Claudia she now had the money to pay for her own and Evniki's passage and all other expenses, and that she would spend it gladly. "I need to get away, Phoebe. I can't stay in Corinth now that Ares will be there with Paul. Your place, too, holds too many memories for me."

So it was that Helena and Evniki agreed to return to Corinth along with Erastos, Alexandros, and Ares. "We'll be there just long enough to say goodbye to Paul and Prisca and to announce my new decision to Claudia," Helena said to Phoebe. "Evniki and I will sail north from Piraeus."

"Before you leave, you must connect with Timotheos," Phoebe insisted. "Paul is sending his young assistant back to Thessaloniki, so you must travel with him. Do this for my sake." Evniki and Helena agreed.

———— ✺ ————

In Claudia's house two days later, Evniki watched with avid admiration, saying, "I don't know how you do it, Helena. You move from one world to the other—from Phoebe's to this villa, with no difficulty." Helena, happy to be hospitable, smiled as she made sure that Evniki was comfortable and asked her to share her room. They talked into the night, Helena desperate to find distraction from heartache, Evniki eager to help her.

"You and Alexandra," Helena confessed to this girl who was becoming her friend. "I've seen how much you love Phoebe. How difficult it must have been for you before she found you."

"She bought both of us when we were children," Evniki said. "But we felt free even before the official manumission."

Helena returned to her lingering regret. "I'll always be sorry for the way I left all of you that crazy day when I received Ares' letter in Kenchreaê."

"Oh, Helena, forget that. Since we met you, all we've wanted was for you to be at peace. Many times Alexandra and I wished for you to wake up. Ares…." She shook her head. "We wanted you to accept Erastos' love for you and to be happy."

Helena was so astonished that she jumped up and pulled Evniki by the hands to stand in front of her. "What did you say? What's that you said about Erastos?"

Evniki swallowed her surprise but wouldn't speak. Helena took hold of her arms and pleaded: "Please, tell me why you said something so outrageous. Erastos despises me."

At that Evniki stammered, "But, but Helena, is it possible that you don't know he loves you? Everyone else knows but you."

"Everyone else knows? Is it possible that you don't know my history, that you don't know that Erastos saw me trying to kill Claudia's husband? Do you think a man like him could love me after seeing me that night? Is he a fool? He doesn't look like one. I wouldn't *allow* him to love me. Haven't you seen what terrible things happen to those who love me?"

Evniki thought this an exaggeration but guessed that Helena believed it. On her part, Helena was trying to make sense of this new intrusion to her emotions. "Erastos?" she kept whispering. "*Erastos? Why did I never notice?*"

But then she was visited with memories of his kindness as he spoke to her in whispers that night when she had stood in a copse of trees wishing for death, and heard again the fear in his voice, the concern that was only for her, not for himself, his hesitancy and diffidence whenever they met. She remembered his worried face as he bent over her when she lay on the sand near the Bath of Eleni and his deep hurt afterwards at her reaction. *I must leave Corinth immediately. I must not see him again. I don't want any other love to confuse my life. I couldn't bear it. I must go away from both of them.*

That night she dreamt again. She was inside a sailing vessel, but Ares had jumped off and she was calling his name. "Come back, Ares, come back. Don't leave me again." She was weeping aloud. She decided to jump in after Ares, to save him. But as she climbed up high on the rail of the stern in order to dive, someone's strong hand caught her tunic from behind and pulled her back into the safety and the shelter of his arms. "No, no!" she cried as she felt his arms around her. She struggled to turn her head to see who had dared save her but, when she managed it, she found that she was dreaming. There was no one there. She sat up on her cot, awake and trembling.

"Helena?" Evniki's voice whispered in the dark. "Are you unwell?"

"Just a dream," she said quietly and tried to take a deep breath.

"A bad dream?"

"I don't know. I really don't know."

Chapter 21: On the Greek Sea

October was still mild and sailing would be safe, but November's uncertain weather would force them to wait until spring; so they decided to leave without delay. They found a ship, booked passage, and made their final preparations before sailing. Helena's sadness while in Corinth remained palpable. In the city, Ares was nearby, and it took all her self-control to avoid him. Claudia declared that Helena was behaving like a fool. "You need to seduce him," she told the girl. "Then he'll forget all this religious nonsense and remember that he's yours."

Helena didn't even bother to respond. She had learned from Alexandros that Paul, when he baptized Ares, had renamed him Aristarchos. Helena listened to Alexandros, pleased to see that he felt so comfortable among the Christians now that he was able to imitate the apostle's accent, bringing a moment of comic relief to the conversation. He even took on Paul's authority: "We cannot have a servant of Christ being called by the name of the idol of war! Far be it from us. From now on we will know our new brother as Aristarchos!" And Helena thought it most appropriate that her Ares was now someone else, Aristarchos who belonged to Paul, not to herself. The end of their love had been confirmed, but she had already shed all her tears.

Helena now found comfort in the company of two former slaves and her respect for them grew enormously. The human psyche is so strong, she mused, that in the best of us, even the humiliation of slavery cannot destroy it. *How I wish I could share this discovery with my father.* She wanted desperately to have Alexandros accompany them on the journey north, but she knew that he would not abandon Claudia and that he was becoming vitally important to Paul and the *ekklesia* of Corinth. Instead, Paul's assistant, a young man named Timotheos, was going with them.

"Timotheos is experienced enough in traveling," Prisca reassured her. "He will take good care of you and Evniki."

They said goodbye to Paul who blessed them lovingly, and to Prisca and Aquila who admitted that they would miss them. Helena avoided both Erastos and Aristarchos. She had said her final goodbye to her love in Kenchreaê and, since Evniki's revelation, she found Erastos an uncomfortable subject. Yet, on the eve of their departure, a messenger arrived from Erastos with a beautiful warm shawl wrapped around her father's dagger. She accepted both gifts and felt the familiar shiver go through her when she saw the dagger.

———— ∽∾∿ ————

Aboard the ship Helena basked in the magnificence that was Greece. She knew that theirs was a beautiful land, but she had never realized the drama that lay at the heart of its beauty. The mountains plunged to the sea—impressive, blue, and craggy —they disappeared and then rose above the purple waters as though at any time they would decide to sail away. The leaves of the evergreen trees, glistening in the sun's light, softened the weight of the Attic mountains, and the rough edges of the rocks looked white in the sun's brilliance. Coves and peninsulas opened up before her eyes. She drank it all in. It was the only metaphor that worked. She swallowed the startling images, becoming drunk with the combined drama of land and sea.

In the late afternoon the mountains became less substantial; they were now ethereal, faint lines of blue drawn on the gentle sky. Helena was aware of Evniki next to her, a still form leaning on the rail. *Is she remembering something?* Helena wondered. *Is she remembering the little girl who knew she was a slave, who knew she was a possession, not a child loved but a chattel being used and ordered around by hard strangers?* She touched Evniki's fingers as they gripped the painted wood of the railing. Without a word, Evniki bent her head and kissed Helena's hand. That spontaneous communion brought tears to Helena's eyes. She became aware of Timotheos somewhere nearby, watching them. *I wonder what he's thinking. Is it always about Paul and his Christ, or does he have moments of desire, moments of being a lonely young man? What is this power that grips these men and holds them so possessively? Is this really what their God wants? Did their Yeesous, their Christós, know loneliness?* From what she had heard of their Yeesous she knew that he was not one to wave some mythical wand of gold that changed evil into good. The magic of the Olympians was totally lacking from this teacher who was adored as a god by minds as profound as that of Paul and loved by great hearts like those of Prisca and Phoebe.

The three of them shared a loaf of bread and briny olives and then drank the cooled wine; immersed in a mood affected by the beauty around her, Helena asked: "Timotheos, do you ever wish for a family, do you ever wish you had not met Paul?" Her voice sounded dreamy to her ears. "No, no, don't protest yet. Think about it. Do you ever wish for a life that is not so difficult, so full of constant travel and worry about the *ekklesiae* and about Paul?"

Timotheos considered her questions; she had already seen that he took time to think before he spoke. "How can I imagine life without Paul? It'd be like thinking of life without Christ. Paul has given purpose to my life. I can't imagine spending it in a different manner. Christ has given me freedom."

"Freedom? But why does Paul encourage young men not to marry?"

"Oh, no, Helena. He doesn't encourage or discourage. He asks us plainly if we can endure being away from families, and being celibate. If we have the slightest doubt, he tells us we must marry, he urges us not to wait."

She thought about this. So Ares had been given every chance by Paul as she had also given him every chance to accept her love. She asked suddenly, and the others must have heard the bitterness in her voice, "Was your Yeesous ever rejected?"

"Ah, Helena, he was rejected in the most bitter way of all. Not just by the people who followed him and then suddenly agreed to the crucifixion, but by his friends, and, at the end, by his God. Didn't Prisca tell you this part? The women who were at the foot of the cross heard him cry it out—'Oh, God, my God, why have you forsaken me?'"

The words ripped her heart. She wept openly, without making a sound. Evniki could not stop her own tears and even Timotheos had to hide his wet face.

"So he understands," Helena whispered and looked straight at Evniki.

"He understands."

"That's why we pray to him," Timotheos added.

Helena thought: *This is the most important secret but nobody remembered to tell it to me before now. It was left to this unremarkable young stranger to reveal the most meaningful detail of the story.*

The winds were perfect for sailing. The boat glided east

on the dark waters. The moon was full that night. It rose as a huge, red, mysterious ball to reveal the awesome promontory of Sounion at starboard. As it rose higher, its white light struck the marble of Poseidon's temple and lit its Doric lines in numinous outline. She caught her breath. She felt the familiar chill that had nothing to do with the weather. A voice whispered in her mind, *The old gods are dead. But this new god, this suffering god, abandoned by his God, who is he? Why can I not feel him? Why can I not approach him?*

She was sitting in the women's section of the deck, a long curtain separating them from the men during the night. Everyone else seemed to be asleep. She knew that the *kybernetes* was watching carefully to make sure no one approached the women passengers. She heard him as he made his rounds and remembered that Julios had expressly asked him to look after her and Evniki. Now Helena allowed herself to think of the dangers that lay ahead.

No journey was ever safe, and yet, she had the strong assurance that they would get to Thessaloniki in safety. When the word safety registered in her brain, something else happened in that mysterious and mystical region of the *nous*, the mind so cherished and respected by her ancestors. For the first time since it happened she remembered, with a vividness that shook her, Demetrius' rough hands on her, his smell of sweat and danger, his ugly voice taunting her. The memory of fear assaulted her until her teeth hurt, but at the same time another part of her *nous* was examining these questions: *Why is it that only now I am remembering that terrible hour? Why is it that when I found myself in Ares' arms I never once thought of Demetrius, or the danger of abduction, the real possibility of violation, of death? Who has been protecting me all this time? Who kept my mind from veering into madness that morning in Kenchreaê as it most assuredly did after Gaius raped me?*

She hugged her knees and willed herself to stop shaking.

She looked at each question carefully as if it hung there before her, highlighted by the moon that had risen and now shone with a brilliant silvery light that reflected itself on the water, an illumined, liquid line that followed the ship as it glided and rocked on the sea. *Who are you, Lord?* she whispered. *Did you hear me that day when I called on you in my anger, terror, and unbelief? Did you indeed come to my rescue in the person of Ares, and were you in the relief I have felt until now from the memory of fear?*

Covered in a long *himation*, she left the protection of the women's section and slipped out to stand at the railing. When she spotted Timotheos who was also admiring the moonlit scene, she moved near him.

"Tell me," Helena began softly, "when you pray to your Lord, do you feel his presence?"

"Sometimes," he answered thoughtfully. "Sometimes I feel the Presence, and other times I feel nothing. I then trust on the promises I know are true. This knowledge is very important. Paul has taught me not to put my trust in feelings. God's reality does not depend on my feeling. God *is*, Helena. One of our writers called God the Alpha and Omega. So when I don't feel anything, I don't worry. At first I was full of excitement and intense emotion. Now I have a steady conviction and much work."

"The work is important then, isn't it? I see that Paul never rests. Prisca is the same. And Phoebe is always thinking of doing something for others. Is this a part of it all?"

"It must be," he agreed. "Almost everything happens in community. We spend very little time alone. Did Phoebe not explain the meaning of the communal meal?"

"Phoebe *showed* even more than she told. If I'm attracted by your Christós, it's because of Phoebe's life; so eating with her is sacred. Is this what you mean?"

"Very close. When we break bread together, we do it in

remembrance of Yeesous' broken body on the cross; when we drink wine together we do it in remembrance of the blood he shed."

Helena remained silent, thinking it would take a lifetime to understand the meaning of this.

Timotheos smiled. "Ah, Helena, you are very close. Don't get discouraged."

And Helena felt his prayers for her, she felt the memory of fear receding. She was enfolded in more than the *himation*; she was now ready to close her eyes and sleep. She returned to the women's tent.

On the day they arrived at Thessaloniki's deep and generous port, Helena felt as if she were dreaming. She had imagined the city, and her imagination for once had not deceived her. They entered the Gulf of Therma, with Mount Olympos a massive snow-covered companion present on their western views, the curved shape of the land opening up like an amphitheater before them, the sea deep and blue, dotted with craft, the houses climbing uphill, the blue of an unknown mountain in the northeast—every sight charmed her and made her feel at home. There was no memory of Corinth in this northern realm. It was cooler here and the land much greener. Next to her Evniki was wrapped in her usual quiet, but when Helena turned to her, she saw that the former slave had been crying. Helena asked, "Are the memories bad, Evniki? Are you remembering anything?"

"My mother's face," Evniki said. "I'd forgotten it, but now here it is, and I can't bear it."

"Hold on to the memory," Helena told her. "This is a gift, don't reject it. Talk to her in your mind, remember her."

Evniki glanced at her with gratitude but continued her silent weeping. "Do you suppose," she wondered later, "that she stood there when they took me away? On the shore? She's looking at me. She's waving a white cloth and crying the whole time."

"And here is your lovely daughter back," Helena cried to the wind, to the shore, to the unseen face of grief before them. "Here's your Evniki, free and grown, and safe. Evniki's Mother, wherever you are, rejoice for your beautiful child!"

There was so much noise around them that no one else heard her. They rolled their belongings in bundles and listened to Timotheos as he pointed to the sights, teaching them the names of mountains and rivers. For a few blissful moments, Helena realized that she had not thought of Ares, and she felt free.

The process of disembarkation had begun. "Going to the house of Jason first," Timotheos explained. "As Paul's host in this city, he's paid dearly for the privilege."

Chapter 22:
Danger in Thessaloniki

Helena liked her hosts and the dramatic setting of the northern city. She had already learned Thessaloniki's history, with all the internecine killings and forced population relocations. As she was shown around the sites she meditated on the tragedy of Greek Corinth when Mummius destroyed it—a century-old disaster that felt so recent—and now on the damage the early death of the conqueror Alexandros had wrought on the course of this northern province. Everyone here called him the *Great* Alexandros; was he? And what about his tragic half-sister, Thessaloniki, who gave her name to this city? *What are we here for?* she wondered, and *why should bad men be allowed to destroy whole cities?* She thought about Paul and the meaning of human ambition. Here was a brilliant man who was devoid of ambition as the Roman powers defined it. A man whose body had suffered almost to the point of breaking but who considered it all as nothing compared to the glory afforded by his Christ as she had heard him say. She remembered the phrase that had made all the difference to how her friend Alexandros saw the world now: *Owe no one anything but to love one another.* She couldn't quite take it in. What was it about Paul that filled him with such passion—a passion that hurt no one but himself?

Claudia had given her letters addressed to her relatives in the city. "Make use of them," she had told her. "My cousin, Sevastianus, is not likeable but he can be of great use to your friends; much to my surprise, he is now the *politarch* of Thessaloniki."

Helena consulted Philothea, Jason's oldest daughter. "How should I go about it?" Philothea introduced her to one of her father's freedmen: "Nikiphoros knows the city better than any of us. He's one of the brothers. A good man. Send a message to Sevastianus through him. Meanwhile, I will organize a trip for us to Pella so you can know Makedonia and her past."

The next day, walking around Thessaloniki with Nikiphoros as guide, she saw a city filled with altars to the emperor. She thought, *They call the emperor their savior. How different Paul's savior is! Maybe this is why they persecuted Paul so severely in this city. Was it because of their desire to flatter the emperor?* When she shared this thought with Nikiphoros he said, "It's probable. But what surprised us was the great hostility from the Jews of the city also. Paul came to a conclusion about his troubles. Do you want to hear it?"

"I always want to hear what Paul is thinking."

"It's the desire in human beings to claim God as their own, he used to say. The gentiles don't seem to know who God is. The Jews know but claim him only as their own, and the new converts to Christós are either too sure of themselves or confused and afraid." Helena listened carefully. She found herself thankful that her father had spared her from believing in any gods. She asked: "And what is the solution?"

"To forget the self, Paul told us, and focus on the resurrected Christós. This is what frees us."

Jason and Philothea had explained to Helena that the people of the *ekklesia* in Thessaloniki, unlike those of Corinth, were being harassed to the point of physical danger. There was much concern about the immediate future and Timotheos expressed this privately to Helena. "If you return to Corinth before I do, Helena, you must inform Paul that all is not well here; his people are suffering."

But she decided to do something now, not to wait. Worried for the safety of her new friends, she would break her resolve about having nothing to do with aristocratic Romans. They held the power, and Helena would go to that power to plead for her friends, as she had done with Gallio. After sending Claudia's greetings by messenger to each of them, she now received invitations to dine with Claudia's friends.

With both reluctance and curiosity, she prepared herself for reentry into the world of the rich Romans. Would Alexandros approve? Would Erastos? *I will not even think of Ares and his reaction. Let's see if I can do something useful for once, something for others, not for myself.* She visited some distant cousins of Claudia's first and a few of the aging dignitaries who had known Claudia's father. The visits were polite and meaningless. She decided that since the politarch held more power than the rest, she would pay a visit to him. Nikiphoros accompanied her to the palace gate and promised to wait outside for her return.

Marius Flavius Sevastianus, the politarch, lived in a splendid palace—this much she saw immediately upon entering; the beautifully kept grounds were easy to admire. When she met the man himself, she saw with amusement that he matched his house in elegance, both in his clothes and manners. He welcomed her with a pleasure that was too apparent—his eyes lit up in a way that made her suspicious and renewed her impression of the power of gossip in Roman society. "Rumors of your beauty have preceded you," he told her. "I was anxious to see you for myself, and now I know that even the rumors did not do you justice." He promptly abandoned all his other guests and offered to show her around the exquisite palace himself, pointing out its views of the sea in the south and the green hills on the north. He received Claudia's greetings as if he had expected them and Helena wondered if he had spies everywhere. She commented politely on the statues and gold ornaments, the engraved golden urns with images of victorious battles by Philippos and his son Alexandros on them. She professed herself amazed to discover that the level of Makedonian art had reached the excellence of Athenian and Corinthian works. She thought the place overly decorated, lacking the restraining hand of a Claudia, but she kept up a chatter, giving him news and humorous descriptions of his cousin's civil activities and her children's precociousness. Sevastianus seemed to be listening avidly, his eyes on her face. She felt uncomfortable near him from the beginning, but the moment he placed his hand on her arm and drew her close to him, she *knew*. Her skin crawled, she remembered Claudia's husband, and a surge of loathing hit her with an intensity that nauseated her. *I must keep a cool head, avoid him at all costs.* When he placed his arm around her waist, she pretended thirst and hunger in order to be led to the *triclinium*, desperate not to be alone with him a minute longer. She was ready to bolt.

But in the dining room he insisted that Helena recline to his right. Over the course of the lengthy meal which she hardly touched, she kept her eyes on the plates of mussels and pheasant and the delectable vegetables of the region as if they were the only things meriting her attention. Sevastianus, mellowed by the Samian wine, laughed and joked with his guests, his eyes on Helena, and she felt she was being devoured as he was now devouring the elaborate sweets. As her acute dislike turned to fear she searched frantically for an excuse to leave early.

After the main course was taken away, the host clapped his hands to summon the musicians. Helena heard the notes with regret, feeling suddenly homesick for Corinth and her own *kithara*. The music awakened her, and with sharpened perceptions she felt herself standing on the edge of a precipice. *I must not show that I love music. Why, oh why, did I come here? Of course: the defense of my friends.* She focused on them, downed a cupful of wine and, grabbing on to courage, she spoke up.

"Tell me, Marius Sevastianus, among the various groups in your city, what do you know about a recent awakening among the Judeans? I believe some call the adherents Christ-followers. I know the ones in Corinth and find them decent and of value to the empire."

He choked on the nuts he was munching. He turned red, and a slave rushed to give him water and to beat him on the back. Helena looked on in alarm and concealed glee, yet instantly regretted her provocation.

"You surprise me, Helena," he said petulantly after he recovered. "These people are not well liked, and the rest of the population looks upon them with suspicion and disdain. How can you possibly be mixed up with those who are of the lower classes?"

"Even Claudia admires them in Corinth," Helena retorted, not quite truthfully. "Here, my host Jason and his family are certainly people of worth and not 'of the lower classes,'" she tried but failed to keep the sarcasm from her voice. "Jason is wealthy and respectable and a valued citizen of your great *polis*."

"My, my, but you're a fiery one! Yes, Jason is a worthy citizen. But still, Helena, you should leave your dubious friends and move here to this palace where you belong. Don't associate with Christians; the emperor will not like it. A strange little Jew, a certain Paulus appeared before me last year, I remember. They chased him out of the city, I heard, and some of those who disliked him the most were his own people. I had to have Jason whipped in order to appease them."

"And that's the worst thing that *your* people and *his* people could have done," Helena responded, angry now, ignoring the shocked silence around her. "Paul is a remarkable man; there's nothing blameworthy about him. Even the proconsul Gallio, when in Corinth, was forced to admit that there is no harm in the man."

Sevastianus could not hide his anger. "He's a rabble rouser, Helena. He's the kind that turns the world upside down. But come, come, let's not argue about foreigners and infidels. Let's talk about you and your beauty and how you can spend more time near me." She thought she heard the other diners snickering.

And now her internal warning bells were deafening. She tried to think about Paul "turning the world upside down"; how strange it was to hear men who didn't understand him describe his effectiveness accurately, despite themselves. Alexandros had felt the revolutionary thrust of Paul's words and he was changed from that moment on. *But how dangerous the words must be for Paul himself.* Her mind called out to him: *What do I do now, Paul? Can you and your Christós keep me from harm this time?* Aloud she said lightly, "Really, Marius Flavius Sevastianus, your invitation is gracious. But I'm indeed very comfortable at Jason's since I've become quite friendly with his daughter. We are planning to leave for Pella soon, so I must decline your kind and generous offer."

He looked peeved, more petulant than before, a spoiled child. His eyelid twitched as he gazed all around to see how the other guests were reacting to this rebuff. Some averted their eyes; others showed their displeasure with Helena in order to flatter him. *I have to get out of here before the other guests leave.* She recognized one of the older women whose family she had visited the previous week to convey Claudia's greetings. When the woman excused herself, Helena followed, pretending to accompany her in order to get some fresh air. On their way to the latrines, she said casually, "I've developed a frightful headache.

Unfortunately, I dismissed my litter earlier. When you leave, may I ride with you? Is there room for me?"

The woman was scandalized. "I cannot very well take you away from the politarch. He seems so interested in you. He'll take it as an insult."

Helena decided on flattery and intrigue. "I'm asking for help," she whispered, woman to woman now. "I am betrothed to another, in Corinth, and he has a very high position in the emperor's court. He's related to Claudia. We've kept it a secret because he's not yet informed the emperor. The situation is very delicate. If the politarch takes advantage of me in any way, my betrothed will protest to the emperor, and Thessaloniki herself might be in danger of his disfavor."

The other woman was hooked by the flattery, the references to Claudia and the emperor. There's nothing more enticing than a conspiracy, especially connected with the rich and powerful and she felt part of one now. "How thrilling! Leave it to me," she whispered back. "My husband can walk alongside, and we two can ride in my litter to get better acquainted. I hope you will be able to put in a good word with the emperor on our behalf. We're very anxious to see Rome."

Helena agreed, pretending that she had every power to speak to the emperor. When they returned to the couches of the *triclinium*, the woman whispered something urgent to her husband who then said to the politarch, "Your honor, my wife is indisposed. We must beg your leave. And since this is a woman's ailment, my wife has asked young Helena to accompany us. We beg your pardon."

Helena had already donned her *himation*; she said brightly, loud enough for everyone to hear, "I will convey your regards to your cousin, Sevastianus. Claudia will be pleased to know that you're as great an admirer of the Greek arts as she is. I'll also tell her what an excellent host you are." She knew that only a fool would accept this pretense, but he didn't strike her as a man with a quick mind. She was right.

The politarch was confused and angry, but he decided not to make a scene in front of important guests. Under his veneer of good manners, Helena heard an ominous undercurrent of hostility in his voice when he responded, "You may leave now, but you must come again, Helena. I'll accept no excuses for refusing my hospitality. If you insist on going to the hinterlands, I will give you introductions to the right people in Makedonia and I will have my men escort you there. You must *not* leave without visiting us again. I will expect you to dine with me tomorrow evening; I will send for you."

Her throat felt dry. "I thank you for your kindness," she said as brightly as she could manage and followed the older couple out of doors to the waiting litters. She motioned for Nikiphoros to follow and continued under the protection of her newfound ally. Outwardly calm, her heart racing, she stayed close to the woman who had rescued her unawares. The older woman walked with the importance of one who was in charge of a secret, and Helena made a show of climbing on the litter and being solicitous, but the moment they reached the more crowded part of the city, and the litter barriers were forced to a stop because of the throng, she said quickly, "I thank you kindly for your assistance. Believe me, it will not be forgotten. Here's where I must get off."

She jumped to the ground and, followed closely by Nikiphoros who had not lost sight of her, she disappeared into the crowd. The woman called after her, but Helena pretended not to hear. The people of the city were out for a twilight stroll by the seashore, so the two of them were able to hide among them without much difficulty.

Helena said to Nikiphoros: "Quickly, lead me to the house of Eirineos, where Timotheos is lodging. I need his help, for I'm convinced that I'm in danger if I return to Jason's." She explained the scene in the palace. Nikiphoros, who knew all the households of the *ekklesia*, agreed that her plan was prudent.

She thought quickly. "Tell all of them at Jason's not to inform anyone of my whereabouts. Ask Evniki to send me my special bundle I brought from Corinth. If she and Philothea would like to bid me goodbye, I would love to see them once more. But tell only Jason that I'm in danger and that he must be prepared for trouble tomorrow evening when I don't show up at the villa of Sevastianus. I must leave Thessaloniki immediately. It's urgent. He'll understand."

Nikiphoros didn't ask any questions. He led her through narrow streets, roundabout, to create cover for her and up a city hill, confusing her thoroughly in the fading light of the city. When they reached the house of Eirineos, Nikiphoros saw her safe inside and then he ran to Jason's house.

Timotheos looked at Helena with surprise but waited for her to speak. She took a deep breath, wiped tears of frustration from her eyes, and tried to keep her voice from shaking.

"Here's where prayers to your God will be helpful, Timotheos," she pleaded. "I must get out of Thessaloniki. The politarch has threatened me with his version of hospitality. I know it sounds strange, but he insists that I leave the house of Jason in order to move into his palace. I've learned from bitter experience not to trust such men. I need to leave for Philippi immediately. Can anyone here help me? What should I do now without endangering Jason and his family further?"

"What did you tell the politarch after he offered his invitation?"

"That I was due to visit Pella. I started to say Philippi but I changed it to Pella at the last minute. I don't know if he believed me."

"Then we must further confuse him. We'll take you first to Neapolis and then to Philippi. Once there, Lydia will know what to do."

"'*We* will take you?' No, Timotheos. I can't endanger any

more of you. I'll escape alone. I now regret courting such danger by going anywhere near Sevastianus, but that visit was well intended. I went to him thinking I could help the people of the *ekklesia*, but I fear I made things much worse for them. Paul will be very disappointed in me."

"Paul knows about the evil of those who still walk in darkness, Helena. Christ doesn't work magic for us or through us. He offers us his love and the rest is really up to us. You'll be protected by the Lord, and all of us will take care."

With the help of Eirineos who knew the north well, they planned the escape route. When Evniki arrived in the early hours of the morning, she was accompanied by Philothea and Nikiphoros; they brought with them provisions, detailed directions, and names of possible hosts along the way from Jason.

"We're going with you," Evniki announced firmly. She explained that Jason thought it best to protect the other girls by whisking them away at the same time with Helena. He assured them all that he was fully prepared for a visit by the politarch's thugs. His exact message to Helena was, "Be at peace regarding me. Look after yourselves."

Stunned with gratitude Helena agreed to Jason's new plan. After listening to all of them, she decided to dress as a boy. Once again she cut her long curls and borrowed a couple of tunics from Eirineos. With her slender, athletic body, shorn hair, and boyish tunic, she hoped she could pass for a male youth. "Except that you are too pretty," Evniki said, "and I fear that presents a different kind of danger. Talk to our men if you don't understand my meaning."

Helena opened the special bundle she had brought from Corinth. The dagger Erastos had returned was in it and she hid it inside his parting gift, the warm shawl that now she wound round and round her waist like a *zona*. To look more like a boy, she donned a leather vest given to her by Eirineos. In turn, she gave most of her money to him for safe keeping, urged as much of it as he would accept on Timotheos for the *ekklesia*, and divided the rest in three pouches. Each one of the girls hid a generous pouch of coins under her clothes.

Before taking their leave of Timotheos she wrote an urgent note to Claudia:

To Claudia from Helena. Greetings. This is delivered to you by the hand of my friend Timotheos. Please welcome him. As you promised, your cousin Sevastianus proved to be courteous and hospitable. But his alarming interest in me brought bad memories of your late husband. I'm leaving Thessaloniki to escape him. For the sake of my beloved father's memory I ask this of you: If there's any influence you can exert upon your cousin, the gratitude of many people will be yours and prayers will ascend for you and your children. Tell Alexandros he is sorely missed. Good health to him and to you, to young Marcus, and young Claudia.

"She will read between the lines," she told Timotheos.

———— ∽⁀∾ ————

At the break of dawn, the three girls, with Nikiphoros as guide and Eirineos as protector, started on their trek east. Eirineos' home was on the northeastern outskirts of the city and that aided their quick getaway. Soon they were outside the walls, heading toward the sun. In a couple of hours this same sun would hit them full force but, since it was October, the heat would be bearable. They took the Via Egnatia, the quickest and safest route east. Well paved by Roman standards it stretched from the Adriatic to the Byzantium. They knew that they had a short margin of safety, maybe three days, before Sevastianus' spies discovered she hadn't gone to Pella. "If they then decide to go east, they will intercept us," Eirineos advised. "In any case, we will have to leave this main thoroughfare no later than three days hence. For now, I trust we are safe." Helena was grateful for his familiarity with Makedonia.

Still, they were young and strong and despite or even

because of their danger their impulse was to laugh and enjoy being together, traveling as they were without chaperons and free of the burden of belongings. The people of The Way all over Greece knew that they needed to carry very little, because everything else would be supplied to them by the communities of faith who would welcome them along the way. In the short time since Paul's first arrival in Neapolis and Philippi, small groups of communities of The Way had sprung up all over Makedonia and Asia Minor, and by this remarkable growing network of the faithful they were beginning to know and recognize one another. The new company of friends shared all this information with Helena as they walked in the coolness of early morning.

They had determined to cover fifteen miles that day, to rest frequently, but to stop with the coming of dark. Out of necessity, on that first night they would have to sleep in one of the inns, but on the following day they would push to reach Apollonia and to find shelter with the faithful who lived there.

The first night Helena was in an agony of fear; having to share a room with young men meant danger—would she be found out? But since they slept fully clothed and she was covered with a *himation* to keep warm, she lay down pretending to sleep. Soon however, because of the exhaustion of the day, she did sleep and Eirineos, who kept watch, had to wake her in the morning. They had survived the first night, so they started on the second day with renewed hope.

The second night was just falling when they entered the city of Apollonia, and, following Jason's directions, they knocked on the door of a Christian home in the outskirts of the town. To Helena, the rhythm *ta-ta-tá, ta-tá* brought back vividly the memory of Erastos knocking on Phoebe's door—the first time she had encountered people of The Way. This time she asked her new fugitive friends the meaning of the rhythm. Evniki explained, "But it's the name of the Lord, can't you hear it?

Y-ee-*sous*, Chris-*tós*," and now Helena, allowed into the secret, felt that she belonged among them.

They were welcomed in the home of a friend—their word for him was "brother"—and Helena took pleasure that he made no distinction between her and the acknowledged followers of Christ. She was treated lovingly, like the rest of the group. For the first time in her relatively privileged life she experienced water for washing off the dust as a supreme luxury. They offered thanks, had a communal meal, and then they were asleep as soon as they lay down.

Their third day and the night that followed in Amphipolis were uneventful and they were filled with hope that the danger had passed.

But on the fourth morning of their flight, very early, as light was breaking and before they started out, the servant girl at the Christian home where they were staying went to fetch water from the town spring; she heard the commotion, the Roman horses, the questions, the demands for information. She rushed home and whispered to her mistress: "There are men on horses asking if travelers from Thessaloniki are housed in the local inns. I heard someone tell them, 'There're always travelers from Thessaloniki in our inns.' But the strangers persisted, describing a young woman named Helena; they said she had been abducted by bad men of a Jewish cult and needed to be rescued. I hurried back to tell you, even though I don't think anyone by that description seems to be here."

The girl was thanked and kindly dismissed to return to her chores. Helena and her friends gathered in one of the windowless rooms of the house to discuss what they should do, and then prayed together. Helena watched and listened. Afterwards, the man of the house took her, disguised as she was with a *himation* and a wide-brimmed hat, and led her through a maze of back streets to the house of an older brother of the *ekklesia*. Their message to her was clear: *We will not give you up.* They led her to a shed in the garden, and she watched carefully as the old man showed her how to plant bulbs for next spring. For the first time in her life she knelt in a garden, down on the dirt, face to face with it. She started digging with her bare hands, her once-elegant long fingers dirty now, buried in the small holes that would house the bulbs which the quiet man had already thrust into her pocket. She concentrated on the moment as if her life depended on it, looked at her dirty fingernails and remembered how once they had strummed the strings of a *kithara*. She saw her hands writing notes on her father's scrolls, she remembered how she had held Ares' hands in her own, but she felt nothing but sadness and an unbridge-able distance between them. She heard Erastos' trained voice in her head and saw his sad eyes as they fastened on her that last day in Phoebe's home. She recalled Paul's dreadful back, his peaceful face as he stood in front of the Bēma while everyone else around him seemed to be going mad. She remembered Phoebe's calm, dear face and realized how much she missed her. But everyone, everyone seemed so far away from her now. What was close was the dirt, the bulbs, the rich earth smell, the worms crawling in its depths, the pleasant sounds of the garden and those in the house.

The interior sounds now increased and became noises. She heard men's loud voices, knocking and shouting, and then her host's quiet voice saying there was no woman, nor anyone else in his household—only a gardener planting winter bulbs. Later, someone stood above Helena and looked down on her, but she didn't lift her face. Her hair, covered under a hat, her hands hidden in the dirt, she remained crouched, and after a while the man, who had expected a glamorous young woman and not a dirty boy, lost interest, kicked at her once and left. Hours passed. She was given water to drink and food to eat and accepted both with gratitude. The old man looked at her with great kindness, and when the others arrived to tell her the danger had passed, she felt reluctant to leave the garden and her work in the dirt. She went up to the old man and kissed him on the cheek, surprising him and herself.

The company of friends walked on not knowing whether those looking for Helena were ahead of them or had given up and returned to Thessaloniki. They suspected that Sevastianus' men had gone east from Amphipolis and then on to Philippi. So they considered their situation. Thirty miles further east was Philippi. If they headed that way, the horse riders would be returning from Philippi as the young people would be approaching the town. What they needed was an alternate route to reach Neapolis, the port city of Philippi.

Chapter 23: Rushing North

Back in Corinth Claudia was huddled with Erastos and Alexandros. She said, "I had an urgent message from my cousin Sevastianus, the politarch of Thessaloniki. It was written immediately after he first saw Helena. I suspect she had just arrived and was paying the necessary visits delivering my greetings. His message reached me by courier a couple of days ago, but then today another courier appeared with a note from Helena, sent by a man named Jason who knows both Helena and your friend Paul. Taken together, the two missives cause me concern. It seems Sevastianus is insulted that Helena is not staying at his palace, but what worries me is that Helena sounds frightened."

Erastos was standing in her exquisite *tablinum*, the familiar knot hardening in his stomach as it always did when Helena's name was mentioned. Alexandros had asked a slave to bring cool drinks and now he was handing them around to cover his own concern.

"What are you going to do about it?" Erastos asked Claudia.

"Well, my dear, directness always helps," she murmured, waiting for their responses to this evident crisis.

Alexandros exchanged a meaningful look with Erastos. "I am sure my friend here wants to go north to help her. I'll go with Erastos. It's time I paid a visit to Thessaloniki after so many years away."

"You should have taken her, and taken care of all this, a long time ago," Claudia said to Erastos and he felt the heat rising on his face.

"The time for 'taking' is past for me, Claudia. Yes, I do admit that I've waited long enough. But it seems she will not marry Ares, after all."

"How intriguing…" Claudia smiled. "And how did you find this out?"

"Paul assured me of Ares' decision not to marry."

"Ah. The competition is removed." She gave Erastos a cool look of appraisal. "Truly, why you should have ever considered Ares as competition is a mystery to me. You are a fine man of rectitude, handsome and cultured, with enough wealth to support her in style—what more could she want? Ares was just a waif."

"A beautiful waif whom she loved. You don't compete with love, Claudia. You ought to know this."

"She may love him still."

"Oh, I have no doubt about it. Helena is not easily swayed nor does she change loyalties at a whim. But now I feel free to struggle to win her love."

"And now, as Sevastianus' letter suggests, you may have another man's lust to compete against."

He was hot with anger, and Claudia, watching him carefully, made a decision.

"Your lover's heart is not wrong, Erastos. Something bad happened to Helena when she was under my roof, and I will not allow my lecherous cousin to repeat the insult to my family."

He flinched, and she said, with pity now. "So you know…"

"About your husband—yes. Alexandros let it slip out one day not long ago."

"For that violation, Erastos, I am truly sorry. It's a bad memory in my life—in my own home—that has caused me more anger and sorrow than I can describe. Gaius finally got what he deserved."

"I suggest we must leave immediately," Alexandros urged.

"A wisp of a girl," Claudia mused, "and she has all the big men longing to go to her rescue. Of course you must go, Alexandros. But Erastos, what will happen to Corinth with you away?"

"I've asked my fellow *aedile* to take over the responsibilities. I've been managing the city without him up to now. It's his turn to shoulder that burden. But what will you do about your cousin?"

"I hardly know him except by reputation, of course. He was much too young when I left Makedonia, but I suspect I know the type. There's only one way to deal with him. Fear. By all means, we must persuade him that Helena is betrothed to another. Sorry, Erastos, you won't do. We need somebody who can threaten his position, put the fear of the emperor in him." She walked around her *tablinum* picking up an art object here, a flower there. She stopped, sure of what must be done. "Yes. We'll say that *Gallio* is interested in Helena. Make sure Sevastianus knows that the proconsul is a favorite of Claudius. You need not tell him that in fact Gallio is planning on leaving Corinth before his time is up, unable to tolerate its provincial ways." She laughed. The proconsul had proved a great disappointment to her, and she could not forgive him for his Roman pretensions and hypochondria. "I won't write much to Sevastianus; just this: *'Gallio met Helena in my home and expressed great interest.'* There's enough truth in this statement to cover all my other…bendings of the truth. 'She considers herself betrothed to Gallio; hence, hands off, Sevastianus.' While you gather your things for your trip north, Alexandros, I'll write a letter that you can deliver to my esteemed cousin." She turned to Erastos. "Is this enough help?" she asked.

"Yes, thank you." Erastos kissed her gratefully.

"Hmm," she murmured while Alexandros prepared her writing desk. "I should be nice more often."

As they took their leave, she offered some final political reminders: that emperor worship was very strong in Thessaloniki, that the Makedonians had been loyal to Augustus, and that now they wanted to please Claudius. She was sure that Sevastianus would not want to do anything that would displease whoever was the emperor.

———— ∽∾∾ ————

Erastos and Alexandros reached Thessaloniki after days of hard riding and fitful nights in the northern region's infamous inns. They went first to the house of Jason, as instructed by Paul. What they heard there about Helena's flight increased fears for her safety. The reason Claudia had received Helena's letter so quickly was that Jason, worried about the safety and virtue of his own daughter, had not waited for Timotheos to return to Corinth but had bribed a government courier to deliver Helena's message immediately after the young people's departure.

With that same astuteness Jason now discussed all possibilities with them. There was no way to know if Sevastianus' men had already found Helena and had forced her back to Thessaloniki. "How can we find out if she has been hauled back here already?"

Erastos was impatient for action and wanted to leave for Philippi immediately, but Jason persuaded them that first they should see Sevastianus, hateful as that prospect seemed to all of them. Alexandros listened carefully and then offered his big surprise.

"I'll go to visit Sevastianus. He's my relative, after all. He'll not be happy to deal with me as the freedman I am rather than the slave I was, but I'll make that even harder for him. I'll appeal to blood ties. It may even help. Believe me, I'll make every effort to find out where Helena is. If he doesn't tell me, his slaves will."

They accepted Jason's hospitality for the present while Alexandros sent word to Sevastianus, using Claudia's name as an introduction, that he would like to pay his respects. The politarch agreed to see him immediately.

Sevastianus was exactly what Alexandros had imagined—a rich young man dressed in the latest fashion, his tunic embroidered with expensive gold thread, his fingers loaded with rings, his sensuous lips smiling but his eyes suspicious. His chin was weak and tending to fat. He looked at Alexandros' white hair and his proud bearing, exaggerated for the occasion, and he assumed his visitor must be a man of the world until Alexandros without hesitation disabused him. "I'm Claudia's steward," he said, "a former slave when you knew me but a freedman now; don't you remember me?"

He saw the disdain on the politarch's features at the word "freedman" but Alexandros continued his prepared recitation: "Your father was my first cousin." Without mercy Alexandros observed Sevastianus almost choking on his wine. "Since the noble Claudia is my niece," Alexandros persisted, unrepentant, "I'm sure you'll be happy to hear a direct report from her to you. She's very concerned about her ward, Helena. We understand she came to see you?"

Sevastianus managed a nod.

"And did she share news of Claudia with you?"

"Of course she did."

"Is she here now? Claudia is anxious for news of her."

"I don't know where she is. Why should I? She refused my

hospitality." Alexandros ignored the politarch's nervousness and pressed on.

"I almost forgot. I brought you a letter from Claudia. You'd like some privacy to read it, and while you do so, I hope I have your permission to walk about your beautiful gardens."

He handed the sealed cylinder to Sevastianus and, without further comments, he exited the library into the atrium and from there strolled to the extensive gardens on the north side of the palace. Keeping a leisurely pace he admired the fountains and the flowers, studying them like an expert, moving gradually out of Sevastianus' line of vision. He stopped the first slave he encountered. "Tell me, have you seen a beautiful young woman, a Corinthian by the name of Helena, on these premises recently? I've just come from Corinth, and I need to give her an urgent message from friends of hers there."

The slave shrugged. "I remember seeing the young Corinthian," he said, hesitant and sullen, "but that was days ago." Alexandros handed him a small pouch filled with coins.

"Can you remember more specifically?"

"It's not difficult," the slave said feeling the weight of the *sesterses*. "The master was furious when he learned she had left town without visiting him again. He sent a group of us to look for her."

"And did you find her? Her good health is of interest to people connected with the emperor. It'll be very bad for your master if any harm has come to her."

"No," the man said, his tongue now loosened. "No, we missed her, though we searched for days. She vanished. I don't like to remember it because my back still smarts from the lashes. Sevastianus was livid at our failure."

After years of dealing with slaves, Alexandros was fairly certain that the man was telling the truth, but he decided to venture further, to the kitchens, hoping that a woman slave would be more reliable and talkative. He spotted a girl cutting herbs in the kitchen garden; she looked young and vulnerable and he said to her, kindly, "I seem to have lost my way in these lovely gardens. I'm looking for a friend of mine, a young woman named Helena, a visitor from Corinth. Would you call her for me, please?"

The girl looked scared. "But, but sir," she stammered, "She isn't here."

"You remember her then," he whispered, trusting her. "Don't be frightened, I was a slave once, I wouldn't do anything to hurt you."

She returned the trust instantly and, with her back toward prying eyes from the kitchen, she pretended to show him the painted tiles of the garden wall, tracing her finger on them. "I saw her at the banquet he gave, a couple of weeks ago it was. She's so beautiful, young, serious, fine, but not mean. Very different from others he invites to the palace. The gossip was that he's mad for her, but she wouldn't have him. He sent men after her, but they say she's just vanished."

Alexandros slipped a heavy coin into her palm. "Thank you," he said. "You have put my mind at ease," and quickly he retraced his steps to Sevastianus who looked angry and impatient.

"Young Marius," Alexandros took the initiative and addressed him with familiarity and a false heartiness. "I congratulate you on the excellent training of your slaves. I've administered them for so long that I cannot help myself—I keep asking questions to see if they perform their tasks to the satisfaction of their masters." Alexandros, just to be on the safe side, in case any of the slaves reported his questioning to their master, was taking care to explain his conversations with them. "Excuse my curiosity, but I see that you've done well." There wasn't much Sevastianus could say to that, so Alexandros continued. "I hope Claudia gave you some good news?"

"She's meddling," the politarch shouted. "What's all this fuss about her ward, Helena? What do I care if she's betrothed to Gallio, or anybody else from the emperor's court?"

Alexandros suddenly discovered how marvelous it was to be free of the restraint he had long practiced as a slave. *What have I to lose now?* He changed tactics. He approached Sevastianus, his face close to the politarch's. "Listen, Nephew, Helena is beloved by many of us. She's not intended to be anyone's *hetaera*. Whoever puts a hand on her will have to deal with me and many like me. Remember this. You frightened her, you chased her, you overstepped your jurisdiction. If we hear of any more attempts to intimidate her or any of her hosts, Claudia will see to it that you don't last long in this position."

"How dare you?" Sevastianus stuttered. "How dare you, you, *freedman*?""

"Remember what I told you. You can't begin to imagine the connections Cousin Claudia has at the emperor's court. Thank you for your hospitality, Nephew." Alexandros walked away, his back straight, while Sevastianus, like a petulant child threw things at the wall.

Erastos felt a wild hope that, away from Sevastianus, Helena was still alive and safe. With warm thanks to Jason, he and Alexandros immediately set out for Philippi unaware of Helena's increasing danger.

———— ◦◦◦◦ ————

Helena is running, running, her years of training in the woods and tracks of Isthmia vivid in her memory and reawakened muscles. Her tunic above the knees like a boy's, her curls close-cropped, her breasts tied with a leather band and pressed flat on her chest, she feels that she can easily pass for a boy. She smells the pines, pungent, strong, utterly familiar. The scented air invigorates her. She's enjoying the run, but her mind never lets go of the fear that gives her speed, of the worry that, despite the beauty around her, something is terribly wrong. She's running to avoid it.

Last night she and her companions had stopped by the beach, on their way to Neapolis, and had been sleeping under the stars, in the woods, away from the road. They had lost count of the days as they took time to visit other Christians and even sometimes, with the joy of the young, to play at the beach. Then Helena had persuaded them that it was her turn to keep watch. Evniki, Philothea, Nikiphoros, and Eirineos had been fast asleep. Despite her desire to stay awake, she must have drifted off for a moment, because she had been trembling when the horror of a dream woke her again; a fire was burning all her friends alive and all she could do was watch and weep, unable to move toward them. In that dream she was being held by Sevastianus and the slave Demetrius who were laughing while the people of The Way burned. It was then, waking fully, that Helena had made her decision.

But at that moment the cry of an owl must have startled Evniki for she had sat up, looking for Helena. She moved silently close to her, and Helena pulled her down beside her. They were at some distance from the others.

"Evniki," Helena whispered. "I want you to swear to me, swear in the name of your Yeesous, that you will not stop me from what I'm about to do, and that you will not wake anyone else up until morn."

Evniki shuddered. "We're not allowed to swear, Helena, especially not in the name of Yeesous."

"Then promise, Evniki, promise! In the name of all that you love, promise."

Evniki nodded, unable to utter another word. Helena said, "I must leave all of you. I'm nothing but a danger and a burden. I won't be able to live with myself, Evniki, if something bad happened to you because of me. I dreamt of terrible things befalling my friends, and it was all because of me. I must go away alone. I have enough money on me to survive. I'll find a place to live where no one knows me. This is why I'm telling you all this, so you know that I have not been abducted. Do *not* try to follow me."

Evniki was weeping silently, huge tears falling on Helena's hands as the other girl grasped them. "None of us was forced to come with you. We came because we love you."

Helena tightened her hold on Evniki and said urgently. "But don't you understand? It's because of this love that I fear harm will come to you. Everyone who has loved me has suffered. It must not happen to you or to Philothea. God knows what will happen to a poor former slave like Nikiphoros if and when they find him."

Helena embraced her friend, and their hot tears blended together in the sorrow of separation. She whispered in her ear. "You've been a good friend, Evniki. You are filled with goodness. Go back and marry one of these good men and be happy." She swallowed a sob.

She picked up her ready bundle and, without looking back, she started running. Enough light from the moon reflected on the sea, and she ran under the pines that grew so close to the water that they almost touched it. The briny smell of the sea and the piercing aroma of the pines mingled and made her drunk with a joy she could not define. Her eyes were still weeping tears, but her heart was free. She had saved her friends. When the pine forest ended, Helena turned north and continued her steady pace. She had left behind everything that was heavy so the weight was light, and soon the burden in her mind would lighten because she had left them to safety instead of danger.

Helena ran and ran and ran, all the time thinking: *So now I run in the dark while a steady light from the moon runs with me. Death. I think of my death. I'll miss the moon, I'll miss the sea. I'll miss the smell of the pines. Tears blind me. But I run. Toward what? Toward whom? I don't really know. I won't think of it. All I know is that I've stopped endangering my friends, and it's enough for now.*

As she continued to run, Helena sagely considered her options. She knew that in any city a lone youth, whether male or female, would not dare go out at night. But here in the open, on this land of exquisite beauty, the Romans as well as the Makedonians mostly stayed secure in the safety of their homes. Her best chance of safety was to stay away from the main roads.

It was daylight when Helena finally approached a populated area which she assumed must be Neapolis. Dusty and sweaty, she was not afraid that anyone would take her for a woman. She skirted the gates of the city and walked northward, approaching farm houses with caution lest any dog come after her. The smell of thyme was her only pleasure now; dry and poignantly familiar, it reached her whenever she stepped on it and its aroma hit her senses. She managed to avoid all other travelers by hiding behind trees when she heard anyone approaching. In the middle of the day she found an orchard full of olive trees and marveled as always at their silvery, gnarled beauty. She stopped under a large aged tree at the edge of the grove. *I'll rest here, eat my bread, and drink as much water as I can absorb.* She knew she was in desperate need of sleep. As she circled the huge trunk, she saw that it was hollow on one side, so she crawled inside it and settled down to sleep. When she awoke her first thought was surprise that sleep had refreshed her so peacefully.

But then she realized that frightening sounds had awakened her. *Is someone being whipped?* She peered carefully through the opening in the tree trunk. No, it was a child's laughter she heard and muted talk in the air, not screams. A ladder was leaning against a tree in the middle of the grove, a child on the top branches jumping and shaking, dark little olives falling in a shower. *Harvest time, of course.* She had seen this often enough in the countryside of greater Korinthia when she walked with her father to Isthmia. She had not been aware that olives grew here also.

Should I show myself? Are there any women nearby? Then she saw her. She was bending down, gathering, and putting the olives in a basket. *A family? Was this the mother? Maybe they will welcome a stranger. I will offer to help with the olives.* It was the woman's tired stance and the closeness of the family group that made the decision for Helena. There may be other harvesters in these orchards, but she has picked this little family as her own.

Helena emerged quietly and walked toward the harvesters. She greeted them in Greek from afar, intentionally dropping her voice an octave, her musical training coming in handy whenever she needed to pretend at being a boy. "Be joyful," Helena called out, "*Kherete*, I come in peace. I'm a traveler on foot—*odhipóros.*" She remembered the ancient dictum of hospitality, hoping they also knew it: "The sick and pedestrians bear no sin." The villagers stopped what they were doing and stared at her. Helena pointed to herself. "I'm Demosthenes from Corinth," she said, remembering that she was supposed to be a boy and thus using her father's name and praying to him for protection.

The little boy on the top branches called out. "Welcome, *Xenos*, stranger. Climb up here to help me?" Helena looked at the others, on the ground. The man had light hair and eyes, but the woman was darker. The one holding the stick was a boy about Helena's age or younger. *He will see through me right away.*

"I'll be happy to help," she said, looking at the man. "But I'm tired, my feet blistered from long miles of walking. Much better if I stay below to help gather the olives."

The woman, who up to now was bent in two, raised herself

slowly and, placing her hand on the small of her back, twisted her aching body right and left. Shyly she addressed Helena: "Welcome, stranger. I can do with some help."

The man now spoke. The words were Greek but the accent harsh; *Thracian*, Helena thought. "I've no money to pay you. But we can find you some straw to sleep on tonight."

Helena nodded her thanks and started imitating what the woman was doing as she gathered the bitter little olives. Her long fingers, expert at plucking the strings of the *kithara*, picked the tiny ovals easily. She was comfortable in the silence, the sounds of the stick hitting the branches to release the olives, the rapid movement of her fingers. The little boy was back at work talking and singing as he moved around up on top. When Helena lifted her eyes from the ground she saw the older boy looking at her sideways as he kept on beating the branches with his stick. Every now and then the mother smiled encouragingly.

They moved from tree to tree. "Is this your orchard?" she asked the woman who made a sound of regret.

"Oh, that'd be too good for the likes of us. No, we're gathering these for master. We do the work. He lets us live on the farm and gives us our bit of food. Been a-trying to buy our own piece of land; but we being neither slaves, nor paid—we just live."

The words registered slowly for Helena. *They are poorer than house slaves.* Pity filled her. "Do you move from farm to farm?" she asked, still unable to imagine living this kind of life day after day.

"We're here at harvest every year. When it's over, we move to find some other work to do," the woman whispered. "Farmers in these parts not rich enough to own slaves, so we do the odd jobs here and there."

Helena looked at the two boys comparing them to Claudia's fortunate children and even her own carefree childhood. *How cruel and unjust this Roman world is.* The thought saddened and surprised her. *Paul's people have affected me more than my father's Stoicism.*

They worked steadily until twilight when, laden with baskets of olives, they headed for home, and Helena followed. *I have run hard, I've been an athlete, but I've never felt so excruciatingly tired.*

"You do this every day?" she asked the woman who answered,

"Only when the gods allow it."

Helena wanted to weep with exhaustion, but she had to keep reminding herself that she was supposed to be a boy. She evidently had a place to sleep tonight, but how safe would she be? They hadn't asked her any questions. *Maybe they are too tired and too used to moving around to be very interested in other people.* She longed to pay them for food and for a bath but she knew this was a foolish hope, the hallucinations of a tired mind. Learning to live with dirt continued to be an unbearable lesson for her. She was about to start feeling sorry for herself, but then she looked at the peasant woman and was ashamed.

After an hour's painful walk, carrying the heavy basket and ready to drop it, Helena saw the outlines of a farm. "That hut near the stables? That's ours," the woman said as the strong animal smell rushed out to meet them. "There's plenty clean straw left in that stable. Sleep there. If you want for company," the woman offered, "big son can stay with you tonight."

The boy, young man really, hadn't said a word to Helena. The little one chattered on non-stop but she didn't understand most of what he said. She was frightened of the silent young man, terrified that he suspected she was a girl.

"You must do as you always do," she told the mother, hoping she would not insist. "Pretend I'm not here. I've been glad for your company today, but I must leave early in the morning, and your son must have his rest."

She waited to see if they would eat before retiring, but they didn't offer her any food. She debated whether to go to the farm to ask to buy food for all of them, but the prospect filled her with all kinds of fears she had just begun to acknowledge. *I have spent so much time recently with good people, I've forgotten how violent the rest of the world is.* She had another worry, sleeping in a barn. *I haven't even been inside one before,* she thought and grinned ruefully. Worn out from the walk and the bending to gather olives, she collapsed on a bale of straw. She had one piece of dried bread in her sack and she munched on that to ease the pains in her stomach. She listened to the animals as they settled themselves for the night, the coughing and sighing of cows, the occasional stomping of a hoof, and she found the sounds rather comforting. Sleep was overtaking her so, for the first time during this journey, she removed her dagger from its hiding place and gripped it in her fist. She placed the shawl, Erastos' parting gift, around her like a blanket. "Help me, God of Paul," she pleaded as her eyes, heavy and burning, closed at last.

She sensed the sound and his presence before she was fully awake. She felt for the dagger and waited, silent, in the dark. She could smell the young man even above the animal smells. "What do you want?" she demanded, grasping the advantage. "Why are you here when you should be sleeping?"

"Who are you?" he whispered in return. "Why're you here?"

"Why do you disturb my sleep and yours to talk in the night? You could have asked me earlier."

"My father, he don't like me to speak to strangers. He's afraid I'll up an' leave."

"But you're old enough to leave. Why don't you?"

"They can't manage without me. Father would kill me if I tried."

She was visited by an immense pity for him, but she didn't let go of the dagger.

"Tell me about the outside," he pled, and his hunger for knowledge added to her pity. "Where's Corinth? How far have you come?"

She was so tired, she could close her eyes and return to sleep instantly but he was pitiful in his ignorance and longing. "I'm running away from a bad Roman," she said, choosing her words carefully and speaking simply to match his halting style. "I'm grateful to your family for letting me join you today. I left Corinth a month or so ago. It's in the south, in Achaia. A group of us traveled together, but in Thessaloniki I ran into trouble with a rich Roman official and had to get away, by myself."

"It's terrible to be a pretty boy," he said, and the bitter knowledge in his voice cut her to the core. "But you're not poor like us," he added suddenly. "I can tell you come from different people. I'm here to warn you. Don't go near the house. The master there is bad, bad; he likes pretty boys." His voice was so dull and the meaning so horrible, that Helena felt like retching; a knot in her stomach, nausea and fear. "Thank you," she whispered. "Thank you for warning me. I'll disappear before full light."

"Let me go with you," he begged and she almost agreed, but then she remembered why she had to leave her friends behind.

"Listen," she said to him, earnest and serious, trying to impress him. "I've some money and I'll give it to you. I want you to feed your family with it. Your mother is kind. Stay near her and help her until she's able to let you go. You see, I never had a mother. It's very sad to grow up without one. Don't abandon yours. Take this money and let me continue my journey. I'm in danger. You don't need to share in it."

She took a small pouch from her *zona*. She kept the *sesterses* divided so that she never had to show the full amount in her possession when she paid for food. There was enough in what she gave him to keep the family fed for a month. He weighed the pouch in his hands and she could sense his surprise and delight at the unfamiliar wealth. "Take it," she said, and in order not to shame him she added, "Do me a favor and keep watch while I sleep. Can you do that? Let me sleep so I can travel in the morning?"

"I'll do anything for you," he said, and she believed him.

He moved away then, and her eyes, accustomed now to the dark, perceived his outline as he sat upright at the barn's entrance. *Can I trust him? I have no choice.* Like a litany she whispered the names of all those she trusted: "Paul, Prisca, Aquila, Phoebe, Ares, Alexandros, Timotheos, Evniki, Erastos. Ask your God to protect me now...." and for the first time since she had heard the story, there was the voice of Ares alive and thrilling in her ears telling all of them around Phoebe's generous table of a baby being born in a stable, inside a manger. Helena smiled at the memory as the animal sounds reached her and sleep overtook her.

The boy shook her shoulder as dawn was breaking. "Wake up," he said, "Master'll be around soon." He offered her a beaker of milk still warm from the goat and she drank it hungrily. She rose and hid her dagger back inside the *zona*. She felt dirty, tired, and smelly. She thanked the boy who pleaded again, "Take me with you."

"Remember your mother," she reminded him, picking up her bundle she had used as a pillow. "Use your money to help them," she urged. Then she secured the bundle on her back and started running toward the north. He ran with her for a while so that the farm dogs would not bark, but soon she left him behind. She avoided the paved road.

Chapter 24: The Presence

As soon as she smelled water Helena stopped and looked all around. The vegetation was thicker here, lush—there must be a river nearby. She listened and soon heard the gurgling of running water so she followed it until she was deeper in the woods, hidden from the road. Ah, there were poplars lining the banks of the river, their leaves, silver and green, twinkling in the early light. Large *platanoi*, their trunks huge, their branches rich with wide leaves, offered her generous shade as she walked around them, searching carefully for a secluded spot where she could bathe unobserved. She found it. Even so, she decided to bathe fully clothed in case someone ventured through the growth. She hid her bundle beneath a large rock, spread her *himation* on top, and stepped into the water. The cold plunge made her shiver, but her pleasure was so delicious that she started laughing through chattering teeth. Ah, to be clean again.

As she treaded water she thought of her father and her carefree childhood despite the loss of her mother. She pictured Claudia's elegant villa where even the slaves were well fed. When Demosthenes was living Helena thought everyone lived as she did—happy and clean and cherished. But now she remembered the woman whose toil she had shared yesterday, her deeply lined face, the hopelessness in her eyes, the way she had of leaning on the hand placed on her aching back. And she thought of the woman's son, the desperate boy who had no hope for his future. *How sad life is,* she murmured, and the stories of the people she now loved took on a specific, now familiar form—the image of a good man going to his unjust crucifixion, carrying his cross. Her eyes filled with tears.

She stayed in the water as long as she dared, without dropping her guard, looking around and listening for danger. Feeling rejuvenated, she crawled to the rock where she had laid her *himation.* Inside the hollowed trunk of a *platanos* she changed into a dry, clean tunic and added her leather vest. She rolled the wet one and tied it outside her bundle, laced her sandals tightly on her feet, and made sure her money pouches were secure inside her *zona.* The shawl Erastos had sent her as a parting gift had many uses. *I wish I had thanked him for it.* She now finished winding it round and round her waist, securing the dagger in its folds at the front. Then she wrapped the *himation* around her. She was hit by hunger pains. Walking rapidly, she soon felt warm enough to remove the *himation* and then tied it to hang like a cape from her bundle. She wondered about yesterday's family. *Were they cold? Were they hungry all the time? And what does it do to a person, this gnawing, constant hunger?* No matter what lay in her future, she would never be indifferent to poverty again.

Feeling warmer by the movement and the rising sun, she stopped at an orchard to look for fruit, but fearing the accusation of theft, she decided to remain hungry a bit longer. Somehow more confident now that she was clean, she moved to the paved road hoping to come across someone who had bread and olives for sale. It was still early and the road was nearly empty of traffic and pedestrians.

It was then that she heard the heavy footsteps running behind her. Who was it? She didn't want to know. Yet she felt the sour taste of fear, much worse than hunger, and she started running again.

This time she ran in misery, weaving away from the pavement, among the trees, her blood pumping, all her energy concentrated on escaping those footsteps. The fear urged her on, but the density of the trees kept her from sprinting. *Hopeless, it's hopeless; I cannot get away.* The man's footsteps—*heavy footfalls, it had to be a man*—came closer, he was behind her, grabbing at her tunic. "Come, my pretty, been chasing you all morning."

She heard the rough Latin and, gathering the last dregs of her energy, she screamed for help. He laughed. "Pretty boy," he said in a most nasty voice, "you sound like a girl. All the better for me," and he dragged her to the clump of pines, his body pressing against her. Desperate at the thought of being violated from behind, she yelled, "Stop. I'm a girl, not a boy. Look at me."

He spun her around. She wanted to be facing him so she could confront the evil. She could deal with the known better than the unknown.

He was now tearing at her tunic, his ugly face bending to her own. With a determination that screamed in her mind, *Never again, never again,* her hands found the dagger. As he tore at her tunic she turned the blade toward him. He pulled her to him with a violence that brought the dagger straight into his stomach. She felt only a thud, heard a swoosh, blood squirted all over her, but his hold did not loosen. His stupid eyes looked surprised but he held onto her left shoulder, all his weight on her slight body. Suddenly he howled like a beast as a large rock smashed on his head and, as Helena wrenched herself free, she heard the crunch of bone, the pain in her shoulder blinded her, and his hand finally loosened its hold on her now useless arm. He doubled over and rolled on the ground. Behind him she saw the farm boy of yesterday looking triumphant.

They stared at each other, her eyes huge with fear. "Thank you," she managed to whisper.

"I didn't do it only for you," he said, and he was crying openly now. "He's abused me for years."

Helena said desperately, "But is this your master? What's he doing here?"

"He saw us this morning and started coming after you, but you're too fast for him, and for me, so I decided to follow him. I can be very quiet; he never heard me. I thought he'd lost you. But then you stopped? Of a sudden there you were coming out of an orchard and he gained on you."

The plunge in the river, she thought, *it slowed me.*

But that didn't matter now; she had escaped an evil attack once more. She would think about this later. Now she considered their predicament. Soon the rest of the world would come awake and the wheeled traffic would begin on the country roads. "You must go back," she urged the farm boy. "He didn't see who hit him, but I don't think he's dead. Run to your parents. And I'll disappear. Thank you for saving me."

"So you're a girl," he said sadly, full of longing. "I've dreamed of girls like you."

"Not now," she said. "Another time," and she looked at her left arm hanging by her side. She didn't know how long it would take for the attacker to recover and follow. The dagger point had probably pierced only the fat of his belly. "I don't even know your name," she said. "Tell me your name and then go."

"Philippos," he answered, and Helena went up to him and kissed him on his dirty cheek. "Helena," she said. They were both crying like little children now. They left the man on the ground with the dagger point inside him. They couldn't roll him over, so Helena said good-by to her father's dagger. *I'm losing everything from the past*, she thought.

"Thank you, Philippos," she said again, and started moving north like a cripple, slowly and painfully, no longer fast and fleet. But she kept going, and thinking all the while:

I'm running like a mad person, without plan, without hope. I've escaped, but now I know myself vulnerable. The breath is leaving my body. It will be easier to collapse. My mouth is dry and bitter, I taste the salt in my tears. Still I run as if someone is pushing me.

In the afternoon, unable to go any further, Helena crawled to the cover of a long line of bitter laurel. She lay underneath. She didn't know how long she stayed there, trying to breathe. Again she heard the sounds of the river close by, and she pushed herself, crawling, to its bank. Nausea rose and choked her. She retched and retched until everything inside her body seemed to rise and stop in her throat. *I'm capable of killing*, she thought. *I tried to do to him what I had wanted to do to Gaius Marius Sylvanus. I'm capable of killing.*

She couldn't stop crying. She washed her face with the water of the river and then saw the blood all over her tunic. She stripped, threw the bloody tunic away from her, slid into the water and came back out immediately. With extreme difficulty, one-armed, feeling the sharp pain, she put on the tunic still wet from early in the morning. Throughout all the struggle her bundle had remained tied on her upper back. She was thankful to have a change of clothes, but she never knew dressing would be so difficult. She hid her body under the shawl and the *himation*. She walked on and it felt more like crawling; she had no energy left. She hid again and waited, listening. Nobody was following her.

Later, far in the distance, she thought she heard voices, but now she was in a sort of cave formed by the wild Makedonian land, the pines, the plane trees, and the river. She felt well hidden.

Helena wept quietly, feeling defeated, in terrible pain, utterly alone. *What am I doing? What's happened to me? Why did I leave the comfort of Claudia's home?*

Yet she knew that she would never go back to that world even if she survived this day. She remembered the olive-gatherers, the kinship she had felt with the sad mother and knew with clarity that helping them was one of the best acts of her selfish life. She thought of Evniki and how sweet it had been to discover the girl's humanity, of Alexandros and his severe goodness. She thought of Ares and understood, without difficulty now, his longing to have a life full of purpose. The quality that set Phoebe apart—her ability to give of herself without reservations—filled her with awe. As she thought of others, her fear gradually receded, leaving her free. The pain remained.

Her body was bruised, but suddenly she felt whole. Her heart ached with loneliness. *"Kyrie, eleison!"* she cried now, and she had no doubt as to who this Kyrios was and is. Something quiet and strong was invading her, calming her. Always eager to understand, to name the feelings, she heard the word clearly —*eirēnē*—peace…It permeated her and covered her and, as if they were being spoken aloud, she heard clearly the words of Yeesous that Paul liked to recite—"Do not be afraid. I am with you always."

"Are you with me, Kyrie?" she asked aloud. "Was it you who protected me back there from violence and slavery? Has it been you all along, and I didn't know it?"

She waited. A strong YES resounded and coursed through her whole being. A powerful, undeniable confirmation: "I am with you always." And to that assurance she uttered her own eternal YES. Almost immediately she became aware of something else—a change within her own mind, the *nous* that she cherished. She forgave Ares for abandoning her twice. That was over, finally. Nothing but sweetness remained. And then with a surprise that amounted to shock she said goodbye to her hatred of Gaius Marius Sylvanus. "Miserable man," she cried aloud. "Miserable man who knew only violence and greed and had no joy," and she forgave him the wrong he committed against her and her father. And then, and this was hard, she whispered, "Let that terrible man down the road live but stop him from hurting the boy. Protect Philippos, oh, Lord, protect him."

And she was free.

Helena emerged from her hiding place. The voices she has only been dimly aware of were coming closer. She stood but could hardly walk. She was exhausted, hungry, and aching, her left arm hanging loose from the shoulder; but she was at peace. She kept by the side of the river, under the poplars that were whispering, their song joining another melody that sounded strangely familiar. She decided to use the last of her strength to approach the people and the song.

By this time Erastos in his sore heart had given up hope, but Alexandros had continued to try to keep him from thinking that they would never see Helena again. Even searching as they had, it seemed she had indeed disappeared. The slave in Sevastianus' garden had told the truth. *She had disappeared...* He choked on the word, but again Alexandros refused fully to accept it.

Yet they had tried so hard, hunted everywhere for her. In Amphipolis their hopes had risen briefly; they found the old man who had sheltered her and heard his report of how Helena had planted his bulbs and how she had fooled the men who were looking for her. "Such a girl," he kept saying, "so fine and so humble, so eager to learn how to plant. God will take care of her."

But as they left that city it seemed to them that the great lion at its entrance held fast its secrets. No one had seen her afterwards. The two men were at a loss. Alexandros had considered the possibilities:

"Maybe the close call they had in Amphipolis forced them to change plans. It's no use, Erastos, trying to look all over the countryside. Let's go straight to Philippi, to see Paul's friend, Lydia. She's the one person Helena knows will shelter her."

Erastos had been forced to agree. He kept telling himself that Helena was too smart to be caught, that she had friends with her. He tried to hold on to that hope because he knew that men were ruthless, that the danger of rape and abduction lurked everywhere for unattended women and often resulted in their being sold into slavery. He knew the realities of the Roman proclivity to violence, especially toward unescorted women. Alexandros kept reminding him that, according to Jason, she was traveling with two men and two other women. Surely the group was large enough to offer her protection.

But at the gates of Philippi this hope too vanished, and there was nothing left for him to hold on to after they met up with the very people who were supposed to be traveling with Helena. Erastos had been riding on a horse so it was easy to see Evniki's blonde head in front of him, her familiar walk; his heart lifted and he searched for Helena, but she was nowhere to be seen. He dismounted, calling out Evniki's name; she turned and, seeing the two men, ran straight into the arms of Alexandros. He held her for a moment, then he looked at her and saw her tears. "Is she alive?" he asked quietly. "I don't know," Evniki said in despair, as Erastos stood by feeling lost. The group from Thessaloniki and the two men from Corinth met on the side of the road and exchanged only troubled news.

The first impulse of both Corinthians was to reprimand the others for losing her, but a moment later Alexandros laid a restraining hand on Erastos' arm. "Evniki," he said to the girl, "it's not your fault. I have known Helena long enough to assure you that once she got an idea in her head you could have done nothing to stop her. I also want to say to all of you," and he looked at Erastos, "that Helena is unusually resourceful and quick, and she can't be easily defeated. Now, let's do what Paul would do in this situation. What do you say?"

Eirineos responded with conviction: "Paul would seek out Lydia, and then everyone together would join in prayer. He believes that prayer is more powerful than the wiles of the enemy."

They entered Philippi and, led by Eirineos, they soon reached Lydia's home. One of the servants told them that Lydia was at work dyeing cloth, and she guided them out of the city gates, near a commemorative arch spanning the Via Egnatia. She turned south alongside the River Gangites to lead them to where Lydia and her girls were washing and dyeing the purple cloth of their trade. "This is the same spot where Lydia first met Paul," their guide explained as they followed her. "She comes here regularly not only to work, but to pray."

The River Gangites was narrow at that shady spot, the forceful water rinsing the precious dye of the mollusk into an even, luscious indigo. The women were singing as they worked. Eirineos ran ahead to greet Lydia. As she leaned over the river, Lydia turned her head and looked at the solemn group approaching her and knew without being told that something was wrong. When Eirineos said, "You have guests from Corinth," she asked, her face losing all its color, "Has something happened to Paul?" He reassured her immediately, so she stood up and said, "My friends, I perceive that you are greatly troubled. I would like for you to take a long drink of water, and then all of us will offer thanks to God our Father through our Lord Yeesous Christós. And after we have done so, I will listen to your stories."

Her strong voice filled them with calm. Erastos thought, *Her faith puts me to shame*, and tried to follow Lydia's example. After they drank, Lydia asked, "Whose is the name we should be bringing before the throne of grace? Who is in danger?" and her phrasing reminded Erastos of Paul's manner of speaking.

"Her name is Helena," he said aloud, and he felt a great weight being lifted.

Lydia said, "Brothers and Sisters, do ask God to protect Helena while I listen to our guests."

Erastos told her of the danger that had threatened Helena in Thessaloniki, of her flight with the young people present. He explained how they had been warned of possible trouble for Helena by her Roman protector, the woman Claudia, and why they had decided to leave Corinth to come to Helena's aid.

And then it was Evniki's turn. She told Lydia of Helena's sudden departure from her group two nights before. "We were hoping that she left to come to you," she added feebly and the others agreed.

"Is this," Lydia asked, "the Helena who interceded with Gallio on Paul's behalf?"

"It is the same one," Alexandros answered and Erastos surmised that Timotheos must have shared that story with Lydia on his last visit to Philippi.

"We have all prayed for Helena," Lydia said. "I have been praying for Helena since Ares first mentioned her name to me." And only then did Erastos remember that this was the woman who had rescued Ares and Dionysos and felt in awe of her. Lydia then turned to all of them. "It's very possible that Helena was indeed heading for Philippi when she left you," and she looked pointedly at Evniki. "Do not lose hope."

And now she lifted her voice in song. It was a hymn they all had heard, a hymn that was spreading throughout all of Asia Minor, Makedonia, and Achaia among the small groups of believers, the *ekklesiae* of Christ, as Paul called them. *"Christós anésti ek nekrón."* "Christ is risen from the dead," they sang, "by death, having defeated death." Erastos was deeply moved. This now was a drama he was living, no longer merely acting on the stage. "Christ, protect her," he heard himself saying, "Christ, protect her."

And it was through that prayer and his tears that he saw the pitiful sight of a slender apparition in the distance, someone walking with great difficulty, limping, one arm carrying a bundle, the other arm useless, hanging on the side as if disconnected from the body, and even in that sad condition he recognized her once proud walk and stance, the lift of the head and the hidden energy of an athlete, the loveliness of an ancient Greek statue that had come to life, his own love, his Helena, who now could barely move. He ran.

"Helena," he cried, "Helena, I'm coming."

When he reached her she whispered, "Erastos, don't leave me, don't leave me." And with what looked like immense relief, she gave herself permission to stop, to collapse, and to close her eyes. He lifted her up and held her while tears ran from his eyes to fall on her, to wash her with his love and prayers.

He carried her to Lydia who moved quickly to dip a cloth into the cool water of the river; she washed the girl's face with it while the rest of the company, speechless, kept their distance and waited. "Her arm," Erastos whispered, "it seems broken."

Helena, from somewhere in the depths must have heard his voice, opened her eyes and asked, "Erastos, is it you?"

"Yes, my love," he whispered. "I'm here. You are safe."

She moved her lips. "I'm so thirsty."

And then everyone moved. The spell was broken. Lydia asked for food, for wine, had them spread their dried cloths on the ground, but Erastos refused to let go of Helena. "She asked me not to leave her," he said, and suddenly Alexandros laughed aloud. "She lives," he cried, "thanks be to God."

As Evniki was slowly, drop by drop, wetting Helena's lips with water, Lydia said, "A young man by the name of Luke is staying at my house. He's a physician. After Helena eats and rests we'll take her to him, and he will look at her arm."

And to Helena she said, "Don't try to speak. Everything can

wait until you are better."

Helena, her head resting on Erastos' breast, closed her eyes, a tiny smile on her lips.

They returned to the city and to Lydia's spacious home. In its well-stocked library, a young man surrounded by papyri was bending over scrolls. His hair was light and his eyes green, filled with a faraway look. Lydia approached him, said something to him, and suddenly the dreamy look was gone. He spotted Erastos with his wounded burden; he became alert, his eyes focused, and he started giving orders.

"Lay her on this couch," he said, but Erastos would not.

"I promised I won't let her go."

"You better obey the physician," Lydia said with a hint of a smile. "Helena is going nowhere."

Very gently, he placed the sleeping Helena on the couch. Luke touched her useless arm, felt it with expert fingers all the way up to the shoulder and said, "It's not broken but dislocated." He looked at Alexandros. "Hold her other limbs so she does not thrash, and you…" he looked at Erastos, "pfft, you may be of no use at all."

"I'll make no sound," he protested. "Let me help."

Luke considered this. "Well then. Go behind the couch and hold her head. Lydia, you know what to do."

She brought the oldest, most potent wine, recalled Helena to consciousness by lifting her head and ordering her to drink as much of the wine as she could and, Helena, hearing that voice, obeyed.

Then Lydia moved aside and the men bent over Helena. Erastos was holding her face, whispering in her ear; Alexandros placed one arm on her knees and the other on her right arm as Luke struggled with her left. He moved it, felt the socket, and then with one great pull and turn, he deftly replaced it. It clicked in place. Helena let out a great cry, and then she was still. Without any embarrassment Erastos wept over her. The other two walked away, but he stayed by the bed. "Helena," he kept whispering, "Helena, can you hear me?"

A long time later she opened her eyes. "Where am I?" she asked. He felt a sudden fear that she would look at him as if she had never seen him before and send him on his way as she had done so many times in the past.

He said, "You're in the home of Lydia, in Philippi. A young physician named Luke has just restored your arm to its rightful place."

She smiled, and he saw in that the memory of a merry girl, the one he had first seen such a long time ago, in another life. "Dear Erastos," she said, "always so formal, so correct. Come around where I can see you."

He moved and knelt by the couch, facing her. She lifted her good hand and touched his face, the deep line between his brows. "Why the frown, Erastos?"

"I'm so afraid you will ask me to leave again, as you did that day in Kenchreaê when we first saw Dionysos."

"How I regret all that. I owe you so much," she said, and tears filled her eyes. "I owe you so much, and I never told you, Erastos, my good, faithful friend. I did not dare think that you would love me after the way I treated you. But there was your voice always accompanying me, full of care and kindness, your beautiful actor's voice. As I walked today towards the sound of your hymn, it was your voice I heard above the others. And it kept me going, even though my body was telling me to fall. I could not believe that it was you, only the memory of your voice keeping me company in a feverish dream. I knew then that I have loved you all along, and that I have been a fool."

He too wept openly, unashamed. "But Ares?" he questioned, "Ares?"

"Aristarchos is my brother," she said. "I simply did not know it before. We grew up together, we fell in love for a while because we were so lonely, and he knew he loved me the way a brother loves a sister long before I knew it. I'll always love my brother. But you, Erastos, you will be with me from now on."

There was a question in her last sentence. He bent and kissed her lips. "I will be with you always," he answered solemnly, and she smiled a radiant smile that filled him with the greatest joy he had known. She made an effort to sit up. "Erastos," she whispered with an earnestness he had never seen before in her, "those words you just uttered…When I was losing all hope earlier today I heard these very words. But it was not your voice that spoke them. It was the voice of the Lord Yeesous. 'I am with you always.' I recognized his Presence. I said Yes to the living Christ and I was finally at peace."

Erastos stood up ready to announce it to the rest of the company. But Helena stopped him. "Not yet," she said, and a transcendent light filled her eyes. "Just this moment, I understood something very important, Erastos. I kept searching for the Christ, longing to know what Phoebe and Paul seem to comprehend so effortlessly. I thought the knowledge would come through a miracle, a sign."

He sat next to her and waited. He wanted to tell her that this was the sign—that she was alive and safe. But he hesitated because something powerful was happening and he needed to understand it also. "Was there a sign?" he whispered at last.

"Not what I expected. He came to me, the Lord Yeesous, only when I was able to feel compassion for the poor olive pickers. And when I found it in my heart to forgive them all— the men who have hurt me—that is when I felt the Presence…" She was weeping openly now. "Do you understand what this means?"

He said, after a while. "I think Paul understands this fully. He would not baptize me until he was convinced that my love for you was true . He was content only when I told him that no matter what happened between us, I wanted you and Ares to be well."

She thought about this. "Yes. And as for Ares, our brother Aristarchos, Paul wanted to see that his decision was not based on a miracle but on a true desire to serve others. Isn't this all filled with wonder, Erastos?" He stood up, and she nodded.

"Come and rejoice," Erastos called out, and his voice filled the house and reached everyone's ears with the good news, and they all came running. Helena was sitting up. She saw Alexandros first and she cried with delight. "Alexandros, dear old friend. Soon we will return to Corinth and, together with Paul, and Prisca, and Phoebe, we will turn the world upside down. Are you ready?"

———— ᔕᗋᔑ ————

The End

Glossary of Greek and Latin Words

Adelphos (sing.) - brother

Adelphoi (pl.) - brothers (may include women also)

Aedilis/aedile - the title of a city manager in Roman times elected for one year (nominative: *aedilis*; accusative: *aedile*)

Agapē - Greek for disinterested love and God's unconditional love

Agora/forum - marketplace in Greek and Latin; gathering place for political and other discussions

Athena Chalinitis - the goddess Athena holding the reins (*chalinia*) of a horse in her hands

Atrium - interior open space in Greek and Roman homes with opening in the roof

Bēma - raised platform in the middle of the Agora for speakers and dignitaries

Caldarium - the tepid pool in the Roman baths

Chiton - a robe-like garment worn by both men and women

Christós - Greek for Christ—the anointed one, Messiah

Diakonos - male/female Greek noun—deacon, a word for servant, used now ecclesiastically

Dourios Hippos - the ancient (and modern) Greek name for the "Trojan Horse"—Wooden Horse

Dynamis - Greek word for power, hence dynamic, etc.

Eirēnē - peace; pronounced *irini* in modern Greek; "*Eirēnē imin*" was the favorite greeting of Christians, "Peace be with you."

Ekklesia/ekklesiae - (singular/plural) a gathering, the calling-out-of people to come together, used also by pagans, then adapted by Paul for congregations of the faithful; in Greek today it denotes both the physical building and the congregation—the church

Eros/Cupid - Aphrodite's son; a love that is based on physical attraction

Frigidarium - the cold-water pool of the Roman baths

Gravitas- seriousness, the weight of a personality

Gymnasion - a place where the ancient Greeks exercised the (naked) body; in modern Greek it now denotes high-school

Hetaera-ae- high class prostitute(s), oftentimes with highly artistic capabilities

Himation - an outer garment worn also like an overcoat

Impluvium - a pool placed under the roof opening in the atrium, it collected rain water

In situ - in place

Kerygma - proclamation or sermon (still used in Greek)

Khêrai/Kherete - the beautiful Greek greeting that meant and still means "be joyful" used as both hello and goodbye (singular/plural)

Kithara - lyre-like instrument, now means guitar

Korē - young woman; girl, daughter

Kyrie - vocative of *Kyrios*, Lord; hence *Kyrie eleison*, "Lord have mercy"

Kybernētēs - the captain of a ship

Mantis - seer—one who foretells the future

Megas Alexandros - Alexander the Great; the adjective precedes the noun in the Greek

Moira - Greek name for the semi-goddess Fate

Nous - the mind

Odhiporos - one who travels on foot (pedestrian)

Oikonomos - the financial overseer of markets

Palestra - a place where athletes wrestled, exercised

Peplos - a short, sleeveless overblouse worn over a *chiton* or tunic

Peristylion - the columns surrounding an open space

Philia - love between friends

Platanos - a plane tree; a large tree found in the Mediterranean region, near water; it can grow extremely large, with huge trunk and large leaves

Plektron - the pick musicians use on the strings of an instrument

Politarch - the leader of a city—*archon* of a *polis*

Praeficae - professional mourners at Roman funerals

Prostatēs - the protector, both male and female usage; used by St. Paul to describe Phoebe's relationship to him

Scholē - more than our word for school; a place of learning, but also of learned argument, discussion; it was usually combined with the gymnasion; hence, today's school and the derivative—scholar

Sesterses - the smaller denomination of *dinarius*, Roman money

Sinus - the part of the toga that formed a kind of hood

Stoa - a Greek word for a covered portico which usually included shops; because philosophers talked to people while walking in these *stoas*, a group of them came to be called Stoics

Stola - a long outer garment worn by women

Strigil - an instrument with a curved blade for scraping the skin after a bath, used by both Greeks and Romans

Taberna - tavern or shop; also served as restaurant

Tablinum - an office space within the *domus*—home

Thalatta - the sea in Greek, now pronounced thalassa

Tepidarium - the warm, tepid-water room of the Roman baths

Triclinium - the Romans' dining space which included three tables and three couches on which the diners reclined

Vigilis/vigile - a Roman official who served like the modern firefighter, or policeman

Yeesous or Ieesous - the Greek pronunciation of Jesus, accent on last syllable

Zona - a wide belt

Author's Note

"Owe no one anything but to love one another."

These words stayed with me as I researched and wrote *A New Love*. How was it possible that a small sect of mostly poor people, insignificant in the midst of the mighty Roman Empire, were able not only to survive and become a church but to conquer, without weapons, this indomitable empire?

The first Christians emerged from Judaism; that seems organic. The others interested me even more: how and why were educated pagans attracted to this new love? The early converts of The Way lived in humility a life apart from the glamour, luxury, fawning, and favoritism of their pagan fellow citizens. And yet "they were turning the world upside down." How?

These were the questions that occupied my mind as I followed my protagonist through her early tentative recognition of Phoebe's active love and her encounters with the dynamic message and person of the brilliant Apostle Paul.

Later Christianity misunderstood and misinterpreted Paul to the detriment of not only the church but the world. Women suffered and were ignored; slavery was excused, and even Empire was justified because theologians and laymen misused the apostle's words for their own purposes. These sins still persist. I wrote this book to emphasize Paul's humanity and the honor he gave to the women who surrounded him.

We need to know how we began. A love story is a good way to teach this history of the faith that is founded on Love.

A Cast of Characters

The persons of *Phoebe*, *Prisca* (*Priscilla*, as Luke calls her) her husband *Aquila*, and *Lydia* are well known from Paul's letters and the Acts of the Apostles. The name of *Erastos* (this is the Greek spelling; *Erastus* is the Latin) is found in The Acts of the Apostles 19:22 and Romans 16:23. The disputed Pauline letter, Second Timothy, also mentions an Erastos. He is identified as an *oikonomos* of the city (Greek), *aedilis* in Latin, a city official responsible for buildings and finances. A plaque was found near the Theater (Odeion) in Corinth, which gave me the idea that, in his earlier life, Erastos was an actor. The inscription reads: ERASTUS. PRO. AED. S.P. STRAVIT (Erastus in return for his aedileship laid [the pavement] at his own expense.)

Ares (out of my imagination) becomes *Aristarchos*, thanks to Paul; the real *Aristarchos* is found in Acts 19:29, 27:1-2. I have been fascinated by the young men who gave up (obviously) all chances of a private life in order to serve Paul and his Christ. What led them to that life? One explanation was what happened to Ares. *Timotheos* (Timothy) is well known from Paul's letters.

The minor characters (in my novel) of *Stephanas* and *Sosthenes* are both biblical. Stephanas' family was the one Paul himself baptized. He is mentioned in First Corinthians 1:16, 16:15, and 17.

Sosthenes is an intriguing character mentioned in Acts 18:12-17, as I describe before *Gallio's* Tribunal, but also later by Paul as "Sosthenes our brother" in First Corinthians 1:1. I am convinced he is the same man in both references—Paul is assuming that the *ekklesia* knows him well—and his conversion experience after the beating seems quite plausible to me. *Gallio*, brother to Seneca, is a historical character.

Titius Justus is mentioned in Acts 18:7, probably a wealthy man with a large house who offered space in his home for the ekklesia.

Helena, Alexandros, and the rest have come from my imagination.

Getting Ready for a Discussion of *A New Love*

Reading the Bible requires imagination. We cannot understand the first century using the perspective of the twenty-first. The first intellectual activity before we even consider the meaning of biblical readings is to imagine the places where the action or the encounter with the divine took place. What did the land or the cities look like? How did the people dress? What did they eat? How were their houses furnished? How did they travel? Why did certain biblical injunctions make sense to them but not to us? And why is it so harmful to claim inerrancy?

Reading a novel set in the first century can be as educational as it is enjoyable. We learn history and see the context without having to read "boring history books," as many students complain. Learning while also being entertained by a love story or an adventure is the reason historical novels are so popular.

Seeing the people in the place where they lived and worked gives a totally new perspective to the meaning of the words. So let's start with Corinth and two exercises of the imagination:

What did Corinth look like in the first century? Even though it was located in southern Greece, it was no longer a Greek city at the time St. Paul visited it. Corinth had been thoroughly Greek (as was Athens) since before people learned to write history. In 146 B. C., two centuries before St. Paul's visit, a Roman general named

Mummius destroyed it as thoroughly as a city can be destroyed. History tells us that he ordered every male killed by the sword, children and women slaughtered or taken into slavery and the buildings and grounds burnt. From 146 to 44 B.C. Corinth did not exist. However, there are always exceptions to a historical reality. It's possible that quite a few managed to escape Mummius. The author assumes that Helena's ancestors moved to the nearby Sykion and continued their tradition of music and the arts. Culture has a way of enduring. A century after its destruction, Julius Caesar ordered Corinth rebuilt and repopulated. Soon afterwards he was assassinated in Rome, but he did leave at least one reborn city behind. Retired Roman officers with their families were ordered to settle it, together with many various citizens from Ionia (what was known as Asia Minor with its long-lived Greek culture) who were attracted to Corinth as were many Jews. This city, with its two excellent ports, came to dominate the maritime commerce, and by the time St. Paul arrived a century later, it was thriving and multicultural. We are now in A.D. 50-51. The city is elegant, with paved roads leading to the two ports, with many springs, especially a particularly ornate water system called the Peirene Fountain, with temples and countless statues adorning it.

Now, imagine yourself living in such an opulent city. If you are lucky enough to be rich, you live in a domus, a single home. Life is good and you don't really care when a Jew from Tarsus tells you that love is more important than money and sacrifice more valued than power. If you are among the poor you live in crowded narrow streets, in an apartment building of poor construction. A fire could cause the whole structure to fail. There are so many gods in this city, you can pray to a whole crowd of them until you find just the right one for your problem. Now here comes a passionate, highly intellec-

tual Jew who tells you there is one God only and that this God cares for you personally. How would you react?

You like what you hear and you start attending the synagogue out of curiosity, as many non-Jews did at that time. Soon, however, they start meeting in someone's house, where Paul preaches regularly. Among those gathered in this *ekklesia*, you see not only folks of your class but also some rich people. Quite a few of the new converts are Jews but more and more Gentiles (Greeks, Romans, Egyptians, and others) are attracted to this new faith. In addition to talking and singing, the custom is to share a meal together whenever possible and to remember the sacrifice of Jesus and his last supper with his disciples. But at this common meal, the rich have meat and the poor do not. Those who do not have meat are scandalized because it comes from animals sacrificed to idols. Paul encourages them to eat if they are hungry and urges the rich to share with the poor. *Imagine yourself in one of the two groups and describe your reaction. Now switch groups and describe your reaction.*

Questions

1. The novel is called *A New Love*. How many layers of a new love are hidden within the story? Has any such love affected you? How?

2. For Helena, what is the crucial point in her life that changes her? (There are quite a few crises, but which one is the most effective in terms of her spiritual growth?)

3. Which other character(s) has a moment of epiphany, of seeing the light and changing? Explain.

4. If you were to live in that first century, which one of these characters would you rather be? Why?

5. Which of the women characters do you admire? Why?

6. Remember that slavery was an integral part of first century Roman society. How are the slaves treated in the novel?

7. The author is convinced that St. Paul honored women. Can you find instances in the novel that prove this conviction?

8. How has the role of women changed between the first and twenty-first centuries?

9. How has the role of women *not* changed? What can we do about it?

10. Before you started reading this novel, you had your own concept of the character of St. Paul. Did this story change your perception of the great apostle? If yes, how and why?

For information about arranging speaking engagements with Katerina Whitely please visit: www.MaterialMedia.com or KaterinaWhitley.net

Acknowledgements

A New Love took a long time to research. I enjoyed reading about St. Paul and having my mind changed about him. In the process I learned to love him and to thank God for him. The most influential of the many books I read was Neil Elliott's *Liberating Paul*. Many thanks to Professor Elliott.

To my dear friend and publisher Elizabeth Cauthorn of Material Media for taking a chance with it, and with me. My immense gratitude, dear friend.

To Laurie Devine for her excellent and careful editing. I rejoice in the work of editors who respect the author's voice without missing a single detail. Many thanks to my new friend, Laurie.

And to Saint Paul who loved the Risen Christ. His passion endures.

"Love never fails."